STEPHEN GRIFFITHS is inspired by his experiences in the Far East, where he taught English as a foreign language. His fascination with people, places and cultures drew him first to Morocco, then to Pakistan and India in the 1990s before landing in Hong Kong, where he remained for the next seven years.

As well as *The Kowloon English Club*, he has written a play called *Civic Duties* and articles for newspapers and magazines in the UK. Aside from work, travel and writing, he keeps himself occupied by rambling in the countryside, playing and coaching football and, just recently, studying psychology.

For the time being, Stephen lives in an unpopular tower block in Stevenage, but he doesn't mind. After all, he's known worse.

THE KOWLOON ENGLISH CLUB

Stephen Griffiths

BLACKSMITH BOOKS

The Kowloon English Club

ISBN 978-988-79638-7-5

Published by Blacksmith Books
Unit 26, 19/F, Block B, Wah Lok Industrial Centre,
37-41 Shan Mei Street, Fo Tan, Hong Kong
Tel: (+852) 2877 7899
www.blacksmithbooks.com

Edited by James Smith

CONTENTS

Preface

CLOSE TO WHERE the dank outflow of the Pearl River was rinsed by the tropical shores of the South China Sea were a smattering of desolate, rocky islands, a small peninsula and a ridge of mountains separating it from the vast mainland plains.

Early British explorers and sailors had long been impressed by this strategic location, with its sheltered deep sea harbour and access to China's coastal ports. That it was considered otherwise worthless, with few natural resources and little habitable, workable land didn't greatly concern the settlers, whose ambitions for it – realised after an unscrupulous imperial aggression – were initially limited to the establishment of a secure opium supply port for the city of Canton, eighty miles upstream.

One hundred and fifty six years later, Hong Kong had diversified and reinvented itself several times over, transformed from nothing to something else by the ingenious wedding of British politics and Chinese enterprise to become the most dynamic colony in the world. Yet, in spite – some would argue because – of its obvious success, the marriage was heading for divorce.

Prologue

HONG KONG, 1996

The final full year of colonial rule, and 'Handover' was the only news story in town. Among the inhabitants of Hong Kong, speculation and intrigue were rife, a sense of betrayal all too tangible. But, as the clock ticked down to the historic date, dissent was giving way to a weary acknowledgement of their own powerlessness. A deal had been done one hundred years ago, and the transfer of their city-state's governance from Britain to China was imminent and irrevocable, regardless of seven million wishes.

Tens of thousands responded by emigrating in order to gain the security of a foreign passport, while those left behind would have to live with their fears and mistrust of the incoming power. The brightness of Hong Kong's recent past and present was about to be eclipsed by a vast red shadow gathering on the northern horizon.

Patriotic Chinese nationals didn't see it that way; instead they were counting down the days to the auspicious date with pride and optimism. One hundred and fifty years of humiliation were about to be wiped clean. Hong Kong was being welcomed back to the motherland where she truly belonged. And nothing could confirm China's re-emergence as a political and economic force more potently.

For foreigners, unburdened by nationalist issues or fears of the future, the situation was less polarised. There was still disapproval and dismay from certain quarters, but the majority seemed determined to make the most of these historic, halcyon days before the sun would set forever on Britain's last great outpost. Tourists and foreign workers arrived in droves; thousands of young people, particularly Britons, would exploit a thriving economy and the privilege of visa-free employment. There were lawyers, engineers, stockbrokers, qualified teachers, journalists and designers from the professional classes. Then there were those who came to experience 'pre-handover fever' and the cosmopolitan social scene, while picking up casual jobs, such as labouring, sandwich delivery, bar work, waiting, and informal English teaching. For these migrants there was a feeling of impermanence and evanescence, as if this were the final opportunity to make something of Hong Kong. There was a greed and a desire, but for the moment as much as the money.

Among the incoming hordes was a young Englishman named Joe Walsh, fulfilling one of his travel ambitions by visiting a place that had always inspired his imagination more than any other: Hong Kong, city of lights and life, of commerce and high-tech sophistication, juxtaposed against old-world Chinese markets and festering back streets lined with traditional herbal shops and dubious animal parts hanging from restaurant windows. If that was his picture, he wouldn't be disappointed. No other place could match its richness of contrasts and extremes; its traditional Eastern conservatism and modern Western pretensions; its opulence and squalor; its jungles, both urban and rural.

Joe had spent nearly six months backpacking around the Indian subcontinent by the time he arrived, excited but burdened by high expectations, low self-esteem and barely enough money in his pocket to afford a flight out. Aware that he was coming to a city of opportunity and fortune, it was time to make good. Having resolved to put a wayward life of drifting and wasting back on track, he felt this would be his time and place. Notions about the energy and enterprise of Hong Kong told him if he couldn't make it here he couldn't make it anywhere, and if he didn't make it now he never would.

PART ONE

Salad Days and Sandwiches

ARRIVAL

The small peninsula to which I was headed was the only flat land for miles, flanked by tropical seas and bordered by a precipitous arc of mountains to the north. Beyond was the New Territories and, further north still, the immensity of mainland China, looming like an impending cold front that, over the century, had blown a million and more refugees south across the border to create the densest concentration of human habitation on earth.

I looked down upon that cityscape: a morass of teeming tenements squeezed between mountain and sea. The prospect of landing, now barely a minute away, was something I regarded with excited unease. The challenge of negotiating the extreme topography and the tall buildings before a sharp, late turn to line up with a runway jutting out into the sea, meant there was no landing in commercial aviation to compare.

As we veered away from a rocky escarpment, then swooped over Kowloon City, below were residential blocks that seemed almost adjacent and close enough to touch. Modern towers appeared in the distance, but here were older buildings, crumbling and blighted by rusty, corrugated rooftop appendages. The angle and height of the aircraft allowed me to see people through their windows, going about their everyday business, quite oblivious to the passing of a one-thousand-ton Jumbo just metres from their living rooms.

Then the city ended, like a wall of cliffs descending from a concrete plateau before the sea. The runway was now below and yet the plane remained far from perpendicular. I felt a fleeting rush of panic, willing the pilot to pull up and approach again. Around me the other passengers had no such concerns, as if it were a routine landing. (I still maintain it wasn't. Later on, I would climb that rocky ridge high over the airport and look down on airliners making their final skewed approaches and marvel at the skill of airmen navigating this great arrangement of man-made and natural obstacles. And I never observed such a late manoeuvre as the one I was now experiencing). Only in the last few seconds did the wings become parallel with the ground and then we landed with a great bump and a shudder, by which time it seemed we had already over-flown half the length of the runway. As the reverse thrust kicked in and the fuselage vibrated, I had visions of the pilot struggling to halt the aircraft before the end of the tarmac gave way to the deep, dark waters of the South China Sea and memories of an incident a few years earlier of an airliner that finished half-immersed, only narrowly cheating catastrophe.

As I disembarked I got my first glimpse of Hong Kong Island across a narrow channel. Although not the central district, the residential towers were tall, shiny and modern, in contrast to the squat, grey structures we had just passed over. Only by looking over to Hong Kong Island on the other side could I feel that I was somewhere new and different; Kowloon City by contrast appeared at first sight to have more in common with Calcutta, from where I had just flown.

After breezing through Immigration and Customs I scanned the faces in the Arrival Hall. There was only one person in the whole of Hong Kong that I knew, but she wasn't there. I walked around in search, then sat down with a newspaper I couldn't bring myself to read. All I wanted was to see Jan. Her absence and the effect it was having on me was stronger than I could have imagined. She wasn't the reason I'd come to Hong Kong (it was my good fortune that we'd both planned on coming within a few weeks of each other) but if she'd gone anywhere else in Asia, I think I would have followed. Sitting watching intently for any signs of her straw-blonde hair and freckles made me realise there was no doubt: I would have followed her anywhere.

I tried her telephone one last time but still it wasn't answering. Disappointed, but not completely surprised since I had only posted my flight details, I left the airport. The environment was all concrete, tangled flyovers, underpasses and anonymous blocks, and as colourless as my mood. A twenty-minute bus ride later I was in Tsim Sha Tsui. Here on the southern tip of Kowloon, amid a proliferation of bright lights, swanky shops and hotels, I found what I was looking for. It may not have been pretty but it was happening, and though the atmosphere was far from clean, metaphorically it was a breath of fresh air. The shoppers, tourists and businessmen were all doing their own thing. I felt assured that nobody would bother me here, and that mattered. India had been a rousing experience but one that gradually wore me down, raising my stress and withering my patience. The modernity of Kowloon's tourist and shopping district seemed just the antidote to those wearying months.

Instead, on alighting, I felt once again as if I was back in the sub-continent, being 'welcomed' by a party of Indian youths, shoving cards in my face, all urging me to go to the guest houses and hostels of their choice. I tried to ignore them at first as I got my bearings, before losing patience and snapping. Half of them dropped out of the race – not as desperate as the touts I was used to – but four or five still crowded me.

"Where you go?" one of them asked.

"Mirror Mansion," I stated coldly, trying to barge my way between them.

"Wrong way, sir. Mirror Mansion is that way."

I thanked them sheepishly amid some mocking laughter. There was no further pursuit – most were keen to avoid creating a scene, since they were working illegally on short-term tourist visas for the cheap hostels of Chungking Mansions. This was where I had originally planned to head, being the one place I knew that provided cheap accommodation. A chat with an 'old hand' on the bus, however, had put me right. He'd explained that it was 'a sleazy, run-down fire trap, a rat-infested cesspool, where heroin addicts shoot up on the stairs and you have to wait twenty minutes for a lift'. Instead, the nearby Mirror Mansion was recommended, which he described as 'a better class of shit-hole altogether'.

I found the inconspicuous entrance squeezed between two small shop-cum-stalls, and took the lift to the third floor. From here I could appreciate the scale of the building. It was constructed in a huge square, facing inward, with great air-conditioners and generators rumbling away on a central podium, pipes and cables snaking in all directions, blackened, dank and litter-strewn. Outside the air was heavy and close, but here it was positively fetid. The podium was open to the sky but the encompassing eighteen floors prevented any breeze or ventilation whatsoever.

Within its concrete parapets I saw hostels; cramped and crowded sweatshops; storehouses; steamy launderettes; private residences; and even a few brothels (so discreet as to be almost unnoticeable). The place was pulsating with people of Chinese, Indian, Pakistani, Nepalese and Western origin. A constant drone of machinery filled the air, while odours and aromas of cooking oil, curries, dampness, mildew and kerosene vied for your senses' attention. And all the while, water leaked from air-conditioners onto a floor frequented by giant cockroaches that scuttled and shimmied to avoid impending footsteps. It was repulsive one moment and compulsive the next, this squalid, sweltering, diverse and industrious block of life. I looked through doorways that revealed a contrast of scenes within each of the gloomy windowless interiors. At one were ten or fifteen women, crammed tightly, hunched over sewing machines. Next door was a pretty schoolgirl eating noodles, watching television. On the other side, a room full of stereos and other hi-fi was being taken apart and reassembled by a group of Indians, while another led immediately into a dormitory of about ten bunk beds, all apparently occupied. Beside this was a little Chinese-run convenience store. Everywhere something was going on. I wanted to be part of it, but first I was going to have to find a bed, which was proving as elusive as a whiff of clean air.

On the tenth floor, having already been turned away by three or four hostels, I came across Craig and Helen, whom I had briefly met at Calcutta Airport earlier that day. Then, they were bright and vivacious; now their optimism appeared exhausted. She was a picture of despondency, sitting on her rucksack with her head slumped towards her lap. He was standing, looking bemused and vaguely lost.

"No luck either?" I asked.

Helen looked up. "Like you wouldn't believe. We started on the second floor and worked our way up, but nobody will take us. Guess we arrived too late."

"Strange." I was thinking of the Indian lads touting for business.

"You're British, right? Should be easier for you. Some places asked if we were British, then turned us away when we said we were Americans."

"How come?"

"Guess they think you'll stay longer. You get a one year working visa, right? We only get a three month tourist."

"Well, if it's any consolation, everyone's turned me down without asking."

"It's not, believe me, it's not." She concluded with a sigh.

At my suggestion, Craig and I went up to check the remaining floors, while Helen kept an eye on the baggage. Despite receiving more setbacks, Craig remained calm. He seemed gentle and passive compared to his girlfriend. And when we were eventually offered a room, on the fourteenth floor, he politely gave me first refusal.

I was holding out for something cheaper. As I walked out, someone called me back. "Hey, you have British passport?"

"Yes."

"You looking for work in Hong Kong?"

"I will be, yes."

"Okay, come, come."

I followed him up two flights of stairs as he introduced himself as Mr Mohammed, the hostel owner. He unlocked a front door and showed me in. The air was musty and stale, the hallway grubby and neglected. There were windows, but only to a lightless, airless shaft. He showed me to the bedroom, which was in an even worse state of disrepair. There were two beds, one a bunk, lying back to back with very limited floor space. The room was dank and gloomy – worse than a prison cell – with paint flaking off the walls and ceiling; there was no window, no air-conditioner, a TV that didn't work, and the only concession to modern convenience was a noisy, filthy fan. Even in India I seldom encountered less salubrious surroundings. But I was hardly in a position to choose. Even the price was non-negotiable.

"It's pretty rough," I complained. "Can you take fifty?"

Old Mr Mohammed was having none of it. "Now sixty dollars is good price for you, my friend, really. This is nice quiet place. No one bother you here. You English, you like reading, no? This is the perfect place for you, very quiet."

"I like television too."

"No problem, we will fix that for you."

"What about the air-conditioner?"

"We will install a new one, you have my word. But for now the fan is very good. More healthy, you know."

I wasn't satisfied but I had no other choice and he knew it. The television would never be fixed, the air-con never installed, and the place would prove anything but quiet and peaceful. And yet, it would be my abode – I hesitate to use the word home – for the next six months.

WILL DO

I went downstairs to sign in, with the assistance of Mohammed's nephew, Akram, who worked the reception desk. Here I was greeted by Will, a short, pot-bellied Brummie with a strong line in vocals. "Hello mate, just arrived 'ave we?"

"Don't know about you, but I have," I said with a smile.

"Ha ha, I like you already. Are you hungry? I betcha haven't eaten for ages, have you? You've got a hungry look about you. Now what can I tempt you with, chicken, B.L.T., club or cheese and pickle? The choice is yours."

I looked into his large plastic box on a trolley, about a quarter filled with sandwiches. "How much?"

"Since it's you, five dollars. Special price for new arrivals. What d'ya say?

My quick arithmetic worked out that it was a mere forty pence. "God, it's cheaper here than I expected. Give us a chicken baguette."

"So, what brings yer to Hongkongland?"

"I've been travelling around India the last few months, but I'm getting low on funds and needed a change of scenery. Always fancied Hong Kong."

"Wise man, wise man. You're in the right place at the right time. This is the centre of the world right now, epicentre of the universe, know whadda mean?"

"No, not really."

"You will. You can be who you want, do what you want 'ere, no questions asked, no barriers raised. I know people who arrived 'ere with nothing – they're makin' fortunes now. It's the new West, mate, land of opportunity, that's what this is. All you've gotta do is knock."

"So how come you're selling sandwiches, then?" piped a Geordie-accented voice belonging to a large, scruffy young man passing down the corridor.

"Bloody 'ell, mate, a man's gotta start somewhere, give us a chance." Then with volume reduced: "Don't listen to 'im, this place is full of cynical bastards, I tell you. And take it from me, it ain't a bad job really: meet plenty of people, get free nosh, pay's okay. So if you're looking for a bit of work..."

"Sounds all right, but how do you make a living when you only charge five dollars a sandwich?"

"No, stoopid, I'm only flogging the leftovers from the main round. We sell 'em for twenty-five or thirty dollars to all the rich *gwailos*, Hong Kong side. Nobody would pay that over 'ere."

"*Gwailos*?"

"You're a *gwailo*. And so am I. Cantonese for ghosts or foreign devils. That's what they call us, yer know. Bloody amazing, innit? ...after all we done for 'em. So, are you in or out?"

Before I could answer, he went on: "You get to keep twenty per cent of all takings, loads of free grub, plenty of nice birds to chat up. What better way to get to know the people and the city? Ideal introduction, mate, that's what it is. And, like I say, I know of people who were selling sandwiches, got to know all their clients – staff and management – and then got offered jobs. Researchers, journalists, stockbrokers. You wouldn't believe it but it's true, I'm telling ya. Nowhere else in the world. No conventions 'ere, mate, no class system or lack of education to hold ya back 'ere. You can just go for it. What do you say?"

His non-stop, breathless pitch was irresistible. "Can't wait."

"Yeah? Start Monday, alright? I'll introduce you to Phil here later this evening. You'll be taking over from him, okay?... Where else in the world could you arrive, not knowing anyone, and still get yourself fixed up with a job without even looking, ay?"

He had a point. I smiled as he trundled his stout frame out of the doorway, the hem of his baggy trousers dragging along the floor, and immediately engaged a passer-by with his unique sales patter.

FIRST PERCEPTIONS

Half a day earlier I had been an object of curiosity or exploitation on the maddening streets of West Bengal. Now, walking down Nathan Road, I was again among flocking crowds and noise, but this time I felt anonymous and free. I strolled past the famous Peninsula Hotel. Across the road the Hong Kong Cultural Centre, a tiled, windowless, municipal monstrosity, now blocks out much of the hotel's harbour view. Just beyond, across the harbour, Hong Kong Island's skyline is an altogether more cogent symbol of the city's strengths and ideals: clinical, uncontrived and functional, but no less attractive for that. What a treat to stand for the first time before that wall of skyscrapers glinting and winking in front of mountains darker and more impenetrable than the night sky. After half an hour, maybe longer, viewing in quiet appreciation, I was back on Nathan Road.

Without even trying I found the notorious Chungking Mansions, a big grey 1960s block, with an entrance teeming with peoples of all colours. I ducked inside and found myself back in a bazaar. A group of touts descended on me again, thrusting cards with the names of various Indian restaurants under my nose. Unperturbed this time, I went on past the money exchanges through to the dim, mouldering recesses of the interior and into a cacophony of alarm clocks and wafts of curry. The traders were mostly Indian, Pakistani and Chinese, selling timepieces, tourist tat and cheap clothes. Their customers included a surprising number of Africans, but local natives were thin on the ground. I stopped to look at the variegated rows of Indian food on display behind glass cases. There were tandooris, curries, masalas, chapattis and sweets, all looking generally more appetising than the typical, authentic Indian fare I had become accustomed to. Until, that is, I noticed cockroaches sauntering around the trays on which the dishes sat. My stomach turned, but the proprietor, ignoring their presence, continued serving his equally unconcerned customers.

Upstairs on the mezzanine floor, there were more hole-in-the-wall type Indian eateries, where you could sit at tables along the passageways. It was hotter and grimier than the ground floor but less crowded. I would eat here later but, for the time being, the real Hong Kong outside was more exotic and alluring to me than this subcontinental transplant.

Almost the first structure to catch my eye on leaving Chungking, however, was a large marble mosque. It would be some time before I would see anything of similar relevance to the local culture such as Taoist or Buddhist temples. Instead, I would realise, the array of shopping malls, designer goods and jewellery stores were the real places of worship in Hong Kong, and the luxury brands within, its icons. But for now I would leave such cynicism aside. After six months in a place deprived of such things, I found the novelty surprisingly attractive.

Lying behind the mosque on Nathan Road, Kowloon Park was a place of spick-and-span orderliness, where nature was controlled and isolated in pockets or tidy rows, behind fences, amid acres of concrete and stone, surrounded by featureless tower blocks. With hardly a blade of grass to be seen, the many water features and twisting banyan trees nonetheless made it a tranquil haven.

I sat on one of the few available benches and observed the passing human traffic along the park's main thoroughfare. All the young people were impeccably clean and groomed, conservatively casual in dress. Most wore T-shirts with English slogans or motifs, some of which they patently did not understand. I saw a girl sporting a garment with the advice *In case of fire pull hose* and an arrow pointing towards her crotch; another perhaps unwittingly warned that *My dick would like to buy you a drink!* Across the T-shirt of a carefree lad was, *I'm not gay but my friend is.* He was alone.

I observed the faces and the behaviour with interest. A girl sat down opposite with her boyfriend. She was sulking tearfully with her head down. His attempts at consolation were met by scorn as she spat and hissed like a cat, before reverting to ground-gazing, with her bottom lip following the same trajectory. The temptation to retaliate, or at least to walk away, must have been tangible, but the boy seemed pathologically patient. Tentatively – ever so tentatively – he stroked the back of her hair. She flinched, then stared back at him with a spite quite undiminished by his gesture. I wondered what awful betrayal he must have inflicted upon his girlfriend to have earned such a fierce response, and indeed which of them was more worthy of sympathy. What interested me most at the time, however, was their total indifference to being seen. For fully ten minutes I observed unhindered. Not once did either of them catch my eye or indeed look up. Such single-minded detachment, I would find, is a very local trait.

A NIGHT OUT

I went up to the lobby to wait for Will and Phil, whose sandwich round I would be taking on. Helen and Craig were munching the last of the sandwiches and Phil was offering to introduce us to the nightlife.

"I'm game," I said gladly. "What about you two?"

Helen and Craig spoke simultaneously. He: "No, we're real tired now, guys." She: "I'm in."

Will and I tried to persuade Craig to change his mind but Helen made little effort.

"Are you still coming then?" Phil asked her.

"Sure."

Craig looked ashen and hurt. I felt uncomfortable for him, but Helen and Phil seemed oblivious.

"What about you, Will?" Helen enquired.

"No, no, love to guys, but you know 'ow it is, the big game takes priority tonight. It's Ajax, yer see. Crunch game in the European Cup, showing at the little Irish pub round the corner. Don't wanna miss it. Pity, though, would've liked to 'ave joined youse. But this is a big one. Used to live in Amsterdam, so I've got a soft spot for them. Great team still, reckon they could go all the way."

"What's he talking about?" said Helen, with a bemused smile.

"Don't worry about him... verbal diarrhoea."

Will was completely unmoved by Phil's slight and Helen's resultant laughter.

"You a footie fan, Joe?"

"Yeah, I like football."

"Who d'you support, then?"

"Barnet."

"Oh," was all he could muster by way of reply.

"Nice one, Joe. *Barnet*. You'll 'ave to remember that, if you wanna shut the little bastard up, all you've gotta do is say *Barnet*. I wish I'd known that nine months ago."

Helen, out of sympathy or curiosity, asked, "So, you lived in Amsterdam?"

"Don't give 'im ammunition, Helen," warned Phil.

"Sure did, five years in all. Great place that, you been there? … No?… You should. Yeah, great place, great times. Only trouble was, dunno why, but I never had any money. I could never work it out, 'cause I earned okay. Must've been the entertainment, I suppose, nudge, nudge, wink, wink. You're a man of the world, Joe, you know whadda mean. Not sure about this fresh-faced college boy, though," glancing at Craig. "You've got it all in Amsterdam, decent beer, hash, women…"

"But you've got a nice little filly of your own waiting for you at home now, right?" said Phil. "Let's go."

Helen was giggling hysterically, quite unconcerned by her boyfriend's lonely retreat to their room. Clearly she had never met anyone like Will or Phil, and Will had probably never encountered anyone quite so impressed by his bullshit. Which he took as a sign of encouragement.

"Got a nice Filly-pina, yeah. I prefer them to the local girls. Cantonese birds take life far too seriously, don't know how to let their hair down. Most don't even wanna know you. No friendly banter, no chit-chat, no nothing. You're lucky if you even get a smile out of 'em. Every other place, I've always managed to pick up a bit of the lingo, in Thailand, Holland, Germany, you name it. Everywhere except here. That's one thing that really disappoints me about me time here. D'you know I learned more Dutch in two weeks than Cantonese here in two years?"

"So you're a bit of a linguistics expert, are you?" I asked.

"What's that then?"

"Languages, mate, languages."

"Yeah, I've been thinking about moving into teaching. I've already done a bit of translation, like."

"What, Dutch?"

"No, I done German a coupla weeks ago, Italian last week."

"You speak Italian as well?"

"Nope."

"You can read it, though, right?"

"No need, no need. It's amazing what you can do with an English-Italian dictionary."

Helen was killing herself again. "What about the different grammar and usage?"

"What's she fucking talking about? Language is made of words, right. Translate the words, you translate the language, right? Dead easy."

"And people pay you for this service?" asked Helen.

"I'm not a fucking charity, yer know."

"Do your clients ever come back with more work for you?"

"Not so far, I admit, but it's early days."

With some difficulty Helen managed to force out a few words. "You're some guy, Will, you really are."

"Gee thanks, gal," he replied with a phoney American accent and cheesy smile.

"So, what did you do in Holland?"

"Oh come on!" cried Phil, finally losing patience. "Do you wanna go out or not? 'Cos if you let 'im answer that one we'll be here till past the bleeding handover. Perhaps you could give us the answer in writing, me old China." He slapped Will playfully on both cheeks. "Come on you two, let's paint the town."

"Hang on, hang on, you don't need to go yet, you've got all night," protested Will.

I ruffled his hair on the way out. "Barnet."

"I can see I'm gonna have a great time here," giggled Helen.

We wandered down to the Star Ferry for the ten-minute ride to Wan Chai. Halfway across, the view surpassed even that from the quayside, as the massive monuments of international commerce loomed ever nearer, casting their bold impressions shimmering across a rippling surface. The old steamer chugged with gentle resolution, just as it had for nearly fifty years. A brass footplate, *Wapping 1948*, made me wonder at the changes witnessed by the venerable vessel, with scarcely any structure except the anachronistic ferry terminals on either side of the shore still standing from that time. Perhaps it was appropriate that one of the most visible legacies of Britain's tenure should be something so transitory and functional.

My nostalgic ruminations were interrupted by a sudden, loud pop as Phil burst a crisp packet behind a couple of old biddies. They gave him a strong and deserved dose of vernacular, while he looked at the bag with an expression of feigned mystification. Helen confided in me that she couldn't believe England could produce such characters as Will and Phil. "I thought you Brits were all conservative gentlemen."

"Depends what class of Brit – not sure you'll meet too many that fit your image in Kowloon."

As we walked away from the dock, Phil's theatricals found another victim in the shape of a youth wearing a baseball cap back to front. Phil tapped him on the shoulder. "Hey, mate, your cap's on the wrong way." The boy ignored him, deliberately looking in the other direction. "Look, wear it like mine, see?"

The boy's face, in equal measure, was a picture of hatred, resentment and embarrassment. Unperturbed as always, Phil lifted the offending headgear and replaced it in the sensible fashion. "*Chee gow seen, chee gow seen* (stupid prick)!" the irate and chastened youth cried, before turning it back.

This was a normal thing to do in Phil's world and was apparently performed for his own entertainment rather than trying to impress us.

"I love the Chinese. I'm gonna miss them so much," he said, before proceeding to call "*chee gow seen*" in a friendly tone to every Chinese face that passed.

Phil's local was a deep, open-fronted bar, full of expats. It was supposed to be an English pub, but it could have been an American bar for all the varnished timber, brass and mirrors. It wasn't cosy or comfortable or 'lived-in' enough to be authentic, despite the John Smith's Bitter and some Portobello Road-type memorabilia. The prices were English but only as long as Happy Hour lasted.

Phil spotted a group of friends, excused himself, and left me alone with Helen. I wondered what to make of her. I liked her, I knew that much, and not just on account of her attractiveness. She had an excitable, carefree openness about her: virtues I appreciate in others for the simple fact that I fail to possess them myself. But still I had misgivings about the way she had treated her boyfriend.

"What's up with Craig?"

"Oh, he's a sweet guy, he really is. But you know he's quite immature and reserved about stuff."

"What stuff?"

"Drugs, sex, you know."

"And you're a rebel, right?"

"Compared to him, guess I am. We both come from the same dull, comfortable, middle-class Minnesota background… difference is I'm trying to break out."

"That's understandable."

"I'm twenty-three years old now and I wanna live, man. Feel like I missed out when I was studying and living in my hometown. There was nothing doing. Couldn't even go out for a drink. Now I wanna make up for lost time, live it up, when all he wants is to settle down. We've got different agendas, you know."

I thought of Craig, back in the solitude of their room, no doubt mulling over these very matters.

"How did you two get on travelling round India?"

"Well, basically, he left everything to me: the travel arrangements, negotiating and stuff, dealing with hustlers. Everything. He couldn't cope with the stress of the place. He wouldn't have survived without me to look after him."

After our second drink, Phil returned, suggesting a change of scenery. Armed with a bottle of whisky, purchased from Seven Eleven at Phil's behest, we descended into a subterranean den of noise and flashing lights. It was smoky and crowded, but thankfully air-conditioned. The ceiling was a tangle of padded pipes and trunking, the walls black-washed and unadorned. "Welcome to the Black Hole of Hong Kong," shouted Phil.

We bought a Coke each, which together cost nearly double the whisky. "It's always Unhappy Hour here," Phil said, as we sat down opposite a group of Filipinas. "All Flippers and *gwailos* here. I'm surprised they let you in, Helen." Then in his best Cantonese tone: "No *gwai mui* allowed!"

He took out his bottle of whisky and poured some into each of the Filipinas' glasses without asking, and was rewarded by shrieks of surprised approval and the kind of smiles you scarcely see in Hong Kong or indeed back home.

"God bless 'em," said Phil, out of their range. "These girls are forced to work from dawn until midnight, six days a week, cleaning, cooking, nursing babies. Then they have to send back the pittance they earn to support their families. But they make the most of a bad job. Just look at them, you won't find them feeling sorry for themselves or anything."

True enough, they really knew how to party. I, on the other hand, would have struggled without the drink, especially in such claustrophobic surroundings with the bass of low-grade Europop pounding out from the speakers.

Phil had no such reservations. Before long he was on the dancefloor, making fun of some huge, lumbering ox of a man whose style of dancing he was cruelly mimicking by transferring the weight of his body from one foot to the other, slowly and awkwardly out of sync with the music. The ox didn't see the funny side. He stared back at the smaller man with features of stone. But there was also something slightly gormless in his expression, leaving Phil anything but intimidated. He stood on tiptoes so they were almost eyeball to eyeball, his countenance now replicating the severity of the uncoordinated dancer's. This time I was sure he had gone too far and I'd soon be picking him up off the floor. Just in time, Phil's face broke into a friendly grin, he gently patted the shoulder of his stooge, and fell back into his dance routine, which involved covering every inch of the floor in the shortest possible time, his head being thrown this way and that, arms all over the place. A couple of girls were bothered by his flicking their backsides as he passed, wrongly assuming it to have been deliberate. He was out of control, a picture of rhythm and madness.

I joined him later, but there is a limit to how much of this kind of music you can take, even when inebriated. I returned to my seat as a Roxette number was unleashed. The Filipina girls had gone and the bottle of whisky was nearly empty, but I necked what remained with abandon, then dozed off, before waking with a spinning head and a compulsion to vomit. On the way to the gents I noticed Phil and Helen dancing closely. By the time I came out they were gone.

I surfaced from the club into the muggy mildness of pre-dawn. Like a plastic bag blown down the street I drifted towards the Admiralty district, with faint notions of getting back to the Kowloon mainland. But there would be no buses, MTR trains or ferries at this time, leaving only taxis, which I could ill-afford. It didn't matter. I was seduced by the calming hush of the big city surrendering to the hour. The only sound was the distant and sporadic hum of traffic. Gleaming glass edifices took on a new aura, almost animate in effect. Distorted vision or not, I found myself climbing to the roof of a walkway shelter for a better vantage. I lay back, almost as intoxicated by the sublimity of the scenery as I was from the alcohol. A futuristic world of upside down overhanging skyscrapers was swaying gently, hypnotically.

When I awoke, dawn had already broken, and with it the romance of three hours prior. I sat up, opposing the drab Kowloon visage and the dark dividing waters. Behind me even the

Hong Kong-side towers had taken on a new, muted hue, almost colourless beneath a pale grey sky. The city was coming back to life, with the noise of traffic building and the first trickle of pedestrians. Memories of pre-dawn abstraction were fading with the onset of daylight and sobriety. And in its wake, the real Hong Kong was about to reveal itself.

JAN

As I climbed the stairs of Jan's building I recollected the shared events of our two months together, feeling tense and excited about the prospect of reunion. It was six weeks since she had left, and I still missed everything from her generosity of spirit and humour to her daring and spontaneous attitude to life.

On the fifth floor I rang the doorbell and waited. And again. No answer. Checking the address on a letter she'd sent *poste restante* to Bombay confirmed this was definitely it. I had to consider that my letters sent from India might never have arrived. Either way, there was no reason to assume she would be home. Still I was quite persistent, about to admit defeat only after my fourth try. Then I heard some shuffling, and the door opened. I was looking forward to seeing her reaction and suddenly regretted not bringing flowers. I need not have bothered, for instead of seeing that familiar, rosy face, I was greeted by a worse-for-wear, bleary-eyed, freckly girl, with wild hair and a Glaswegian accent.

"Hello, I'm looking for Jan."

"She's nae here. She won't be back till late."

"What about tomorrow?"

"Well, she's usually up aboot one."

"Okay, will you tell her I'll be here at two tomorrow?"

"Sure."

Next day I went through the same routine and with the same outcome. "You just missed her," I was told.

"Well, didn't you tell her I was coming?"

"Oh aye, I did, aye," she said, in a tone so casual it grated.

"Do you know where she's gone?"

"I do, aye."

"And…!"

"Ugh? Oh, sorry. Hong Kong-side, out for dinner, I think."

I wrote a brief note for Jan, asking her to contact me, and gave it to her flatmate. The ball was in her court now. I trusted it would be returned soon enough, but instead found myself left on the sidelines once more. It was disappointing but there had to be a rational explanation. It was probably just a matter of crossed communications: she hadn't seen her friend and missed the note, or perhaps she had rung when I was out and was too busy to ring again. Either way I remained confident we'd soon be reunited. A watched phone never rings, though.

I returned to the flat a day or two later and the Scottish girl told me that Jan was out again.

"Didn't you give her my note?" I asked impatiently.

"I did, aye."

"Well, do you know why she didn't contact me?"

"I don't kno', maybe she had better fish to fry."

It seemed as if she was hiding something.

"Where is she now?"

"She's working."

"Where?"

"She works at Harry Ramsden's in Wan Chai."

"I geddit… Better fish to fry, right?"

She looked confused. "No, I was talk'n' aboot last night actually, which was her night off. Anyway she's a waitress."

I couldn't tell whether she was being deliberately provocative or just plain stupid; either way, prospects were definitely looking down. I thought of making my way over to Ramsden's to find Jan, but decided better of it. She wouldn't appreciate it if she was busy. Meanwhile I had a couple more questions.

"Has Jan mentioned me before?"

"She mentioned somethun aboot a friend she met in Calcutta, who was maybe gonny visit. Is that you, is it?"

A friend! "I suppose, yeah. Do you know Jan well?"

"Aye, she's my best pal in Hong Kong."

I cleared my throat. "Is she seeing anyone at the moment, do you know."

"Aye, she is."

The direct and unequivocal response caught me cold.

Then I asked, "Is it serious?"

"I think it is, aye."

I felt demoralised, not knowing where to look. The Scots girl seemed not to notice; or more likely she did but didn't care. If she had, she might have offered me a sit down, a cup of tea – or preferably something stronger – and a sympathetic shoulder. All I got was a cold, vacant stare. Not wanting to display any weakness in front of her, I just muttered something like 'good for her' and turned around.

By the time I reached the bottom of the stairs I was so deflated that anybody passing could hardly fail to notice that here was a young man seriously down on his luck. I gave thought to tracking down Jan, but it would be awkward at best, humiliating at worst, and in all likelihood a lost cause. But maybe it wasn't so surprising that she had looked elsewhere and succeeded. In this tight-knit expat community, where everyone knew each other and everyone was young and available, the opportunities were ample. Perhaps our paths would cross again in the future or I would phone her when I felt calmer and more confident. That would have to wait. I wanted to find somewhere tranquil to be alone with my thoughts – not an easy task in Hong Kong – and remembered a place I'd stumbled upon a couple of days before. Signal Hill was a secluded little park tucked in such a position down a dead-end street that few people were even aware of its existence. Last time I'd had it virtually to myself, but today, being a Sunday, it was taken over by Filipina maids enjoying their one day of the week off. I couldn't begrudge them, but the last thing I needed at this hour was to hear their chorus of chirpy singing. I kept my distance, trying to ignore the revelry, which only seemed to deepen my sense of melancholy. I was surprised at the strength of my feelings, but rejection and loneliness in a far-flung land is an isolating experience, in this case compounded by the sense of losing something that I'd taken for granted. I wanted to believe that her flatmate was wrong, when I knew she was just being brutally honest.

I thought back to my first meeting with Jan at a curd shop along Sudder Street, Calcutta, where we'd had to sit on a table to avoid the rapidly rising waters of a monsoon flood, then wade through it holding each other as we struggled to avoid potholes. The experience brought us together and we became close friends and more. Jan had all the typical virtues of the Irish contingent in Calcutta – warm-hearted and humorous – but without any of the barriers of Catholic piety. Originally she was attracted to the city by altruism – she worked voluntarily with mental patients and street children – but it was also the social scene and her love of the city that kept her there so long. She introduced me to some of the seedy local bars, including one where the evening's entertainment included observing rats running across the apex of wall and ceiling. Such things never bothered Jan, whose easygoing tolerance meant she was made for life in the subcontinent. She also impressed me with her simple candour and absence of any materialism, ego or greed. We were on the same wavelength, laughed together, had similar tastes in music and literature, and generally shared opinions about other people, which is a useful, if often overlooked, indicator of compatibility. I started falling for her, and wasted little time in acting on it, persuading her to climb through the window of my backstreet hotel, whose puritanical (in the Hindu sense of the word) management did not allow cohabitation of unmarried couples. Another time we made love in the girls' dormitory at the Salvation Army one afternoon while all the other girls were out doing their voluntary work. I was anxious about being caught with my trousers down but nothing fazed Jan. We went on trips to Bodhgaya and south to the coastal resorts of Orissa, cycling and swimming by day, getting stoned or drinking by night. All great times, great memories, but now they counted for nought. It hurt that these things appeared to mean less to her than to me. Still I continued the self-inquisition, wondering whether I'd upset her, or failed her in some way. Had I, in my own satisfaction, neglected hers? Certainly I had complacently and smugly assumed I was good enough for her. Even allowing for the fact that my physical appearance had been affected by disease, diet and climate, I was sure she would be there for me. She wasn't the flirtatious, seductive type: she always wore trousers or shorts, seldom made up, and kept her hair tied up; she was well-built also which, along with her crumpled, baggy attire, meant she looked more like a stout farm girl than a pin-up. To be with someone like that may not do wonders for your ego but it makes you feel secure. I had hacked it north to Darjeeling and Sikkim with an easy conscience and few qualms while Jan was winging her way to Hong Kong. The prospect of the hill station and the secretive mountain state had been too alluring to resist, but now I was finding it had come at a cost. And I was feeling anything but secure.

From my bench facing eastward down the narrow channel that separates Kowloon from Hong Kong Island, the end of the runway was visible. My eyes followed the progress of each plane soaring skywards every couple of minutes, trying to match the indistinct livery to an airline. It was difficult from this range but it hardly mattered. They were leaving and I could scarcely acknowledge that fact without a deep and irrational envy. I wondered where to, but again it was of no consequence. They were flying away from the cruel greyness of this lonely place and that is all that mattered, while I was tied down by limited finances, debts at home and, indeed, by any other options. Logic told me it was no bad thing, as running can only ever be a short-term solution. Better to stay and confront the fact that I was a failure in love and life wherever I was.

An hour or two of abject contemplation had passed by the time I found myself drifting down to the seafront at Kowloon's southern tip. Darkness had descended and the city's drab daytime countenance had been transformed once more by the neon wall of illumination across the harbour. But this time I was unmoved. Courting couples were strolling hand-in-hand along the promenade, where crafty hawkers offered red roses and only served to reinforce my loneliness. I leaned on the railing, turning my back on the procession of young lovers and camera-wielding tourists. Gentle currents lapped at the quayside below as a ferry and then a police craft passed by. Ignoring the kaleidoscopic reflection further out I gazed down into the dark waters, as the wavelets reverted to ripples. Deep through the surface my stare penetrated, trying to lose touch with my world until I refocused and decided there was a better place to be.

CONTEMPTATION

As I headed for Mad Dogs – The Pub, I saw Craig trudging heavily in the opposite direction. Even with his body slouched forward to counterbalance the weight of his oversized rucksack, his head was above the crowds. I wanted to acknowledge him but there was something in his demeanour that deterred me. With vacant, red-ringed eyes, squinting to prevent tears from flowing, he appeared more forlorn than I felt, which meant inconsolable.

I felt for him. He had come to Hong Kong with similar aspirations as mine, and had also seen them dashed. It was worse for him, though, being made a cuckold of by his longstanding girlfriend, and then virtually banished. His sense of isolation was heightened by his inability to cope with the city bustle and disorientation on the streets of Hong Kong, where he repeatedly got lost. He couldn't stand his sandwich delivery job and knew his time was up. Earlier he'd confided in me that he was disillusioned with the place and worried about his relationship with Helen. She, on the other hand, had really taken to Hong Kong to the exclusion of her boyfriend, revelling in the social life, fixing up bar work and securing teaching jobs in this her first week. Their contrasting personalities and ambitions may have been reconcilable back in small-town America but here in this place of Occidental decadence and Oriental discretion you had to make your choice. One way or the other, this was no place for compromise. Craig and I had both learned that lesson too late, although the circumstances of his despair seemed to put my own experience into perspective. His loss was more tangible, more bitter, certainly more final. The thought went some way to assuaging my feelings of self-pity. But still I needed that drink.

After a couple, my thoughts turned to Helen. I wondered what she was feeling. I hoped it was shame or at least remorse. She had cast Craig aside at a time when he was unsettled and lacking confidence, which was bad enough, but worse, she had humiliated him before doing so. I had another drink, then another again, and the more I drank the more I felt like taking out my own frustrations and grievances on her (Craig clearly wasn't up to the job).

I knocked on Helen's door, which opened almost instantaneously. I hadn't planned to rush in and make any accusations in case she was belatedly upset at Craig's departure.

I need not have concerned myself. "Hey Joe!" she spurted, brightly. "Come on in."

The enthusiasm of her greeting was not reciprocated. "I've just seen Craig. He looked in a bad way."

"I know, it was awful, he was blubbing like a baby, almost made me wanna cry."

"Almost?! How sensitive of you."

She wasn't really listening. "He had to go."

"You kicked him out?"

"No, I agreed it would be better for him to go. He just doesn't fit in here. But it was his decision."

"Sounds like you didn't do much to convince him to stay. He probably just needed reassurance."

"And what if he stayed and wasted more time and money and still left, how would I feel then? I had to let him go."

It all sounded more fair-minded and reasonable than I had imagined. Which was not what I wanted to hear.

"Do you think you'll see each other again?"

"I said I'd be back at Christmas."

"Will you?'

"I don't know, Joe. That's another six months. I wanna go Korea or Japan before that."

"Meanwhile, Craig'll be waiting with his torch."

"I guess… it'd be better if he just forgot about me and found someone else, but I know he won't."

"It's called loyalty."

"My oh my, you're a romantic ol' idealistic kind of guy, aren't you." Her tone sounded more admiring than derisive. "Do I detect some bitterness in your words?"

I thought: *I'll ask the questions, you're the one who's on trial.* I said: "Where did you go with Phil the other morning when you left the club?"

"Back home here. He went to his."

"Really," I said in disbelief. "It's just that, talking to Craig the other day, he said you didn't get home till half eight. What happened to the other four hours?"

"Quite the little detective, aren't we. What did you tell Craig?"

"Don't worry, I didn't let on."

"Thanks."

"It wasn't for your sake. I was thinking of him. How did you explain your way out of it?"

"Oh, I can sweet talk my way in and out of any situation, especially where Craig's concerned. But I'm touched by your concern, I really am." This time the sarcasm in her voice was unmistakable.

"Why is it that when women are unfaithful they are so bloody unperturbed? At least we have the decency to feel guilty afterwards."

"It's because we're in control of our destiny. You take orders from your dick without thinking of the consequences until after the dirty deed is done. Naturally then the guilt sets in."

"So you planned to screw Phil, is that it?"

"Don't be a jerk. But I just had the feeling I would be sleeping with one of you guys that night. It just seemed, I don't know, fateful and symbolic somehow." I almost gasped at her candour, a reaction not lost on Helen. "You know, you're such a sweet guy. The sweetest guy I've met here actually. Your concern for Craig is just so touching. And all those questions… I do hope you don't feel bad about me, do you Joe?" Her voice had taken on a smooth, seductive quality. I didn't respond. "Fuck it, Joe, we're not property, we're not tied down, we're young and free. Celebrate it, don't deny it."

I swallowed and said, "I still think you treated Craig like shit." But the conviction was gone.

Now I was sliding from contempt to temptation. The male weakness to which she alluded was becoming all too apparent, and she knew how to exploit it. She handed me a glass of wine from a bottle that was already half empty, then gazed at me through large, wide, hazel eyes, unblinking and piercing. Her lips assumed a thin, sly half-smile. The next stage of seduction was underway and already I knew that I had no intention of resisting. I didn't like her, I certainly didn't respect her, but fuck her, I thought, I'm going to fuck her.

When it happened it was mechanical and clinical, devoid of real passion, never mind tenderness. I thrust forcefully and aggressively, but she could take it, rhythmically hitting me halfway time after time. I drove on swiftly, not wanting to prolong it and having no real wish to satisfy her. There was no foreplay, no real embrace. No sweat. Just a quick ram with minimal upper body and oral contact. But she was in heaven. Now wasn't that typical? If only I'd had that effect on Jan.

With misty eyes and a smug grin across her flushing face she mumbled, "Feel guilty now, Joe?"

I didn't, mainly due to the lack of affection, which made it more a process than a personal experience. I also felt vaguely disappointed that I had made her night.

"I would if I were you," I uttered.

"Why do you say that?"

"Well, Craig's probably not even on the plane yet, is he? And look at you."

"Hold on there, hold on. Look at me! Excuse me, you were not involved? It was you who professed to care so deeply about poor Craig. You're the fucking hypocrite, not me."

"I wasn't his girlfriend."

"You should have been. You would have made the perfect couple."

It wasn't her intention but I couldn't help chuckling and immediately the tension dissipated. She sat up, putting her arm around my shoulder. Then we kissed properly for the first time. And it was more meaningful than anything that preceded it. She was still bad, she was wicked, untrustworthy and promiscuous, but in that moment she was nonetheless appealing for it. We touched and tantalised each other for some time before tangling once more. And this time it was personal. Jan and Craig might never have existed.

We had a couple of replays in the next few days, one at home, one away, with each time actions taking priority over words. Then on my third visit, Helen suggested we go out together. Until that point, our lack of social intimacy meant we had a raw and uncomplicated relationship, unfettered by commitment, love or personal politics. Part of me wanted it to stay that way, but equally I was interested to learn more about this vibrant and almost recklessly carefree young woman.

We went to a local bar packed with mainly young Brits, a juke box belting out indie hits. Strangely, Helen seemed to feel even more at home than I did. "I love it here, man," she shouted. "This is just the coolest place, don't you think?"

I agreed, but not quite with Helen's enthusiasm.

She then strode confidently over to the corner of the bar, where sat a squat little geezer, sucking self-satisfied on a cigar. He looked pleased to see her, patting her backside before some kind of exchange took place. She gave him a peck on the cheek and then returned to me, beaming.

"You look like the cat that got the cream."

"I am, I did. Check it out, man." She held between her thumb and index finger a couple of pieces of blotting paper.

"What is it?"

"Acid. Tried it before?"

"No. Can't say I have."

"No shit! Me neither till I came here. Hope you're not like Craig, afraid of a little experimentation."

I probably had more in common with Craig than with her – not that this was the time to admit it. "I'll try if you do."

"That's my boy."

By the time it started to kick in we were well into our second drink. I hadn't noticed any effect until I surprised myself by mouthing a sentence of such garbled syntax that I burst into a fit of laughter. She soon joined me and for the next twenty minutes or so we were irrepressibly convulsed. Hilarity poured from any source: Craig, some guy's eyebrows, the merits of hamburgers versus fish and chips. Basically anything that wasn't really funny.

We learned to control the giggles and came through that phase with a renewed empathy, as if we were finally getting to know each other on another level. I was aware even at the time that our relationship was moving in a paradoxically perverse direction. It started with a fuck, continued with a kiss, progressed to a date, and was now graduating on to diffident flirting. My God, if it continued like this we would soon be having polite conversation, say goodbye with a peck on the cheek and never see each other again.

I didn't want that to happen. She seemed more beautiful and cherishable than before. Her eyes were in unerring contact with mine as we sipped our drinks. She was about an inch taller than me with her heels on, but didn't stand straight to accentuate the difference. She complimented me on my dress sense and hairstyle a couple of times, and she was tactile in her gestures, rubbing her nose against mine, playfully touching, squeezing and prodding at any opportunity. And I seemed to have discovered a weird new level of perception. I focused on her face and the delicacy of its features and the purity of her complexion with a keen clarity, a three-dimensional glow, while all else was a blur. Her voice was powerful and gentle, like an omnipotent angel's. She was adorable, and innocent of all prior charges. How could I ever have doubted her?

Then, while we discussed our Indian travels for the first time, my feelings started to mutate. It was okay as we reminisced, almost affectionately, about the hardships: competing to find who had had the worst journey (she won that, being stranded when her train halted between stations in the middle of nowhere at midnight for a 24-hour strike that had just been called); the worst food, and the worst toilets (both too subjective to call). Memories of poor hygiene, pollution and hustlers were generally ignored or reduced to minor inconveniences. We concentrated on the strength of the culture, architecture, history, value for money. We recalled the rogues without bitterness: nosey, rude individuals became harmless eccentrics, as did officious bureaucrats. Unpleasant experiences at the hands of such people were now cheerfully cited as evidence of the quirky charm of Indian life.

It is easy to reform your opinions when you're clean, well-fed, comfortable and remote. At the back of my mind was my declaration on leaving Calcutta that I wouldn't be back, and the joy and relief arriving in Hong Kong to see clean streets, modern shops, orderly traffic, people who ignore you, and all the other trappings of First World civilization. Not wanting to spoil Helen's illusions, nor our intimacy, I tried to keep these feelings to myself. She clearly had a genuine love of the place and a desire to return. How much of that enjoyment was down to Manali hash and its distorting effects I didn't know. I just wanted to flow with her, but it wasn't easy when she was spouting so effusively about how spiritually impoverished we were in the West compared with India. I was brimming with scepticism. I'd heard it all before and it seldom failed to provoke me – *Do you want to swap places? You think 900 million wouldn't?* Normally I'd relish such a debate, but something was stopping me this time. My senses were stimulated to a degree that I was being distracted by music, hearing it in a new aura with all its various sounds coming at me in distinct layers; a group of tourists sitting nearby were irritating, their shrill, upper-class tones and horsey laughter becoming unbearable; and then there was Helen with her idealistic, hippy ramblings. All this was hitting me in slow motion, enhancing the clarity of its impact, overloading my beleaguered brain and making me so edgy that I seriously worried whether I could utter a coherent sentence, particularly in view of a flashy-looking, large and overweight Indian man, decked out in a white sports jacket and denims, who was standing close enough to hear. I had already decided he was listening but was still shocked when he abruptly introduced himself, which Helen welcomingly reciprocated.

"So you liked India, eh?" he said as he flashed a toothy grin at Helen. "I'm Rajiv from Bombay."

"Loved it. So, what are you doing in Hong Kong?" she enquired.

"Oh, you know, trading."

I decided it was time to give my voice a test run. "Trading in what?"

He smiled again, in a manner suggesting he would rather I hadn't asked that. "Oh, jewellery, watches, this kind of things."

I didn't believe him and had already decided I didn't like him.

"India's just the greatest," gushed Helen. "There's nowhere in the world can match it. It's just, like, unique, man."

I could tell Helen was getting high but clearly she was having a smoother ride than I was.

"It's that, alright," I agreed sarcastically.

"And I love the people," she gushed. "They are just the warmest and friendliest in the world."

I was getting bolder. "You told me you'd only ever been to three countries before going to India, so how would you know that?"

She whispered in my ear, "Shut the fuck up," without any hint of jocularity.

"And how is it that people who have so little are so generous?"

I might have heeded her warning had she not kept dropping such juicy bait. "Because they've got nothing to lose?"

"Yes," agreed Rajiv, with a long, drawn-out vowel and pensive expression, in reply to Helen. "Indians do indeed have some special qualities based on sharing and caring in the community. I fear you in the West have lost touch with this side. Ours is indeed a much more harmonious society than your North American and European models."

Helen was nodding keenly, her face a picture of sincere solidarity. I was thinking of communal violence and the caste system, but I bit my tongue this time. I didn't feel quite up to the challenge of taking on Rajiv yet. He continued, "Also we are more open, we talk to anyone. We're always willing to make new friends."

"Sometimes a bit too willing, mate."

"I beg your pardon?"

I tried to depersonalise it. "Well." I took a deep intake. "In India you can't go anywhere without people pestering you, wanting to know where you're from, what you do... are you married? If not, why not? You can't get any peace or solitude anywhere. And on top of that, all the Western girls get endless sexual harassment."

"Joe." He placed his hand on my shoulder, while his face wore a look of affected concern, regret and even sympathy. "So you had a rough time in India, did you? Of course it's not like a holiday in the south of France, my friend. You know, when you go to the Indian subcontinent you have to open your mind and soul, as Helen did; you have to adapt to the conditions and the customs. Only then will you truly have a rich and beneficial experience. It seems to me that you weren't equipped to cope with the experience and that you suffered a chronic bout of culture shock, you poor chap. Let me buy you a drink."

I felt humiliated as the condescension rained down, but too insecure to respond, which only compounded the shame. I could remember word-for-word what he said, dwelling most uncomfortably on the terms 'my friend' and 'you poor chap'. But I couldn't formulate anything like a cogent response, and certainly not with his calm assurance. I knew if I spoke, my words would be disproportionately bitter and unconvincing, and I'd end up looking even more pathetic. If only he could have been a bit more hostile I think I might have coped. You see, at that moment I despised Rajiv, not for what he said but for what he made me feel. I was powerless and paranoid, and while I bore an irrational hatred for him, he felt only pity toward me.

I refused his offer of a drink and tried to let the argument lie; after all, my grudge was against him, not his country. But he wasn't so prepared to let the East v West morality conflict drop.

"I hope you don't mind me saying this, Helen, but it seems to me that in America the people are only interested in money. Nothing else matters. Where is the spiritual enlightenment, the self-improvement, the charitable ideals? All lost on the road to economic prosperity, I fear."

I don't know if I really expected Helen to raise a spirited defence in honour of her maligned homeland, but I still found myself surprised to witness her nodding, with a grim, rueful frown, and then: "Yes, materialism is America's God now."

I've lost count of how many times I've heard gutless English sell-outs denigrate their country to foreigners, but it's unusual to come across a spirited American in the same vein. Usually they are more protective of their nation's reputation, often indignantly so. Far be it for me to defend American values, but I still couldn't help feeling he had gone too far again. I would nail him this time.

"What are you doing here if it's not for money?"

He looked at me for some moments before speaking, with a coldness in his eyes previously absent that told me I had at last touched a nerve. "You have to understand, Joe, I come from a poor country. I have to find a way to make a living. If I don't, my family won't eat and I won't eat."

I pointed at his fat belly and laughed disparagingly. "You're in no danger of starving, *my friend*." (I was pleased with that).

"Oh," he chuckled self-consciously. "It's just my genes, you know."

"It's got nothing to do with your trousers!" I burst into giggles at the perceived brilliance of my wit, while Helen and Rajiv made mutual signals of resigned disapproval, as if to say, 'what are we doing with this prick?'

It is not easy to maintain mirth in such an atmosphere, and as my laughter waned I had the terrible feeling I was going to lose face if I wasn't careful. I wanted to continue throwing insults but he was thick-skinned and composed, while my insecurity was mounting again with the thought that they were ganging up on me. Although I couldn't stand another second in Rajiv's company I hadn't quite given up on Helen. Nothing would have given me more pleasure than striding out of the door with Helen at my side and Rajiv left in our wake.

It was a long shot. "Shall we go now, Helen?"

Rajiv answered, "No, no, please stay here as my guest."

"I wasn't asking you," I said sourly.

"My God, you're a rude little shit sometimes," Helen said.

"Are you coming or not?"

"What do you think?"

I needed to escape from the scene, but I wasn't going to skulk away with my tail between my legs, that much I had already decided.

"Alright, alright, you think I want to stay here listening to your fucking phoney, sentimental Eastern philoph... philo... philophosising? You can stick it up your arses, you precious pair of... huh... huh… hypocrites."

I felt spent, the exit was beckoning. I couldn't stand another moment of this, confirmed by my mispronunciation and slurring of the words. As I walked off, I heard Helen's voice strike me again. "My God, just when you think you know someone."

I turned around smartly. "Think on, then… think on… and… fuck off!" The expletive was uttered almost for my own benefit and I don't even know if it was audible to them, but as I trundled off with addled sensibility, I was satisfied that I had landed a fitting response. What's more, I had got the final word. That mattered. Losing Helen didn't. She could indeed 'think on' and 'fuck off' with Rajiv for all I cared.

SANDWICHES

"What does a girl have to do to get a fella in this place? I haven't had a shag for months."

I looked around. The speaker's appearance was hardly appealing, but nor was it as unattractive as the voice behind it (loud, unashamed and Australian).

You might stand a chance if you kept your mouth shut, I didn't say.

Another conversation was going on on my side of the room, in which Dave was complaining that he couldn't find any condoms that fit.

"Okay, Dave, so you've got a big cock, congratulations," said a pimply girl.

"Wahey! We're all gonna be down Dave's house tonight, aren't we girls?" said Michelle, the manageress.

Dave beamed and quietly went back to chopping cucumbers.

"I don't bovver wi' those poxy fings if I can 'elp it," chimed a cockney from the kitchen.

"Don't worry, no one'd have yer," said the Australian.

"You would, by the sound of it," countered Dave.

"Sex wi' johnnies is like swimmin' wiv a raincoat on," the cockney continued, seemingly unaware of the two prior exchanges.

"Yeah, right," said Michelle dismissively. "How often do you go swimming with or without a raincoat? Not very often, I bet."

"I wouldn't be without them," said a tall and fey, freckly Canadian. "I mean, you don't want all that nasty lady juice over your dick, do you?"

There were a few chuckles, which is something I rarely heard in this place. The banter was always hard-edged and scathing, only occasionally laced with humour. I found the atmosphere stifling, such was the general lack of goodwill. When I did speak I generally found myself ignored or discouraged. I soon realised that to gain any kind of respect or acceptance here you had to be a bit of a bastard, for these were the meanest, street-wisest, most grudge-bearing bunch of individuals I'd met since leaving English shores. But I couldn't quite match their cynicism, so usually I let them get on with it, while the conversation moved on, referencing 'Chinky bastards', inter-racial shagging, and 'sniffing coke', none of which I felt qualified to comment on.

There was a group of ten – half of whom were English – making sandwiches and then selling them on their own rounds. The business was quite lucrative apparently, and therefore competitive, with another half-dozen or more operators on the go. It was essential for me to leave on time to be on the 21st floor of the Jaymark Centre before the Hong Kong & Kowloon Sandwich Co. got there and cleaned up. I waited impatiently for someone to finish making a cream cheese and avocado bagel, which was a special order. Ten minutes late, I seethed gently, cursing them under my breath for talking instead of working. At last my basket was full and I was out of the door, making a point of not thanking anyone or saying goodbye. I knew it was a futile gesture, but it was the nearest to protest I could muster.

As I walked down the stairs with my heavy load I was called back by Gerard, a busy-body with a posh accent and a stiff manner. He had nothing in common with the others but was equally objectionable. He didn't do a round himself, his duties instead concerning accounts and logistics, as he put it.

"What is it?" I called back. He told me that he wanted me to come back upstairs so he could count all my items, implying that I might eat or pocket any potential sales. "Bugger off, I'm already late!" That was more like it. Maybe I was starting to fit in after all.

Down at the taxi rank there was a shapely red-head from our firm struggling to get a large plastic box and trolley on to the back seat of a taxi. The driver was not having it, though, insisting, not unreasonably, that it should go in the boot for which a small extra fee would be charged. She dragged the box out in a fury, slammed the door and screamed, "Fuck you!"

I felt some shame – in the absence of any from her – and wondered what her response to a London cabbie would have been in the same situation. *What is it about this business that attracts such stressed-out low-lives?* I wondered. Sure, they (we) were in the lower half of the food chain in the Hong Kong hierarchy, and young Brits in Hong Kong had even been dubbed 'latter-day coolies' by one of the British broadsheets. But the analogy was erroneous, as almost everyone on the sandwich round was only using it as a stepping stone. Only a month or two was the average span, and one company gave bonuses to workers that lasted more than three. So why all this chip-on-the-shoulder bitterness? There was no excuse or explanation I could find.

When I entered the large open-plan offices of a stockbroker's firm, the competition, in the shape of a Danish girl called Mette, was already doing the business. She was surrounded by men, so I busied myself among the female staff. There was no real rivalry between Mette and me – we flirted with each other as much as with the customers – and I had a better relationship with her than with anyone in my own firm. She didn't even need the work, as she made a tidy packet working as a nightclub hostess chatting up mainly Japanese businessmen. But she seemed to enjoy the ego boost of having the office lads – sometimes literally – eating out of her hand. She told me she wasn't considered particularly good-looking in Denmark so she wasn't used to the attention. "It must be the blonde hair and big tits," she suggested with a giggle.

"That's good-looking where I come from," I said, and she giggled some more.

My regular customers were mostly established British and American expats who, in contrast to the negativity of my sandwich-making colleagues, were generally approachable and welcoming. Amongst them I detected a classless attitude and a sense of camaraderie and togetherness, the shared experiences and aspirations of compatriots in a far-off land. Occasionally I got the impression that their warmth towards me stemmed from sympathy, but as long as it translated into sales I hardly cared.

One of my favourite calls was at a British advertising agency, where on a good day – provided I got there before Mette – I could sell about ten sandwiches. With my cut at five Hong Kong dollars a sandwich this was a fair deal. But it wasn't only for the rich pickings that I enjoyed being there. The presence of a group of female researchers and secretaries, who chatted and flirted freely, had something more to do with it. I suppose they gave me the same feeling that the boys gave Mette. Girls back home didn't behave like this, but then the gender demographic was different here. Not that expat females outnumbered expat males – far from it – but that a large proportion of Western men were, as Phil put it, 'drinking from the local well'. And after my experiences with Jan and Helen, as well as the girls in the sandwich firm, it was a prospect to which I was increasingly drawn.

The Asian branch of an international newspaper seemed to have potential in this field, with several glamorous, westernised

Chinese and Indian office girls in attendance. But they were mostly too polite and reticent, and not regular customers. The journalists could usually be relied on to buy, although among them were a few too many egos. When one of these stuck-up hacks ignored my cheery greetings I usually comforted myself with the thought that they – Hong Kong's expat journalists – had been nicknamed FILTH (Failed In London, Try Hong Kong). It may be crude but it seemed apt enough, if a quick perusal of the morning papers, or listening to the television news, was anything to go by. Still, it raised the question, if they were FILTH, what the hell were we?

This was a question that nagged at me the longer I was on the job. Hauling baskets all over Central and Causeway Bay may have been a good way to network, earn pocket money, get fed, stay fit, maintain your suntan, improve your navigational skills and knowledge of the city, but it came at a price. Saturated in an all-over, never-evaporating sweat, you would wend your way through steaming, crowded, polluted streets between the cool, sterile civility of glass towers occupied by fragrant secretaries and smart executives who were all clean-cut, well turned-out, bright and rich: everything in fact we were not. The contrast doesn't bother you at first, as you are only concerned with finding your way, honing your sales technique, or counting your money. But around the time the job's novelty begins to fade, you start to feel inadequate in comparison. It's nothing they say or do: they are all too well-mannered for that. It's just a creeping uneasiness at the disparity between success and failure, and the realisation of which side you are on. The symptoms hit home after six to eight weeks and then there is only one remedy.

PART TWO

English Teacher Exploits

LANDING THE JOB was easier than anticipated: five-minute interview, virtually no questions, start tomorrow. The money wasn't much better than on the sandwiches but I didn't care. It was a real job, with prospects of betterment, something approaching a career and respectability.

My new employer called itself The Kowloon English Club (the 'Club' bit appealed to me, suggesting something of informality, fun and amateurism). I'd heard about the job from Stuart, an austere Yorkshireman, whom I met by chance one day at the hostel. He sought to convince me it would be anything but fun by attempting to dissuade me from taking up the position.

"Now let's get this straight," I said. "You get paid for sitting on your arse having cosy conversations with friendly young locals?"

"There's nothing cosy about this place, let me tell you, and who said anything about friendly? If you think it's gonna be a picnic you're heading for a rude awakening, pal. When you've worked here as long as I have, you'll understand it."

I wasn't convinced. I wondered if he had ever done a proper day's work. Put him on a noisy production line or doing roadworks or even a spell of unemployment and then see where he would rather be. And he was taking home over HK$10,000 a month to ease the 'trauma' of the job.

Arriving on my first day I didn't have any second thoughts, but pangs of anxiety and self-doubt were starting to manifest. I was stepping into the unknown. What would the students be like? What would I teach? How would I cope? I could have done with some words or gestures of encouragement, but the first person I saw was Stuart. "Starting today," I told him cheerily.

"Is that right? Yer fuckin' crazy," he uttered abjectly, before climbing the stairs, head bowed, with all the vigour and alacrity of a condemned man.

Once again I was amazed at the defeatist aura that Stuart exuded, especially in his last week before heading off to Malaysia to take up a scuba diving course.

I approached the proprietor, Maxine, hoping that she at least might provide me with some advice and assurance, but got precious little of either. She was a vaguely attractive woman with a pale complexion, high cheekbones and narrow eyes: features more suggestive of a Korean or Northern Chinese than Cantonese (which she was). When she spoke it was in fluent English, but her manner was disconcertingly offhand, as if I wasn't worthy of her time. All I got was a couple of simple exercise sheets with pictures, phrases and dialogue, and the somewhat ironic advice to "be polite".

I was shown to my classroom, which was actually more like a closet, only big enough for six or seven students, with no window, no pictures, no furniture, no bookshelves, only a whiteboard and pen. I felt quite at home – it had much in common with my own hovel – and was relieved it was so small, meaning I wouldn't be overwhelmed by students on my first day.

I sat down on a bench that was built into the four walls, and waited. Five minutes, ten, fifteen, still nobody came in. A few students looked in from time to time, decided what they saw wasn't for them and scuttled elsewhere. All ten classrooms were open to the corridor, which gave the students the freedom to come and go as they chose, without interruption. They could move between classes or stick with their favourite teacher. I got up and looked down the corridor. It didn't surprise me to see Stuart's class was as empty as mine. At least I had the excuse that nobody knew me, while he'd had nine months to acquaint himself.

I couldn't see into the class beside mine but it sounded like a full house. The teacher's voice was pounding out phrases with the tonal consistency of a metronome, which his students repeated in chorus. This was maintained for nearly an hour, making me wonder if it was just a recording. Surely this wasn't what teaching was about. Even with my limited experience I could tell that none of these students was learning how to think in English or interact in anything like a real situation. And yet they seemed to be flocking to this teacher and his methods, so what did I know? It concerned me because my students were likely to be of a similar elementary level, and if they weren't up to simple conversation what else could I do?

Despite these apprehensions, my first day and indeed week went surprisingly well. Usually I had only four or five in my little room for the evening sessions, and although most of the students were of limited ability, they were inquisitive and lively enough to maintain some sort of conversation. One girl even had the confidence to ask me out. I deferred, without turning her down flat, trying but failing to avoid hurting her feelings. She was an immature eighteen, but could have passed for a twelve-year-old, and she wore creepy emerald contact lenses.

At the time I found teaching the housewives in my morning session a far more rewarding proposition. These were real women, who knew about the birds and bees, and weren't afraid to talk about them. There were few egos or negative influences in the class, and all were confident enough to speak without fear of making mistakes despite the relatively poor standard of their English. All I had to do was introduce a topic or situation and let them get on with it.

It was a different story when I started a new evening class. After one week in the closet I was transferred to the big classroom next door – the 'metronome', a diminutive (metro gnome, perhaps?) American called Robert having gone away. It was the biggest challenge to my teaching credentials so far. Every evening there were at least ten students already in attendance on my arrival. I was straight in at the deep end, and from then on it was a struggle to keep afloat. The students, used to another style, were wary and suspicious of this newcomer and his methods. I didn't meet any hostility but there was mild resistance to anything that required a little spontaneity, initiative or exercise of the grey matter. I felt frustrated that role-plays and exercises that had been a success with the housewives in the morning would fall flat with this group. I knew that most of them wanted nothing more than to read dialogue sheets or chant mantras all lesson, so I put my creative plans on hold and gave way.

Despite their reticence I grew to like almost everyone in the class. They may not have been easy to teach but they were generally cheerful and courteous. I also liked the mix of ages, genders, classes and professions, united only by their desire to speak English. One person in particular, though, stood out, literally and otherwise.

JOSIE was her name. A tall, elegant young woman from Shanghai, she had a soft round face, the smoothest, purest white skin, rosy cheeks and dimples. Her thick, raven hair was centre-parted and tied back in the classic Chinese style. She was simply striking. But it wasn't only her looks that gained my admiring attention. She had a cheeky, playful manner that was equally alluring, and it took some will to stop myself flirting with her. When my resistance (and professionalism) failed, her response was enigmatic. I was hoping that the attraction was mutual, but she always kept enough in reserve to keep me guessing.

Her knowledge of English was limited but her pronunciation was something to behold. I found it beguiling to listen to her bizarre combination of flawed sentence structure and pure vowels. Her potential was obviously great, such was her ease of enunciation, in contrast to the laboured Cantonese tongues. I asked if she had been taught by a British teacher before – sometimes she almost sounded like an upper-class Englishwoman – but she said I was the first native English speaker she had ever met, and she hadn't even had any English lessons before. This underlined her ability further. Here was a young woman to whom I would have gladly given free one-to-one-tuition. I was enchanted by her mellifluous voice and natural beauty, and found myself thinking about her more than was right or proper. I had to remind myself that I was a teacher – albeit a scarcely qualified teacher at a cut-price learning centre – and of the responsibility that entailed. I became conscious of trying to avoid giving Josie too much attention, mindful that I might irritate the other students, particularly female. Sometimes, though, it was impossible not to be drawn to her, not least because I knew she would participate, which was more than could be said for the majority of her counterparts. She came almost every night and was my saviour on more than one occasion when I was struggling to elicit any response. On one such occasion I announced, innocently enough, "I like Josie." There were gasps from my audience, who had apparently interpreted it as 'love' or at least 'fancy', which certainly hadn't been my intention, even if it was true.

"But she tall dan you," shouted one of my bolder students.

"No, no, you don't understand," I protested. "When I said 'like' I didn't mean…"

I was cut short. They weren't listening anyway. "Stand up, stand up," Josie was urged.

To my surprise, she didn't need much persuasion. She strode confidently up to the front of the class to face me and then measured with her hand horizontally from the top of her head over mine. I looked down to check her heels but was dismayed to see they were as flat as mine. "You win, you win," I conceded.

The wag still wasn't satisfied, though. "She stwong dan you, also."

I could see Josie nodding, with that mischievous grin across her face, while everyone else was in raptures of laughter. I decided to play the game. "I like strong women."

My tormentor-in-waiting hit back in a flash. "But stwong woman don' like weak man."

The place erupted again. I hit back with what I thought was an effective riposte – "That rules you out then!" – but nobody was listening or understood. Most were still laughing at my expense, and all I could do was pretend it didn't bother me.

I was learning more of the ways of the Cantonese. In future I would be wary of providing them with such opportunities for putting me down. Perhaps it was just their way of getting back at me for favouring Josie, and her way of showing that my interest in her was not reciprocated. Either way, at the end of the month I was relieved to be transferred again to make way for the return of the 'metro-gnome'. No doubt the feeling was mutual as far as the students were concerned. They could revert to rote learning once more, and I could hopefully build up a more receptive and compatible audience. Few if any of the old class members followed me, although I did still occasionally receive visits from Josie. She would sit quiet and subdued, lacking all the old impudence. There was a wistful air about her, but I never got the chance to relate to her and find out what was on her mind. She came too seldom and left too early, before she stopped coming altogether. The last time I saw her I could tell she was tense and unsettled, wanting to say something (goodbye?) but instead slipped away with a diffident glance and a rueful smile.

That first month had been more of a lesson for me than it had for my students, and the one thing I had learned above all others was to tread carefully around the female students. Compared with their Western counterparts they seemed more immature and less worldly, although nonetheless endearing for it. But in a place where casual sex is not the done thing and boyfriends are chosen with as much care as husbands in less conservative lands, I realised that few of them would welcome any lurid topics or flirtatious attention. The ones that might have been the object of my attention could relax, and those that weren't need not have felt resentful to those that were. It wasn't my intention, but as a result, my class was soon full of young women who seemed to appreciate my approach. They compared me favourably with certain other teachers who weren't smart enough or sensitive enough to recognise that single women in Hong Kong were not comfortable discussing or listening to topics such as contraception or oral sex. Most students lacked the knowledge to participate even if they had wanted to. *Hum sup lo* (dirty old man), they called the sleazy teachers, who were largely complacent, middle-aged, overweight and unkempt. I, on the other hand, was clean-cut, slim, young, pretending to be respectable and getting away with it.

'THE INNOCENTS' was a tag I gave to an agreeable but demure group of young women who formed the mainstay of my new class. With regular attendance their early inhibitions were being shed as they came to know and trust me, occasionally even emboldened to flattery. I was beginning to enjoy the comments – 'you are nice teacher', 'you are handsome' – and the attention. With a dozen or so attractive Oriental girls in eager attendance every night, listening attentively and looking on fondly, how could I not? But if I was wanted I was also wanting. Two months into my new career, however, the opportunity still hadn't presented itself. I may have quietly wished to exploit my position of respect and responsibility but equally I was aware of the potential of losing it all. Many other male teachers had dated students and most who hadn't had attempted to. But they were brazen and shameless, while I was still maintaining a modest front. I refused to embarrass anyone in public, including myself. All I needed was a bit of time and space with one of my favourites, which in such a busy class was proving a rare luxury.

Meeting local girls in the bars and clubs would have been preferable, but it wasn't the way in Hong Kong. Most of my students never went clubbing and some had never even set foot in a pub. So I waited and bided, hoping for a signal or a moment. But I suspect there was an unspoken code between the 'Innocents' regarding teacher-student relations. To cross that line would be a step too far and an automatic exclusion from the group. They had too much discipline and self-respect, and nobody would dare risk disloyalty or loss of face. Until, that is, the arrival of a woman who went by the name of Zero.

ZERO had nothing in common with her classmates. They were mostly hesitant and timid, conservative in dress, style and manner. She was loud and flamboyant, an eccentric, extroverted, sometimes recalcitrant student with a sleazy, rebellious look that belied her years and a gravelly, tobacco-tinged voice that didn't. An impressive command of English to go with that domineering attitude meant she demanded to be heard and noticed. She may have been nearer to mutton than lamb but she had the dress sense of a rebellious teenager: black DMs, leather mini-skirt, dyed hair and mascara. To the other girls, the image and presence of this newcomer in their domain was about as welcome as a whore to a nunnery. But, as is typical of the arrogant, she was oblivious to the contempt in which she was increasingly being held.

She maintained her pariah status in class by continually answering my questions before the others had had the chance to register their meaning, or by interrupting and even correcting them. Their confidence was so undermined that few had the courage to speak up in her presence. Sometimes she wasn't so vocal, but the effect was hardly less disturbing (at least as far as I was concerned). When she was bored or tired and the lesson wasn't proceeding in a style to her liking she would simply stare morosely at the floor for several minutes at a time. Her silence was oppressive and judgemental, and always seemed to come at a time when an interjection would actually have been welcome. Instead she would more likely just look up again during an awkward pause, with that penetrating glare.

As a rookie teacher with limited training I wasn't totally equipped for the job. Four-hour sessions were sometimes stimulating, but on a diminishing tank of energy and inspiration, more often draining. Minutes dragged, hours blurred. I learned to ignore my watch and I learned to listen and concentrate. More than that, I learned to act. I was passing myself off as a teacher, pretending to be in control, putting on a show of approachable authority and, as far as I could tell, pulling it off, although on occasions I was suffering internal turmoil, grasping for topic links, or writing slowly on the board with my back to the class to disguise a mental blockage that thankfully few students gave any sign of recognising.

Zero, being no awe-struck teenager hanging onto my every word, was the exception of course. She alone could see me for what I was. With her overpowering persona, patently superior English and disruptive classroom influence, she didn't belong. I wanted to tell her to go upstairs to the conversational group where she could compete with the other egos, but I never found the necessary courage or tact to do so. She was the one in charge, a black sheep maverick challenging me and my teaching methods. And, though

I was loath to admit it, I was starting to find her interesting. Not so interesting that I was prepared to put her interests above those of my 'Innocents', however.

One evening Zero was being disruptive even by her standards. I didn't look at her and pointedly ignored her interjections. A tension was developing between us and she became spookily silent, staring intensely, unblinking, gazing through me from her seat of prominence at the centre of the group. And when our eyes inevitably met it was an uncomfortable experience. After that I decided to try to contain rather than confront her. She was too thick-skinned to be influenced, though, and the discomfort I felt in her presence was not in any way mutual. But my new tolerant approach only led to her calling me 'cute' and 'sweet' in a way that smacked of seduction and condescension. She went further whenever I mentioned beer or Indian food – both of which she knew I had a typically British respect for – and she would invite me to 'a nice bar I know' or to the Indian Club. She was far from the delicate, feminine Oriental ideal, with her unsubtle manner, slightly pock-marked complexion and that coarse voice to go with her overbearing, supercilious manner. I found it impossible to be at ease in her company, and yet back in my hovel alone I would find myself thinking and fantasising over her. The contradictions were immense and made me wonder about the juxtapositions of lust and repulsion. She was ten or fifteen years older than me – pushing forty – which in no way diminished the attraction. She was experienced, she was rough, and she was ready. I felt the stirrings of temptation quite strongly but only when I was away from her, safely in my own space. As soon as I found myself back in the classroom in her company all the resolve and attraction seemed to vanish.

Partly, no doubt, this was because I had the 'Innocents' to consider. They would not have been impressed, perhaps even regarding it as a betrayal, had I arranged a date with Zero in front of them. And ultimately their wishes and contentment were more important to me than the feelings I had towards Zero. Such high-mindedness would have been superfluous had she just had the good sense to collar me after the class or any time I was alone. Then it would have been harder to resist even if I had wanted to. I was expecting it to happen, anticipating even, but such was her conceit I believe she had no notion of the dilemma she was causing. She never seemed discouraged by my lack of response to her propositions, and continued to tease me ("I think you're shy. Is that right?"). But after a month or two of being chilled by my cold shoulder she finally wearied and her attendance faded. I heard that she tried to latch on to another new teacher but when that didn't work out she was not seen again.

At the time, despite the prospect of another loveless, sexless month, I was mostly relieved to be rid of her. And fortunately I didn't have too long to dwell on it before someone sweeter and more personable came along.

WENDY wasn't in the gang of 'Innocents' but nor was she aloof from her classmates as Zero was. She impressed me immediately with her unusually open, cheerful disposition. This was in welcome contrast to the general passivity of her classmates, charming though they were. They rarely asked questions or showed much initiative, whereas Wendy was full of inquisitiveness and enterprise. She brought spice and vitality where it was missing, plus she was outgoing and cheerful, with a refreshing self-deprecating sense of humour.

Her attitude meant I was able to reintroduce role-plays, which had often been a flop with my more reluctant students. Wendy was not only willing to play any part but relished it, despite her woeful use of conjugation and pronunciation. This lack of ability meant her extroverted nature was happily tolerated by the 'Innocents'. They would have hated her – or at least resented her – had her English been up to the standard of Zero's. Instead she became a positive influence, emboldening them to speak up, with the understanding that a lack of competence need not deter communication. She quickly became my favourite student, so much so I would almost have paid her to attend. When she was absent I missed her because she brought ideas, introduced topics and suggested situations for the role-plays. One such occasion would prove a stepping stone to reality.

Wendy had suggested something about arranging dates. "Do you have a boyfriend?" I asked. (I still hadn't cottoned on to the fact that when Hong Kong people talk about dates they were referring to any inter-personal arrangement).

"No, why you ask dis fing? Of course not. Why I come here ev'y night if I have boyfen?"

"You want to find a boyfriend, then?" (I wouldn't have asked the other sensitive flowers anything so personal, but there were few limits where Wendy was concerned).

"Yes, yes," she boomed. "You have nice fen?"

"Yes, I'll introduce you."

Thus commenced the role play:

Me: Hi Wendy. You look nice today.

Wendy: (big, hearty, laugh) Oh, fank you, Joe. Me too.

M: You too, you mean.

W: You too?... Oh, yes.

M: By the way, I'm not Joe. I'm Joe's friend, remember?

W: But you nook nike Joe.

M: Look like.

W: Nook nike.

M: Oh never mind. Are you doing anything this weekend?

W: I go my grandmother house.

M: Oh, that's a pity...

W: Why you want to know?

M: I was wondering if you'd like to go to the beach on Sunday.

W: Beach on Sunday? Wiv who?

M: Me.

W: Ony you?

M: Yes, only me.

W: Er... er... I remember I not go to grandmother this weekend. It nex' weekend. Where... where...? (Classroom erupts with laughter)

M: Where shall we meet?

W: Yes, where shall we meet?

M: At Central bus station.

W: (With great eagerness) What time, what time?

M: Is half past ten okay?

W: Any time, any time!

It was flowing so easily that I couldn't help advancing it a step further: On the date, at the beach.

Me: It's hot today, isn't it?

Wendy: Yes, it thirty two degree, I fink.

M: Do you want to go swimming?

W: Yes, later.

M: You must be hot with your shirt on. Why don't you take it off? (Nervous murmurs from the audience – Have I gone too far this time?)

W: Oh, good idea. (Pretends to undress)

M: You have a sexy body!

W: (hysterical laughter) Yes, I know. Many men say dis fing.

M: Would you like me to put some sun lotion on your shoulders?

W: Oh, yes please.

M: (pretending to rub it on) How does that feel?

W: Very good. You have... er... soft touch. Now I put on you. (She actually rubs her hands over my shoulders, arms and back) How is it feel?

M: Perfect. You have a good touch.

W: Thank you, you nike Chinese massage?

At this point I thought it prudent to progress it towards the end of the date...

M: Would you like to go to the park?

W: Yes, why?

M: So we can be alone together. Somewhere quiet.

W: What you want to do?... You want kiss?

M: Er... Why not!

(Uproar in the class, but Wendy remained composed, puckering her plump, scarlet lips in readiness).

M: How was it for you?

W: What?

M: The kiss. How was it?

W: I don' know, I still waiting! (Great, infectious laughter)... Okay, I know I mus' preten'... The kiss was very better!

M: You mean, very good.

W: No, better dan good!

M: Oh, thank you. Would you like to come to my house for a coffee?

W: Okay, fanks.

….At home…

M: Do you take sugar?

W: No fanks.

M: What would you like for breakfast tomorrow?

W: Bekfas?… Bekfas?… Why you ask..? Oh, you *hum sup lo!*

I suppose I had let my professionalism slip, along with my non-flirtation policy, but as a result of the students' encouragement I had got carried away. It didn't matter. They didn't take Wendy seriously despite all these blatant, sexually-charged signals that Wendy and I were sending out to each other. It had a lot to do with her image. Wendy was unpretentious, down-to-earth, and to the female eye, I suppose, unprepossessing. On this day she was wearing thick-rimmed black glasses, suede pixie boots with a long flowery skirt and a red beret, which is about as near as you can get to original dress sense in this part of the world. She didn't conform to the standard Hong Kong style of luxury brands or the irritating, cutie kitsch of Hello Kitty, Snoopy and Disney. For that alone she had earned my respect. But I suspect as far as the other girls were concerned, she was unsophisticated and uneducated and not to be reckoned with. If they assumed that I was of the same opinion they were mistaken.

In fact my encounter with Wendy, despite starting as a frivolous tease, was loaded with potential. It wasn't as much of an act as everyone supposed and it was surely mutual. There was an undeniable energy between us, intensifying with each candid expression and knowing glance. All I hoped was that we would get the opportunity to build on it. But on the subsequent few days I didn't take much notice of Wendy, wary as I was of giving her so much attention that the class wise up to my intentions. However, when I found her waiting alone in my classroom on Saturday afternoon I knew the chance was nigh. For some reason I never got many students on Saturday morning, which suited me, and none of the weekday faces had ever shown up. Word hadn't got around and I certainly hadn't publicised it, but Wendy had obviously gone to the trouble of finding out my schedule. Seeing her broad smile on my arrival was a real boost. It was like meeting a friend more than a student (or prospective lover).

As a rule, I didn't like having to face a solitary student – particularly one of limited ability – at the start of a session, as I would often sap mental energy before the bulk of the class turned up. Some would eye me suspiciously, especially new members; often they couldn't understand, or wouldn't talk, through shyness or incompetence; sometimes they were unfriendly or even hostile. Only occasionally did someone like Wendy come along, and it was like oxygen.

As with Jan, Wendy had impressed me with her personality before her looks. She was the sort of girl to whom I wouldn't have given a second glance had I seen her on a train. But after getting to know her it didn't take long to realise that I was being drawn. Ordinarily, plotting to ask a girl out, while in a sober state, would induce some symptoms of tension. Yet face-to-face with her, I could hardly have felt more composed or natural. It was all down to Wendy's easygoing persona, which made it virtually impossible to feel awkward in her presence. Her simplicity and open charm were entirely disarming. Perhaps I had not learned my lesson from Jan, for I had an almost fatalistic sense that we were about to be together. I had hardly considered the possibility of rejection, the spectre that usually haunts insecure men. Confident or conceited, I felt sure she would not turn me down.

We chatted idly for a few moments about our families and her job, but I was anxious to get to the point before anyone else arrived. "What are you up to tonight?" I asked.

"Up to... up to? ...What is 'up to?'"

"Doing... what are you doing tonight?"

"I go out with Kenneth."

"Oh, I see (confidence diminishing), who's Kenneth?"

"You know Kenneth, he your student."

"The old boy, you mean?"

She laughed. "Yes, the old boy, he come here later."

"I didn't know you were friends with Kenneth. I've never seen you together in my class before."

"We meet last year in other class. Sometime he phone to me."

"Where are you going tonight then?"

"I don' know. We go nice restaurant, I fink. Hey, Joe, you want come?"

"No, I don't think so."

"Why?"

"Kenneth invited you, not me."

"He don't mind, he don't mind. You know Kenneth is gentleman."

"Gentlemen are still men."

"What you mean?"

"Oh, nothing."

Maybe it was nothing. Kenneth was about twenty-five years

older than Wendy, I reckoned, and married as far as I could recall. Also friendships between the sexes are quite common in Hong Kong and usually innocent enough. But he was a dapper and well-groomed so-and-so, exuding smooth charm from every pore and fitting the profile of a Lady's Man to a tee. I was just contemplating a response to this unwelcome development, when Wendy's mobile went off.

Interspersed between her gabbing Cantonese dialect, I heard my name mentioned two or three times. "That was Kenneth," she announced, after hanging up. "He say you come tonight. He will ask a girl come too, name is Angela. She beautiful."

This seemed to confirm my suspicions of Kenneth's intent. But never mind. We met him later that evening at a third-floor Chinese restaurant in the neighbouring district of Jordan. He looked as urbane as ever, if not more so, suited out, receding black hairline slicked back; and he seemed genuinely pleased to see me, which was something of a relief.

With him was Angela, an elegant, fragile feather of a girl, with delicate features, impossibly long thin arms, and ivory complexion. She was one of those powdered, snow-white waifs that seem to abound in this part of the world, and whose appearance just doesn't equate with the tropical climes and the wealthy, gastronomically-renowned city that spawned them. Kenneth must have reasoned that bringing along this doll-like vision of femininity would distract me from Wendy. She was a young upwardly-mobile career girl, with the requisite uniform of Prada bag, Gucci shoes, Rolex watch: all the symbols of high-class mediocrity. Her English was good and she knew it, but she spoke in a dull monotone, talking a lot but saying little. Clearly, as is often the case with attractive people, someone who prioritised physical appearance over personality. All evening she sat sipping jasmine tea, only occasionally and fussily picking food off the shared plates. Meanwhile, across the table was Wendy, not pale and preened or delicate and restrained, but tucking unceremoniously into a plate of chickens' feet and a bowl of snails with her fingers, then laughing boisterously as she made a mess. No contest.

Kenneth, observing that I was failing to feed myself with the zeal of Wendy, politely told me what each dish consisted of (such as jellyfish, shark-fin soup and abalone). He was indeed a gentleman, treating me like an honoured guest throughout the evening. I remained unimpressed by the food, however, which was at worst gross, at best bland, and quite unlike anything I had seen in Chinese restaurants back home (conversely, the more expensive and exclusive the menu items in a Chinese restaurant, the more unpalatable they tend to be to Western tastes).

After dinner we wandered over to the Holiday Inn bar, where a cabaret was playing to a largely uninterested audience. There was an awkwardness about our little foursome that wasn't apparent earlier with the distraction of food. Angela and I weren't hitting it off, while Kenneth's attempts to relate to Wendy were scuppered by her insistence on answering him in English. His English may have been better than hers, but he wasn't as confident using it. What's more, he must have been frustrated that her tactic was ruining his chances of getting through to her. I appreciated that she was doing it out of deference to me, rather than to spite Kenneth – and she had no inkling of his irritation – but I could feel his unease, no doubt exacerbated by the realisation of chemistry between Wendy and me. When Kenneth suggested we all leave after just one drink it was no real surprise.

"But the night is young," I protested. I was enjoying the

ambience and comfort of the place, albeit not the entire company, and the first drink had merely whetted my palate. Then there was the matter of Wendy. "Who wants another drink?"

"Yes please," exclaimed Wendy.

As Kenneth rose he shot in my direction a look of genuine hurt and resentment. It was only brief and surely unintended, but in that moment his motivations were laid bare. Angela had little choice but to join him. My guilt impelled me to persuade them to stay, but they made their excuses and left. I sat back, with a sigh. I felt some pity for Kenneth, but I wasn't going to let it spoil my night. He had a nice home and wife no doubt awaiting him, while all I had was a small, empty, airless room.

Alone with Wendy at last, the rest of the evening was mellow and warm, the only contention between us being Wendy's continued insistence that Kenneth's interest in her was nothing more than platonic. I told her she was naïve; she told me I was dumb. It didn't matter. We had a couple more drinks, which brought on a radiant flush and increased giggliness in Wendy. Then I walked her to the bus stop. "What are you doing tomorrow?" I asked.

"Going to the beach," she replied, in a flash.

"Who with?"

"You tell me!"

FIRST DATE or not, she was over half an hour late and my impatience was giving way to concern that I was about to be stood up. Five more minutes had passed when I heard my name being called and looked up to see Wendy bounding towards me with all the grace of a baby elephant. Her face was reddened and there was more than a touch of desperate relief about her as she awkwardly embraced me and expressed her gratitude for waiting, just when I was thinking she was playing it cool by being fashionably late. I should have known she was too genuine an article for that. It wasn't her style. Instead she was full of apologies about how her head was hurting and she couldn't find any clean clothes available.

It showed. She was wearing a brown cord skirt – long and crumpled – and a plain, cheap T-shirt, making me wonder if her sometime Bohemian image was more by chance than design. Truth is, I felt slightly disillusioned by her unstylish arrival. I would have preferred a touch more insouciance and enigma, but the knowledge that she was at least as keen as I was enough to put my misgivings to rest.

Sitting on the top deck of the bus, it wasn't long before my musings seemed to be confirmed. "Joe, you have girlfen in Englan'?"

"No."

"In Hong Kong?'

"No, I don't."

I may not have appreciated her desperation, but once again couldn't help admiring her openness.

"So, what about you… do you have a boyfriend?"

"You know I not have boyfen. I tell you before."

"Have you had a boyfriend before?"

"Yes, we finish three years before."

"Any others?"

"No, only this one." She looked doleful at the thought.

I wanted to cheer her and was close to asking if she would like to be my girlfriend. The fact that I had come so close, so early in a relationship, to blurting something so indiscreet was telling. I would not have considered uttering anything like this since my school days, and even then it sounded puerile. Yet in this intercontinental arena, where cultural conditioning, preconceptions and semantic considerations don't count, I was liberated from the old baggage: free to say and act as I chose without the risk of cynicism, suspicion or judgement. And it was a two-way street. I had already been on the receiving end from Zero, and many of the housewives had also flattered me in a manner they wouldn't have dreamed of with a local man. Equally most Western men were a lot less guarded in their dealings with Asian females than with their countrywomen. And therein lay the attraction. It was a bit like turning the clock back to your first relationship, but without the anxiety.

Wendy, perhaps perceiving my pensiveness, asked what I thought of her.

"I like you, of course." To the English female ear this is almost damning in its faintness, so I expanded: "I like you very much."

She didn't answer but took my hand and squeezed it between hers. Moments later she was dabbing her eyes and sniffing, though I pretended not to notice. I belatedly realised I had made the same error I had with Josie, by failing to take account of the lack of Cantonese distinction between *like* and *love*. And, touching though Wendy's reaction might have been, it made me wonder what I had let myself in for. I was looking for an experience – a romantic, exotic, erotic experience – and probably nothing more. A Hong Kong girl in her mid-to-late-twenties, of limited experience, would likely have a different agenda. It was already evident that this was a very big deal for her. If only I hadn't mentioned that word I might have been able at least to keep some pretence of a casual relationship. But the 'L word' made it serious to her, particularly when uttered with such haste that it gave the impression she was the only one for me. The only mildly alleviating fact was that I wasn't Chinese, so the rules were different. I was a foreigner, an easy-come-easy-go foreigner, and she had to know it. But then she put her hand on my upper thigh and squeezed firmly, and I stopped thinking so much.

The afternoon was spent at Shek O, on the south-eastern extremity of Hong Kong Island. After a sun and sea bathe we strolled away from the crowded beach and dined at one of the open-air restaurants set back from the beach. Afterwards, through fading light, we followed a narrow, winding street that took us past shops and homes with darkened, gloomy interiors but pleasant low-level facades, whitewashed and randomly positioned: just the antidote I needed to the towering hulks of the city. Continuing, we passed an area of shacks that several hundred people call home. With some attention it could have been quaint, but instead it was pervaded by decay and malaise. Where there could have been brightly coloured roofs and window frames there was rust, and where there could have been gardens there were concrete yards blighted by tons of junk. It had the potential to be a charming fishing village but more resembled an abandoned refugee camp.

A large, top-of-the-range Mercedes, with tinted windows, glided past us to an exclusive neighbourhood nearby, where mansions with great gates and high walls sell for tens of millions in Hong Kong currency, and I wondered if there was anywhere else in the world where such conspicuous wealth and poverty could exist side by side apparently without disharmony.

We continued downhill onto a path fringing a rocky promontory, and at the bottom, to a causeway and bridge leading to a small island. There were surprisingly few people in this pleasant spot as we stopped and kissed properly for the first time. As usual with Wendy, it was spontaneous and totally devoid of self-consciousness. But there was still a slight tentativeness and withholding of passion, which could wait for the moment.

At the top of a small hill on the island we sat beneath a pagoda overlooking the sea, whose surface reflected golden orange then turned black as sunset rapidly gave way to dusk. We were alone with the sound of sea on rocks and nothing else. For the first time I felt something close to tension – albeit with a strong, underlying excitement – in her presence. I touched her knee and gently caressed upwards until she shivered and gasped. I felt in control having turned her on so easily, but it didn't last. Standing up, feet either side of mine, she held my head and pulled it towards hers. I saw that large, sensuous mouth homing in, felt the motion of her plump lips and pulsating tongue and found myself captivated by the intensity of her lust. I couldn't possibly compete with it, and truth was, I didn't want to. I was aroused by her aggressive abandon, but when she took my hand towards her thrusting pelvis she seemed ready to explode. I could see where this was leading, but she wasn't going to be denied. She eased open the fastener and flies with one hand, looking with wonder, kissing, sliding onto me, gentle at first, then fast, then frantic.

A short while later I sat back in awed marvel, hardly believing what had just happened. Me, a *gwailo* of the world, sexually subjugated by a supposedly inexperienced Asian girl. The incongruity of it all was a fantastic and stunning revelation.

On the bus back, however, I was starting to worry. And if I was worried, Wendy was positively distraught. I waited a while for her sobbing to stop, but when it didn't I insisted she tell me what was wrong.

"We should not do dat fing," she moaned.

"No," I agreed. "Wrong time, wrong place. Pretty amazing, though."

"Ugh, I hate it, I hate it!"

"What! You enjoyed it as much as I did."

"It don't matter. Now I feel dirty. Maybe have baby. Oh no!" She wailed again.

I suggested getting a Morning After pill, but that hardly lightened her mood.

"I not want sex before marry, unnerstan'? I am Christian, you know. I should wait for good man, right man."

"So, I'm not a good man?"

"No, you bad man... My God, if my fens in church know, or my family know, I die... I die."

"That's enough," I said, my patience withering. "How old are you, Wendy?"

"Twenty-nine."

"Christ! You're a couple of years older than me. You're old enough to decide how to live your life. You've been an adult for eleven years!"

"You don't unnerstan', you just don't unnerstan'. You are foweigner, I am Asian. You have sex anyone, any time. Don't matter wiv you."

"Why does it matter so much to you?"

"I am Chinese, I am Christian."

"So you keep saying, but Chinese people have the same feelings, Christians have the same feelings. We're all human."

"But for Christian is sin."

"Yes, I understand that, but why do you think God gave you these feelings? Is it a test, or is it a joke? There must be a reason."

"Maybe is test. But I fail… I fail… oh, no!… I fail."

I was beginning to consider giving up on her, but I tried one more line of reasoning. "Look, Wendy, you only followed your natural instincts, you didn't hurt anyone."

She was quiet for a time, suggesting that my point had hit home. But then she whined, in what was becoming a familiarly irritating tone, "I want first time wiv somebody I love, wiv husband."

I almost choked with amazement. "Excuse me, if that was your first time, I'm a Chinaman."

She protested, "It was, it was."

I was dumbfounded after such a performance. I asked about her ex-boyfriend.

"We do ev'yfing, but not dat fing. He want but two years I always say no. But now, wiv you, first time, boom, boom!" She added, despairingly, "Oh, I hate you, I hate me."

"But Wendy, you must have been with someone before."

"No… not… someone…"

Breaking down in sobs, she never completed the sentence.

FLAT BROKE was as good a description of my accommodation as it was my financial situation. I'd had the flat to myself in the first weeks of my stay, which was the nearest thing to luxury afforded me and, in such an overcrowded place as Hong Kong, not one to be underestimated. But in time even this was denied, starting when the laundry man opposite started coming in to use the toilet. I didn't mind, but then I didn't know this was the start of the unsanitary conditions that later would prevail.

Increasingly, the other rooms were let for a day or two and I even shared my room on the odd occasion. Nothing I couldn't handle. But when the stays became longer and more frequent there was a disturbing increase in noise and filth: an increase quite disproportionate to the number of people staying there. The maximum was only about twelve, yet judging by the mess, the banging doors, shouting and phone calls it might have been housing a medium-sized army. Many a time I was awoken in the middle of the night by incessant knocking on doors. Usually I would get up and tell the offender that no one was there. "No one there?" they would ask, as if the possibility had never been remotely considered. "Well, could you sleep through that?" Looking at the expressionless reactions I had to conclude that they probably could.

Sleeping in a windowless room was also unsettling. I would wake clueless to the time and disorientated. Once I got up to remonstrate with somebody who was noisily hacking and clearing his sinuses outside my room at what I assumed to be an uncivilised hour. I returned to my room sheepishly after discovering it was nearly 10am.

Sometimes during Ramadan a group of men would be camped all night in the hall, feasting, smoking and drinking. They were also partial to other pursuits of which I suspect Allah would not approve. One room in particular was frequently used as a knocking shop, plied by three lumpen, curvy, middle-aged ladies in saris, with extremely dark complexions plastered with make-up. The only feminine thing about them was their curves, but nonetheless men were beating a path to their doors. The knocking and ringing, followed by banging, sometimes continued for hours but thankfully not every day.

Meanwhile the bathroom was like a pigsty, with remnants of piss and excrement everywhere but in the toilet, and the familiar sight of footsteps on the toilet seat. I was provoked into making an ironic sign, stating: 'How To Use Toilet', reminding the user to lift the seat when pissing and to shit *in* the toilet, preferably with feet on the floor. Then I pinned it on the wall, right behind the toilet where, to my surprise, it remained for the duration of my residence.

Disgusted and sickened though I was, I endured. My tolerance had been strengthened by spells in India and Pakistan. But even there I'd never had to put up with such anti-social behaviour. Nor had I encountered such a foul-mannered, discourteous and downright obtuse set of individuals. In Pakistan I had been impressed by the hospitality, honesty and warmth of the people, but here it was the reverse. The apples were all spoilt. They left behind the best of their native land and seemed to have happily adopted the vices of Western society without any of the virtues.

But they were not responsible for every disturbance. Every weekend a giant African and his tiny, pretty Indonesian girlfriend rented the room next door. Instead of getting straight down to business, they spent most of their time engaged in fierce verbal exchanges of which I could hear – though not always understand – every word. Usually he would complain that they didn't spend enough time together, she didn't love him sufficiently, didn't care for him or generally treat him in the way that he desired. His voice would rise and fall in volume and pitch, full of emotionally-charged paranoia.

Once he screamed, "You seeing someone else, is it?" I waited with him for her denial. It didn't come. I sat up transfixed, unable to do anything but listen. The fact that I couldn't see only heightened the sense of drama and suspense. I didn't have long to wait and wonder for his response before there was a series of bumps and thuds as stuff was flung round the room and against the walls. Violence seemed inevitable. I feared for her, and with my nerves on full alert, I feared too for myself. How far would I let it go before being forced to confront this potentially psychopathic giant?

She cried out, more in anger than fear, "What you doing, you crazy, mad man. I'm going, let me out. Let me out!"

Now he was silent. "Let me out! Get out my way!… We're finished. Understand?"

Still nothing from him.

She continued, not a flicker of intimidation evident in her tone, "You don't own me. I'm not your property, not your television, just here to entertain and please you… you selfish bastard."

"Why don't you answer my question?" he asked coolly.

"Because you asked it, that's why. You are sick and you make me sick. You don't trust me, that's okay. You don't trust me, we have no future. We have no future, I have nothing to say."

"I'm sorry," he blubbed.

"Sorry, sorry, sorry! You always sorry after, never before. This time it too late. I can't stand you no more. You are just pathetic. Now, excuse me, I want to go." After some pause: "Please, let me out."

"No, you're staying here."

"Get out! I'm going… hey!… put me down, put me down!"

"Shh, baby, just let me hold you one last time."

"No… no… put me down. Aghh! Take your hands off me."

I was standing now, fearfully poised to intervene.

"It's okay, you know I never want to hurt you."

It was music to my ears, but the doughty little Indonesian's protests were not yet suppressed. "You're hurting me now, you bastard."

"Don't struggle, you're hurting yourself. Relax."

"Hey! Don't touch me!"

"You like it, you know you like it."

"I don't. Don't touch me there."

"Surrender, darling, surrender."

She groaned loudly, but the 'ah's and 'no's were becoming 'oh's, and the protest was fading with every second, with every touch. He may have been a bully and an emotional wimp, but he could really turn her on. Just like his television, after all.

I had been psychologically involved, caught between voyeuristic and Samaritan intentions. Fortunately, my instinct to stay out had been vindicated. Now, with the pair of them engaged in a full-blooded session, the show, for me at least, was over. Until next week.

One day, during what had been a quiet week domestically, I came home to find the hall occupied by a small band of Nepalese youths. There was something about them that disturbed me: a kind of listlessness beyond lethargy. I was never directly threatened or endangered, and we maintained an uneasy peace by ignoring each other, but I was bothered by their slovenly, indolent ways and their recurrent lounging and hanging around, smoking, drinking, talking in loud, slow voices, and listening to some kind of Nepalese punk.

Sadly these lads were not untypical of a generation of Nepalese who have failed to adapt to life in Hong Kong, with lives blighted by poverty, drug abuse and violence. It is remarkable and sad that the offspring of Gurkhas, the proud and distinguished soldiers of the British Army, should end up like this. But, unlike their parents, they are rootless and disaffected, brought up in a place where they don't belong, isolated from mainstream society, physically, culturally, linguistically and economically.

The group festering in my home – I considered it *my* home since I was still the only permanent resident – may have been socially deprived but my supplies of tolerance were starting to run low after some four or five days. And when arriving home in the afternoon I found them all shooting up in the hallway, quite oblivious to my appearance, with another needle discarded on the bathroom floor, I could take no more. I went to Mohammed, with the ultimatum: them or me.

"But my dear chap, you are alone upstairs, no?" He checked his guest book. "Nothing. They are intruders. We will get rid of them and change the locks. Don't let anyone else in, okay Mr Joe?"

For once, he was true to his word, and the 'intruders' were ejected and not seen again. A sudden hushed tranquillity descended like a blessing, as I once more had the place to myself. Privacy was restored, I was able to sleep at any time without being constantly awoken, and the bathroom could once again be used without fear of contamination. Best of all was waking with natural daylight: keys had been left in the deluxe rooms, and I didn't ask for permission to vacate my gloomy dungeon every night for these windowed chambers. After what I'd been through it was bliss. The stress I'd been under was only fully appreciated on its removal. I wondered how I had failed to notice it before and how adaptable I must have been to live with such daily squalor, disturbance and deprivation, so that only now did I recognise what I had been missing. I was rejuvenated by brightness and ventilation, and settled back into the natural rhythm of the day/night cycle. Never mind the traffic noise, lack of television, stereo, or any kind of cooking appliance. I actually felt privileged.

During this time the other rooms were only sporadically occupied, by the odd backpacker or Bangladeshi or Indian businessman. They seldom stopped long and I hardly knew they were there. It seemed that old Mr Mohammed was at last becoming more selective in his choice of guests. It was too good to last, of course.

THE COMMOTION broke out and filtered into my dream-world before stirring my consciousness. A banging, creaking and some moaning sounds were coming from the direction of the room opposite. My dazed head tried to make sense of what was going on. I knew the room had been vacant when I went to bed at twelve o'clock. In fact the whole place had been empty but for me. I had no idea who it could be, or even what time it was. I briefly wondered if it was the African-Indonesian couple up to their antics again, but it wasn't their time of day. My senses were in a state of rapid transition, from drowsy torpor to high alert. I sat up, straining my ears, tensing my muscles involuntarily. The noise, which was quickening violently, sounded like a creaking bed thumping rhythmically against a wall, behind which I heard the unmistakable plaintive cries of a female: "My god... please stop... stop!"

This time there could be no conflict of intention. I got up without further ado and banged against the door. The action within ceased immediately. The door opened halfway with a creak. Before me was a thick-set man pulling up his trousers in a hurry. Behind, a girl cowered on the bed, crying, "Please help me… he is crazy… he is crazy!"

"Shall I get the police?" I asked urgently.

"Yes! Yes!" She sounded desperate and frightened, sitting on the bed, wrapped in a sheet, with her knees pulled into her chest. "Hurry please."

I went to the phone and started to dial 999. As I was doing so, they both appeared in the hallway before me.

"Do you still want the police?" I asked.

She thought a moment and then shook her head.

As I put the phone down, the man started aggressively asking her for money. I was astonished. He was getting bold and defiant when he should have been defensive. I had no idea about the details of their arrangement, nor the events that led to them being together in that room in this shabby doss house at 2am. But I saw a violent thug who had assailed and traumatised her; I saw a shameless bully, still not satisfied with the abuse he had inflicted, pouring vitriol onto inflamed wounds; I saw a vulnerable, distressed young woman. I saw red.

I grabbed him by the collar, ignoring his distinct physical advantage, and asked him if he would like to repeat that to the police. The impact of that word on him was more forceful than my physical attention. He panicked and made desperately for the door. I managed to check his progress, holding him briefly against a wall. He turned and swung his body violently away from me, extricating himself with the loss of his shirt buttons, before darting out the front door.

Privately I was relieved, knowing he probably could have flattened me if he had wanted; and clad only in boxer shorts and flip flops, I was hardly dressed for the fight or the chase. More important than that, though, I was safe, she was safe, and he was on the run. I felt some satisfaction that his arrogant bullying had been reduced to panicked flight and that he would have to live with that fear on his conscience for some time to come. I hoped he would suffer. I already hated him for the bedroom attack, but his subsequent reaction: his shamelessness, his disdain and disregard for her was just as unforgivable.

After his exit the girl hurried to the bathroom gasping to suppress her sobs. I knocked and asked if she was okay. After a few moments the door opened and she was standing in her underwear still, flustered and animated as she looked towards her crotch. "There is no blood. Is that okay?"

I was confused. "What? You mean you're a...?" I stopped myself. This was getting stranger. "No, it's not alright. That bastard tried to rape you. Who was he, anyway? Do you know him?"

"I meet him tonight."

"But who was he? What were you doing with him?"

"He said his name is Abdul. He said he just wanted to talk."

I looked at my watch. It was 2.20am. "You went to his bedroom at two o'clock in the morning to talk?"

"It was one o'clock. What you thinking? I am bad, I am stupid, I am deserve it?"

I answered, "No, no, I don't think that at all." I had been sceptical but her hurt tone was persuasive.

She forced a weak smile. "Thank you. You are so kind. I am lucky you found me and help me. Where are you from?"

"England. What about you, are you from the mainland?"

She looked offended at the suggestion.

"It's just that you don't sound Cantonese." That was one reason for my assumption, but subconsciously I was presupposing that no local girl would find herself in a place like this, with a man like this, at a time like this. And to her it was an affront. (In retrospect it still amazes me that someone who had been through such an ordeal could be bothered by something as trivial as having their nationality mistaken).

A tremor broke in her voice as she asked, "Do you think he will come back?"

"You're safe now."

She was close to tears, her face bulging with sorrow and gratitude. I hugged her in what was intended to be a brief and spontaneous gesture of empathy, but she responded by gripping me with almost intimate intensity. I was the gallant gentleman, emotionally in touch while physically detached. I had to be. She was in need of moral support, nothing more, nothing less, and that was all I intended to offer. Any other thoughts or urges would be a disgrace. The fact that she was so feminine, with a softly-rounded figure and skin as smooth as cream shouldn't have mattered. The fact that we were both half naked did.

Her breasts were pushed and spread against my upper abdomen, her tender cheeks rested against my shoulder. Then her grip tightened, and what I had vowed to suppress was starting to revolt. I yearned for her to release me lest my desperate ardour become evident. I couldn't cope with that, and I suspect nor could she after what she'd been through. I was supposed to be her saviour, and it was a role I had been happy and proud to assume. But now I was perhaps seconds away from being revealed as another dodgy bloke with a primitive lust quite at odds with the sympathetic, caring, gentlemanly image I had cut. I suspect she was clueless about the forceful tendencies that lurk within the male species and indeed of her own ability to unlock them. She was innocent and trusting, I was innocent and trusted. I hated to shatter the illusion. Then she loosened her grip momentarily to cough, and I was away, exiting the hallway to my bedroom, relieved and reprieved. When I came back wearing trousers I was surprised to see her still in underwear. Then I saw her trousers, which had been reduced to unwearable rags, ripped apart in the frantic attempt to get at her. I felt my anger toward her attacker return. Only moments earlier I had been wondering if she might have somehow spurred him on before spurning him. But this was different. This was startling proof of the nature of the crime. And the beast. I felt angry, with notions of revenge starting to manifest. I wouldn't forget his face. His community was small and I could find him if I really wanted. But that could wait for now. The girl standing before me, pathetically clutching what remained of her trousers, was of more concern. I invited her to sit down on the bed, which she unhesitatingly did, holding my hand in the process. I felt quite proud that she was able to relax so easily in my company, particularly after such anguish. And she was ready to talk.

She told me she had met Abdul along the harbour that evening and had gone to a café and met some of his friends. She liked him, and said he behaved like a gentleman, so she trusted him when he invited her upstairs, "only to chat". She admitted, "I know I am stupid to go with him but maybe I was lonely. I trusted him because I wanted to trust him." She paused, looking to the floor in sad and painful reflection, and as I waited for the tears, preparing for another awkward, commiserating embrace, she sat upright, struck by an unpalatable thought. "My God!" she moaned, then spoke of the dread and shame if her family found out. "I can't go home tonight, I cannot face my family now. Can I sleep here?" she asked, gesturing to the other bed. "You don't mind?"

"You can stay as long as you like, but first you must tell me something."

She looked a little grave.

"What?... What is it?" she asked nervously.

"I can't share a room with someone I don't know... what's your name?"

The tension vanished from her face, and I saw her smile properly, and enchantingly, for the first time. "I am Annie, and you?"

"Joe."

"Pleased to meet you, Joe. Very pleased to meet you."

We shook hands and laughed. With or without an introduction the ice had been broken and now it was starting to melt.

As the laughter died down Annie looked at me, her eyes seeming to shine with gratitude. Her gaze remained fixed for some seconds and she held my hand, suggesting something more momentous. I allowed my imagination to marvel at the circumstance and justice of Abdul's desperate departure and the irony of a would-be rapist turned matchmaker. If my feelings were akin to my reading of hers it would be folly to reveal them now. If this was indeed the start of something, it could wait.

I accepted that tomorrow, minus the emotion and adrenalin, everything could be different. In the morning, tonight might feel like an embarrassing aberration. If she wanted to get away from this wretched place and never return, who could blame her? If she wanted to expunge from her mind everything that had happened and all its connections, including me, would it be a surprise? Perhaps so, since she was sitting so serenely in her underwear, holding hands with a man she knew less well than her attacker, on *his* bed, and giving the impression there was nowhere else she would rather be. I don't know if it was the release of tension or her general nature that resulted in such calmness, or whether it was my influence. I often had cause to begrudge my sensitive side – a lot of girls see no virtue in it – but this was no such occasion.

As we sat I became a touch anxious, reflecting for the first time on the suddenness and strangeness of the night's events. I was also slightly unsettled by Annie's apparent peace of mind, which seemed so incongruous in light of what had preceded. What was she thinking? She seemed in no hurry to move to the other bed and go to sleep. With my heart beating at the pace of my thoughts, I had a suspicion that she wanted to get into bed with me – to satisfy her yearning for comfort and protection more than anything else. The sexual chemistry between us was undeniable but unacknowledged, and it was better that way. To act on it now or even allow temptation would be a step too far, too soon. From my perspective, the mutual appreciation and affection needed to be curtailed for the night. It would be, but in a way neither of us could have foreseen.

There was a loud rap at the front door, just as I was about to suggest going to sleep. Annie's state of peace was abandoned. "Oh God! Oh no, he come back. He leave his watch here." She retrieved it from the other room. "Look, he come back for this."

The watch was a Rolex, but almost certainly one of the ubiquitous fakes that his countrymen hawk down Nathan Road. I couldn't imagine him risking a return even if it was real, but who else could it be at such a time? I had to accept that her explanation was most plausible, particularly in view of his unsavoury character. He wouldn't be getting it back, I decided. No fucking way.

I went to the door. "Don't open it," she pleaded. I paused. Maybe I should have heeded her advice (I'll always regret not doing so) but my ire had been provoked once again – this time multiplied. He had violated not just anyone but someone I had, in the interim, come to feel something for. Now it was personal. My blood was racing to feed every cell in every muscle. I could feel the throb of pressure in my chest and my arms were tensed, ready for action. I picked up a fire extinguisher with one hand and turned the door handle with the other. I was poised to smash the butt end in his face, but instead of encountering the expected dark, square, stubbly mug of Abdul I was met by a couple of uniformed policemen with clean-cut, callow heads. My first response was one of surprise, the second relief, and the third was affected by diminished judgement on the grounds of the first – meaning that owing to their unexpected arrival and a train of logic already derailed by a flood of adrenalin, I was unable to act in the cold, clear-headed manner that would have best served the interests of Annie and me.

Standing like a Ninja Turtle with a fire extinguisher primed for attack I was asked, "Any problem, sir?" I could hardly say all was well, even if I'd had the foresight to do so.

In fact in the preceding moments I had dearly wanted to see Abdul pay. Now I had the chance but by a different method, so I blurted with barely a thought for Annie and the potential repercussions. All I cared about at that particular time was to bring down Abdul and see him punished. So I spoke out: "No, everything's not okay. There was a man here who attacked and tried to rape a girl."

"You rape a girl?"

"No, not me!"

"Where is she?"

I pointed to my room. One officer went to see her, the other stayed with me. I stared at the floor. The realisation of my admission was coming down. Fuck, who cares about Abdul? Annie was the one that mattered and I had landed her in it. She hadn't wanted this and neither had I, not at this time at least.

The policeman before me was a puny, young stripling, kitted out in an oversized uniform. He stared at me with what I took to be fear and suspicion, making sure he kept himself between the door and me. "How did you know about this? Did you trace my call or did someone else call? I thought I had only dialled the first two numbers before hanging up."

He averted his gaze but didn't reply, his nervousness more apparent than ever. *He thinks I did it!* I almost chuckled to myself at the pathetic sight of this wet-behind-the-ears copper in an oversized uniform, almost shitting himself. But with his hand twitching over his gun holster, and the consequences of inquisition looming, it was the bleakest of black comedies.

His colleague came back after a few words with Annie and confirmed what I had said. My 'minder' visibly relaxed and smiled at me for the first time. The other policeman spoke. "Do you have trousers for the girl to wear?"

I went to my room, picked up a pair of tracksuit bottoms and handed them to Annie, which she took without comment, looking a deathly shade of misery.

"Are you okay?"

"Don't speak to her please," I was told.

"Why, what is this?"

"Police standard, that's all."

Annie didn't answer me in any case. No doubt dumbstruck at

the prospect of more pain, she hardly registered my presence and perhaps didn't even hear me. She had recovered from the original shock remarkably quickly but this would be a longer, drawn-out ride in which she would be endlessly required to relive the horrid incident. Then there would be the physical examination and, worst of all, the domestic repercussions if her family got wind of it. There would be those ready to condemn her for bringing it upon herself and she would be accused of promiscuousness. Few would believe her naïve explanation; fewer still, that she was a virgin.

If I was downcast, Annie was bereft. Her head must have been full of impending dread, anguish and shame. The loss of me would be as nothing in comparison. In fact, how could she even feel the loss of something so fleeting? To her I was probably just a nice guy, a good Samaritan, no more or less. But now I feared she might see me as the saviour who had betrayed her. I felt appalled with myself, and more than a touch guilty. It was a cruel paradox that my tactless utterance could end up doing her more harm than the attack itself. I may have prevented the full awfulness of the assault being realised, but that was scant consolation.

For something approaching two hours I was made to stand in the hallway as a procession of officers, including an inspector and plain-clothed detectives, as well as a forensic team decked out in whites, came, saw, examined, questioned and left. Some of them were puzzled – unbelieving even – as I told, then retold, the sorry tale and my part in it. I tired of answering the same old lines, time after time, to each new arrival. My patience was extended to its limits with exchanges like this:

"Did you know the girl before?"

"No."

"The man?"

"No."

"Why did you help?"

"I could hear she was in trouble."

"Did she ask for help?"

"Yes."

"She shouted 'help?'"

"Yes... no... I can't remember. All I know is she needed it."

"Why you get involved if she don't ask for help?"

Whatever their attitudes, judging by the time and manpower employed I couldn't deny that the police were treating the incident with the utmost seriousness. Presumably they were satisfied that each of my statements was consistent with the previous ones and were corroborating with Annie's, for they became progressively more relaxed and sympathetic towards me.

During a lull in the interrogations Mr Mohammed, the landlord, arrived. His white beard trim, his eyes bright, he looked fresh and alert despite having been woken in the early hours and summoned here by the police. He was wearing his usual demeanour of affability and charm with a remote sense of reality, apparently not a care in the world. I heard him telling the police that hundreds of people had stayed here over the years but nobody had checked in tonight. He said he'd had a problem before with tenants who made copies of keys. "I have to change locks regularly. It is a big problem, but what can I do? What can I tell you? It could be anyone, you know. We don't know everybody who comes here."

It was a convincing performance but I was surprised that the police were so easily taken in that they didn't question him further. After all, Mohammed and the suspect were of the same nationality and same small community: if he didn't already know him he could surely have assisted the police in their search. This obviously never occurred to the 'professionals', who were equally unconcerned when Mohammed turned his attention to me. To them he was probably just a harmless eccentric with no idea what was going on, but they were only half-right. Beneath that vacant, slightly dotty façade was a wily thinker who knew more than he let on.

As he approached, I knew he had something of earnest to impart. "Joe, listen to me. We don't want any trouble with police here, you know. You didn't need to call police, no need to speak to them now. Just say you didn't see the man, okay? You don't know what he looked like. The police don't need to know. Let's keep everything simple."

"What!" I couldn't believe what I was hearing, especially as he was speaking with the police in such close proximity. But his tone was calm and casual, conversational, so it aroused no suspicion. He must also have presumed, rightly, that none of them would understand his strongly Urdu-accented English.

"Look Joe," he continued, "You are okay, no? The girl is okay, no? Everything is okay. Don't get involved. Don't say too much. All is well."

His brazenness was astonishing, as was his trust in me. It was virtually an admission that he knew the perpetrator but seemed to have no doubt that I would willingly toe his line. I was incredulous that he could be so confident that I wouldn't immediately tell the police of his flagrant attempt at subverting me, the only witness, right under their noses. I owed Mohammed nothing and would have had few qualms about implicating him, and I knew he could help the police find Abdul. The latter prospect was certainly an appealing one, but something made me bite my tongue this time. It had nothing to do with Mohammed's plea – in fact I had already provided the police with a reliable description and account of events – but everything to do with preserving Annie's dignity, or what remained of it. I wondered how she was coping, what she was thinking. If only I could have gauged whether she wanted justice or anonymity, I would have known how to act. My intuition suggested she would be in agreement with Mohammed, though for entirely different reasons. I would say no more. I had already said enough. This time it was her call.

Eventually the police were satisfied that they had garnered enough information and evidence, and started clearing out. I looked forward to a desperately needed three or four hours' sleep, before discovering that I too was required at the station. I accepted with weary resignation, walking out behind Annie and five or six officers into a volley of flashbulbs on the landing outside. The press had been tipped off or, more likely, heard about it on the police radio. Fortunately, Annie had had the foresight to cover her face with her jacket, while I was ignored, perhaps in the presumption that I was a detective.

In contrast to the attitude of the photographers, I sensed for the first time that my deeds were being acknowledged somewhat heroically by the officers at the station. But to me it had been a spontaneous reaction. To have done nothing in response to those cries of distress would have been shameful. That I'd proved I was no coward hardly made me a hero, yet I got the impression that it was quite unheard of for a civilian to come to the aid of a stranger. Even an English detective congratulated me on my intervention. Whilst I didn't buy it, I certainly had no objections if that was how they chose to judge me.

Between the compliments and backslapping I once again had to undergo questioning in order for them to prepare a painstaking statement. By the time it was completed, the first glimmers of daylight were filtering through the blinds. I was taken to a dark room to rest until Annie's examination and statement had been completed. I was fatigued but not sleepy: the excitement and coffee had seen to that. I felt a touch of self-satisfaction as I sat back in the chair, persuaded by all the acclaim that perhaps I had done something worthy. But then I concentrated on Annie and how my 'good deed' had affected her, and I was drained hollow, subdued and exhausted.

No sooner had I fallen asleep than I was awakened by the door opening and the figure of a female inspector requesting my further assistance. I recognised her as one of the faces that had interviewed me at the flat. She had been one of the doubters, saying that Annie was a very foolish girl. She didn't go as far as to say she got what she deserved, but that was her allusion. I remembered her saying in her strong Cantonese accent, "She go to a stranger man's room at one o'clock, what she expect? He read a bedtime storybook?"

She took me back to the office, where she asked me to verify Annie's statement. She was translating and typing it into English, and constantly asked me to correct her spelling and grammatical errors. After a while I volunteered to take over the typing while she dictated to me. It surely wasn't legitimate practice but saved us both time. As to the legal and moral grounds of my reading her statement, I didn't know and she didn't seem to care.

From it I discovered that Annie had met Abdul down by the harbour that evening and had been wooed by him with flowers. His romantic touch deserted him in the bedroom, however. After a cup of tea, he became impatient and suddenly demanded sex, which Annie unsurprisingly refused. Frustration turned to anger and the rest was history. Had he taken lessons from the African lodger he might have had a chance, but seduction obviously wasn't in his lexicon. One other thing confirmed by Annie's personal examination was that the crime was classified as 'attempted rape'. "She is still a girl," the inspector announced. I didn't need convincing, but this evidence seemed to convince the police of her innocent gullibility over reckless allurement.

At last, with my work time approaching, I was allowed to leave. As I walked down the corridor, Annie and a couple of female detectives came from a room. We stopped and exchanged glances. I clasped her hand in passing but nothing was said. Nothing could be said. She gave a brief and painfully forced half-smile, but it couldn't disguise the depth of anguish or the taint of humiliation. We looked at each other ruefully. She was the saddest, sorriest sight of greyish pallor, with dark sacks beneath stinging red eyes. Her clothes were baggy and crumpled, obscuring those feminine curves; she looked dilapidated and haggard, hardly recognisable from the fresh, vivacious young woman I had seen earlier. She was jaded, spent, and defeated. Defeated by Abdul, defeated by the police, and defeated by me.

FROM POLICE STATION to classroom I went that morning, hoping there would be no early students in attendance so I could get a bit more rest. Instead there were half a dozen or so housewives who cheerily agreed amongst themselves that, with my dark, sleep-deprived eyes, I resembled a Giant Panda.

I gave them a full rundown of the night's events, knowing that it would provide a lengthy topic of conversation, when I could think of nothing else and was in no mood for teaching. The housewives were almost unanimously critical of Annie for leading Abdul on. They couldn't accept she was a virgin because a virgin would never find herself in such a situation. The consensus was that she was no better than a cheap tart who must have known what was in store and I should have just left her to her fate. My defence of her was met by a row of sympathetic faces and shaking heads.

Even Wendy, who was still showing up in class, shared what seemed to be a universal cynicism regarding Annie's conduct. To her and the other women in my class I was a well-meaning but naïve and reckless fool. To me they were callous and uncaring. And it hinted at our different ways. "You don't scratch my back, I won't scratch yours" was the philosophy they seemed to be advocating. And in a place with little sense of community – my students told me they never say hello to their neighbours – and where pleasantries between strangers are rare, I shouldn't have been surprised. I had also received enough suspicious looks and defensive attitudes from new students to appreciate what they were getting at. With this background of single-minded independence, looking the other way and ignoring the plight of the less fortunate becomes second nature. As a survival mechanism and as a way of avoiding physical confrontation it works; as a way of building trust and unity and faith in your fellow man it fails miserably. But in a city of homes stacked like concrete rabbit hutches, where the streets squirm with humanity and the population density is ten times greater than that of London, would any other attitude work? In Hong Kong nobody may come running to your aid, but nor are you likely to find yourself mugged, attacked or burgled, while car crime is uncommon, drugs and alcohol abuse rare, and vandalism almost unheard of. You may be jostled and irritated by antisocial habits on occasions, but that is it. Hong Kong Man and Woman possess a streak of self-reliance and personal responsibility that is admirable although the consequences can sometimes be pitiable.

The neediest of all are the mentally ill vagrants who lead solitary lives, divorced from human contact, friendless and unloved. You see the same wretched characters in the same dingy areas, sitting with vacant expressions, talking to themselves, or sifting through bins for half-finished lunchboxes. They wear clothes unfit for rags, sometimes shoeless, usually filthy. One in Causeway Bay has lank, matted hair like dreadlocks, all the way to the floor. He is blind in one eye, and with the other he scans a newspaper from a distance of about an inch, on the steps outside a cinema. A character around Shanghai Street in Yau Ma Tei smokes dog ends quite contentedly while the tumour under his chin seems to swell daily. Not far away, another hobbles around in a manner suggestive of a terrible bout of haemorrhoids. Few have the wherewithal even to beg, never mind seek the public assistance and healthcare they are surely entitled to. Another all-too-common sight is the old ladies, tiny and hunched, shoving their trolley-loads of discarded cardboard and old newspapers to sell for a pittance.

When I mention these examples to my students, suggesting that such poverty in a rich city like theirs is unacceptable, they are unconcerned. They tell me it's okay – they can beg and most beggars get well paid, while everyone knows that the trolley women are really rich old spinsters who don't want to spend. They are bored and choose to spend the last few years of their lives in self-imposed drudgery rather than relaxing in retirement. As you would.

In their defence, what the Hong Kong people lack in social concern is at least in some way offset by their relations with family and friends. Filial ties are stronger than in the West, and friendships appear more genuine and more permanent. Once you penetrate that defensive façade and earn their trust it would be hard to find friends more loyal and generous.

Annie, coming to terms with her ordeal, would need those friends more than anyone now. I hoped she would number me amongst them. Every day for the next week or two I came home directly from work to avoid missing her in case she called. I wanted to see her and comfort her and perhaps help restore her trust in men and belief in herself. But every day brought disappointment. I wondered if this was evidence of disaffection; proof of her sense of betrayal. More likely, her memories of the place were too haunting and the ghosts, including myself, too real. And could only be exorcised by avoidance.

I had no way of tracking her down. All I knew was that she lived somewhere in the New Territories. My only glimmer of hope was that the police might provide me with the information I sought. I approached the front desk of the police station and explained to the officer who I was and what had happened, then requested Annie's telephone number or address on the pretext of getting my trousers back. He seemed to recognise the case, and I perceived a rueful element in his response. But he rightly refused. I was disheartened and resigned.

DEALING WITH DIFFICULT STUDENTS was not a problem I'd had to face on anything like a regular basis. But these were changing times. I didn't realise at the time that the Annie affair would be a watershed in my new 'career'. Until then it had been an experience and an education as much as a job. All the while I was exploring ways I could improve my technique, find relevant new topics and relate better to the students. I had undergone a hands-on, unaided crash course in teaching, and passed the test when mere survival would have been an achievement. I had taken to it like a fledgling to the sky: wobbly and unsure at first but growing in confidence with the realisation that I wasn't about to nose-dive. The satisfaction in the job was derived from the transfer of knowledge, positive feedback and ultimate respect from students, which provided some compensation for the meagre wages. When things are going well – when you are on top of your game in front of a receptive and appreciative class – there are few more rewarding jobs than this. The stimulation of working with people with different cultural attitudes and customs was another plus. I was teaching them English, they were showing me their way of life. And I had no reason to suppose this happy mutual arrangement could not be sustained. Presumably with the benefit of experience the job would get easier. But now, seven months into the stint, it was becoming increasingly wearing, and the rigours of a 48-hour week were shrinking my reserves of inspiration.

One tired, desperate afternoon I decided to try humour. I knew this was the riskiest and potentially most thankless of undertakings, but in the interests of educational experimentation, and with nothing else in mind, I went ahead. I told a few childish gags and explained the odd puerile pun, none of which remotely hit the mark. My final hapless attempt was the simple play on words: *I'm on a seafood diet – everything I see, I eat.* I didn't expect it to bring the house down but it would surely be transparently comprehensible and an opportunity for me to show how homonyms are used in jokes. I anticipated the odd chuckle or perhaps murmurs of appreciation. Instead, twenty-four eyes fixed on me, apparently still awaiting the punchline.

"That's it," I said, and repeated: "I'm on a *see* food diet – everything I *see*, I eat. Do you understand, seafood, see food?" Then I wrote it for emphasis, but was only rewarded by a row of faces unchangingly blank. *What's wrong with these people?* I thought. "What's wrong with you people?" I said. My frustration was building by the second. "It's very simple. Seafood, see food; that's the joke. Why can't you get it?"

It was left to a no-nonsense local girl to explain.

"But sir," she started, wrinkling her brow in earnest, but speaking in a clear, authoritative and ultimately damning voice. "Of course we understand. It is just that… it is not funny. That is all."

I could understand what a comedian, 'dying' on stage after failing to deal with an awkward heckler, was going through – only the heckles were now silent, which was worse – and the only joke was me.

Much safer ground was classroom conversations on food, minus the puns. Eating and cooking are cultural obsessions in this part of the world and the Cantonese appetite for food is only matched by their willingness to discuss it. By this time I'd heard all I needed to hear about exotic Chinese foods and aphrodisiacs, which were among the topics most favoured by students. I tired of being asked if I'd tried snake soup, a winter delicacy in Hong Kong (I saw one writhing as it was being skinned on a Kowloon pavement once, so the answer was no). They relished telling me about other more nauseating items served in mainland restaurants, such as live monkey's brain (the skull is removed and the monkey is restrained while diners tuck into its brain, which is all they can see protruding through a hole in the table); or how the rump of a live donkey is doused in boiling water before being sliced off ready to eat. And I was surprised how many people cheerfully admitted to eating dog in China, which is illegal in Hong Kong. I expressed my disapproval, of course, asking them how they could eat the best friend and most loyal servant any man could have, to which they replied, "It tastes good."

If finding that some of my students had eaten dog was disillusioning, it was nothing compared to the disgust I felt when one of my erstwhile favourites told me she had been to a bear farm in China and bought the bile, which is bled agonisingly from the bear's bladder using needles and catheters, which are often infected, while it is confined for years in a cage so small that the wretched beast can neither stand nor move. I found it hard to reconcile that an apparently decent person could so cruelly disregard such suffering and be so shameless to admit it. You can only make so many concessions to cultural differences.

With these inhumane demonstrations, along with the response of condemnation and condescension towards Annie and me, the respect I had felt for my students was souring. This, at the same time as the pressure of my workload was beginning to tell, was making me increasingly tetchy and discourteous. Even in the earlier, more pacific, times I'd had the occasional run-in with students, but now they were becoming almost commonplace. Usually the causes were rudeness from a student and stress on my part, a typically flammable combination which most teachers would recognise. Comments like 'this is boring, change the subject' would really earn my ire, particularly coming, as they invariably did, at times when I was already faltering. Such cutting remarks stop you cold and leave you with but four appropriate responses:

1. Heed the comment, without complaint, smoothly change tack and introduce a new, thoroughly interesting and universally appealing theme. (Flaw: If you had a new, thoroughly interesting and universally appealing theme in mind you would have already introduced it, but inspiration doesn't come easy when you're tired and strained, faced with a lethargic audience and pissed off with some upstart student).

2. Ignore the comment and continue. (Flaw: you've lost your thread, can't remember what you were going to say in any case, and if everyone agrees it's boring why bother?).

3. Tell the upstart to introduce a fresh topic himself. (Flaw: he tells you that's your job).

4. Blow your top and tell the student to get out and find another teacher – and there are plenty of those – if he's not satisfied, then storm off to the photocopier or the toilet for a cooling sulk. Usually the offender will be sufficiently stunned to get the message and be gone by the time you get back. (Flaw: It alarms the other students and, in theory, could get you sacked).

It probably says much about my background and lack of professionalism, but it was no contest. Only number four prioritised saving face – important in this culture – even if it meant losing a little dignity; only number four allowed the release of pressure. Getting sacked was hardly a deterrent. We were already the lowest form of life in the English teaching world, and finding decent new recruits would be harder for them than finding new positions would be for us. Only truly inept or troublesome teachers were expendable. I may not have had a contract as such, or any benefits such as holiday pay or insurance, but I had more job security than most in Hong Kong.

Which wasn't enough, of course. At last I could understand what the professional pessimist from Yorkshire was on about and I could appreciate the high attrition rate – ten weeks was about the average span of new recruits, with a few barely lasting a day. Comments from some of the 'old hands', like "Survive this and you can teach anywhere" (you've survived but you're still here, I thought), and "This place can make you or break you," took on a new light of pertinence however much they may have lacked in substance. I was determined not to become another burnt-out casualty of the Kowloon English Club and I still had enough loyal and friendly followers – even if it did include a group of misanthropists and a contingent of dog-eaters – to sustain me. I needed them one evening when a row broke out between me and a particularly large and brutish young man, who bore a facial scar as menacing as his temperament.

He called himself Brett and fancied himself as something of a ladies' man. At first we got on fine despite a level of self-assurance and standard of English on his part that was out of kilter with the rest of the class. He was entertaining on occasions and his attendance was erratic, so I saw no need to expel him from my class, even though I was obligated to insist he go to the higher level. He always sat in the corner near the doorway, where he could watch all the students – especially the girls – coming and going through the main hallway. When one caught his eye he would be up and gone and we wouldn't see him again for the rest of the night. A more sober and scholarly teacher might have put a stop to his antics right away but I didn't see any harm so long as he didn't affect my class, which he seldom did, so busy was he studying the female form. In a way I found his attitude quite refreshing. It was obvious that this was a potential place for pick-ups, with such an abundant supply of single young women and the opportunity to meet them and really get to know them over the days and weeks in a relatively relaxed and informal atmosphere. Aside from the lecherous teachers, Brett was one of the few people who openly acknowledged this fact, and I was hardly in a position to disapprove. Most other lads were as reticent about talking on the subject of sex and girls as the girls were on talking about sex and boys. I heard little, and saw less, evidence of romance flourishing between classmates. So I had no grudge against Brett for his talent-spotting ventures into my classroom – in his situation I would probably have done the same – but once our dispute kicked off I didn't hesitate to use it against him.

The reason for my anger had its roots in an exchange with Maxine, the proprietor, a couple of days earlier when she rebuked me for failing to use the teaching material provided. I told her in the politest possible way that it was crap and I preferred to use my own. This was perhaps not the most tactful of admissions – in view of the fact that her husband had personally designed and written the papers, which featured ridiculous pictures (for example, a picture of a man in Nazi uniform to represent the national dress of Germany) and laughably unrealistic dialogue – but the woman needed to be told. She countered by telling me that the students liked them and had complained I never used them.

"Why is my class usually full every night, then? Why do they keep coming back?" I demanded to know.

She didn't answer, only iterating that I should use the prepared papers. I was confident that none of my 'regulars' could have complained. It could only be a malcontent operating independently. My suspicion fell on one or two 'outsiders' who didn't really jell with the other members. I continued to disregard Maxine's precious material, all the while looking for indications as to the identity of the snake in the grass. I never suspected Brett. For one thing, his level of English was far in advance of the childish papers in question, and for another, he never showed any inclination to study. But when he declared aloud that my teaching was too easy and suggested using the set papers, he condemned himself. I was angry enough to employ tactic number four, telling him if he didn't like it he knew what he could do. The other students appeared stunned by my outburst, but they didn't know what I knew. The only one unflustered was Brett, who remained seated, staring coldly at me.

I continued with the lesson. I was giving answers to questions while the students in turn had to provide the question. It was a challenge for most of them, with only Brett replying immediately without hesitation. That was okay when it was his turn, but then he started interrupting others by answering their rounds. He was mocking them as well as me. And I wasn't having it.

"If this is too easy for you, you should leave now!" I said firmly. "You're disturbing everyone. You don't belong here, you shouldn't be in this class. You only come so you can look at the girls, I know your game."

If I was irate, Brett was enraged. "Fuck you English man, you fucking whore's bastard."

I was shocked and provoked into countering his obscenities with some of my own, though without quite matching his vitriol. We were ranting at each other, to the horrified bemusement of the 'Innocents' in class, none of whom thankfully could have understood much.

I realised we would be at each other's throats if this thing escalated any further. To avert such a scenario I had to get out. "If you are still here when I get back, I'll have you removed." With that I escaped for a breather and a glass of water.

It was no surprise on returning to find Brett still entrenched in his corner position. The three-minute break had done a little to quell my anger, so instead of laying into Brett again, I walked out and told Maxine of my predicament. She was the last person to empathise, but I had no other choice. She told me there would have been no trouble if I had used the papers. I told her that wasn't the point. Brett shouldn't even have been in my class, such was his mastery of English vernacular, and he was upsetting the other class members. I also let her know that the classroom wasn't big enough for both of us. That at last spurred her into facing Brett, who agreed to be quiet for the rest of the lesson. I wasn't satisfied but I accepted for the sake of peace, whilst warning Brett that I wouldn't tolerate his presence in the future.

I knew Maxine would easily dispense with the services of any teacher who dared cross her, for she had done so on prior occasions and her disposition was sufficiently strident to override concerns over staff shortages. After the lesson, so I later learned, she was asking questions of my students regarding the incident and the calibre of my teaching material. If she was looking for evidence against me then she was surely disappointed. The faith I'd placed in my 'Innocents' was vindicated, and my will to teach strengthened. I never saw Brett again. I don't know if he was banned or had taken to using the club's other branch instead, and I didn't much care. It had come to my knowledge that the only reason Brett had made a fuss about the sheets was that a girl he had fancied preferred to attend another class so she could study the repetitive papers in question – and he had already been banned by the teacher of that class.

From these incidents I took the hint and cut ten hours from my schedule. When work's a chore and you're weary and tense and agitated, a cut in pay is a minor trade-off for the extra freedom and the return of job satisfaction. But I was aware that this may not be the only change to my schedule. After denigrating her teaching material I knew Maxine would be flexing her muscles, anxious to reassert her authority. This she did one evening by switching me to one of the higher-level conversational classes upstairs without warning.

UPSTAIRS, my new class was a touch more sophisticated, the students more confident, educated and vocal than I was accustomed to. It was also more cosmopolitan, with Japanese, Koreans, Mainland Chinese, even the odd European in quite regular attendance. I looked forward to teaching in this new and more stimulating environment. Downstairs the topics had been necessarily routine: family, shopping, travel, work. Now I could determine attitudes and opinions on weightier issues.

Since arriving I had been looking forward to speaking with articulate local people about the handover situation. I imagined provoking heated debates between pro-China and pro-Britain factions. The majority of my students had at least one parent from across the border – many of whom were among the hundreds of thousands that fled the appalling upheavals of Mao's Cultural Revolution. So there was little affection toward the mother country from these refugees, even less from their offspring. Their roots, language and culture may have been Chinese but it was hard to find any young people to speak up for China and reunification. Hong Kong was so sophisticated and Western-orientated in comparison to the mainland, and the disparity in living standards and human rights between China and Hong Kong so great, that few were looking forward to the transfer of power with anything less than alarm. It wasn't a contentious subject to them: Hong Kong was Chinese but it wasn't China.

More remarkable than these attitudes was their contempt for what they regarded as the coarse, vulgar people living over the border, and their disgust for the country itself, which they saw as dangerous, dirty and tawdry. Most of my students only ever crossed the border to visit relatives (who were presumably exceptions to the stereotype) or to go shopping in the bootleg markets of Shenzhen. Scarcely did I ever hear any appreciation of the history or scenery of China. Occasionally I would come across individuals who defended China politically, but they were usually lonely, grudge-bearing cranks, who would invariably be shouted down by their classmates.

Anti-British tirades, though rare, were tolerated more easily. Generally I sensed some withholding of opinions regarding Britain's role in returning Hong Kong. In classes taught by non-

British teachers there was less reticence in slating the UK for abandonment and betrayal. I was often asked what I and other Brits thought of the loss of Hong Kong, as if it must be another sore point symptomatic of my nation's decline. When I told them that few people back home saw it that way, there were usually looks of disbelief, even sympathy, as if I were just putting on a brave face. I didn't encourage debate on the political situation for long, as there was little enthusiasm for it. It was too challenging, too controversial and too painful, usually only resulting in gloom and despondency.

They wanted escapism. Few came to study. Newspaper articles were just about acceptable, but any attempts to introduce anything more academic were usually rudely dismissed. I also found that the reticent style that had found favour downstairs was not so popular in this environment. It was also an unwelcome revelation that simply making conversation and encouraging debate was often a more trying task than actually teaching.

Of all the students in the upstairs class, Rhoda was the most demanding of my attention and assertive in expressing her own. She didn't have the force of a Zero but she did at times hold sway over the class in a way that I didn't always manage. Inquisitiveness poured from her on any subject, but particularly with regard to sex and relationships, asking me about my 'first time' – who with, where, and when – and how many girlfriends I'd had, how many one night stands, and did I have a girlfriend at present? The fact that she wasn't asking flirtatiously didn't make it much easier to answer. I had no wish to discuss my most intimate experiences with a classroom full of strangers, especially when Wendy was in attendance, but Rhoda didn't care.

"You are not like other young foreign teachers. You are more conservative."

More normal, I thought, but compared with the *hum sup* 'teachers' and their sleazy agendas she probably had a point and I was beginning to see why the serious teachers at the Club tended to avoid these advanced-level evening classes.

"You need a girlfriend, I think," continued Rhoda.

"Excuse me, how do you know I don't have a girlfriend?"

"Because men with girlfriends are more easy."

"More easy?"

"I mean," Rhoda said between giggles, "more easygoing."

The main contributor to my unease was not Rhoda herself – although she was doing a pretty good job – but Wendy, sitting stony-faced in the middle of the group (we had remained on friendly terms since the regrettable first date, albeit with an underlying tension).

I feigned indifference nonetheless and smiled mischievously as I said: "Maybe I don't want a girlfriend... maybe I have a secret girlfriend."

Rhoda squealed with delight. "A secret girlfriend, how exciting! Maybe someone we know?"

I shrugged my shoulders and noticed Wendy was trying, but failing, to conceal the biggest grin. "Maybe, Rhoda, it is none of your business."

She wasn't discouraged. "Don't be so uptight! You know many teachers date students here and they don't care."

I replied, "Maybe they should."

Rhoda again: "I want ask you, do you have any female friends – not girlfriend."

After brief consideration, I told her there were plenty of females with whom I was friendly.

"But," she said, warming to the theme, "do you think it difficult for you to have platonic relationship with women?"

"No... but I suppose if there's physical attraction it can be an issue."

She looked at me and shook her head slowly, glanced at a girl beside her, before expressing something in her mother tongue that had the rest of the class, except Wendy, rocking with laughter at my expense. (Later Wendy would tell me that she said something about foreign men being too horny).

It wasn't only teachers who were subject to Rhoda's interrogations, at least. She always liked to acquaint herself with any new members, particularly non-Chinese students, and she had her own way of doing it.

To a Korean girl: "Korean men are so ugly. Did you come to Hong Kong to find a new boyfriend?" And to a Korean businessman: "Did you fly here with Korean Airlines? You are lucky to survive."

They never came back.

To a Japanese lady she said, "Japanese people are different from Chinese people... very two-faced. We are more open and honest."

"Sometimes too honest," I said.

"What do you mean?"

"Well, polite people normally consider the feelings of other people before opening their mouths."

"Why?"

"Why? Well, you don't want to upset the other person, do you?"

"No… no, you Western people and Japanese are too sensitive. In our culture we say what we think always. This is what people expect. If I say you look beautiful but I don't mean it I am not sincere… it is not acceptable. For you it is okay, but is worth nothing. In Chinese, a compliment means something… it is real."

"Okay, I can appreciate you don't like to give false flattery, but that doesn't mean you have to insult people."

"Give example, please," she said firmly.

"Erm… well, what about the other day, when Mary came to the class? The first thing you said to her was: 'Oh, Mary, you are so fat now!'"

"She was fat."

"So? You didn't need to say it in front of everyone! You embarrassed her."

"No, no, only you was embarrassed. She is used to this thing in Hong Kong. It is good for her to know she is more fat, anyway. It will help her lose the weight. This is why there have not many fat girls in Hong Kong, you know."

"So you were helping her?"

"That's right."

I cleared my throat and picked up a newspaper.

I didn't like teaching newspaper articles. The language was too formal and much of the vocabulary too specialised. For the average student – even in this relatively advanced class – it was irrelevant to their needs and I felt an ineffective tool for teaching. But, as I had discovered downstairs, anything that involved passive learning was popular.

One evening, as an alternative, I introduced an article I had written myself on India. I expected it to provoke some interest and inquisitiveness but, as usual, I could not have been more wrong. Afterwards Rhoda said, "Why don't you tell a funny story about your time in India?"

I thought for a moment. I recalled the time I was in Ranthambor National Park, the tiger reserve in Rajasthan. I told how I decided to go on a lone foot safari around the park's fringes – foolishly assuming I would be safe, well away from the interior – after missing my tour vehicle. I described the crack of a twig, feelings of complacency replaced by vulnerability, looking through the bush and seeing movement… something large… something orange. I recalled the advice of what to do if you come face to face with a tiger (don't turn and run, for they prefer to attack from behind) but admitted to being too paralysed by fright to move, regardless. I let the suspense build further and then I revealed it was all a false panic as a large grazing stag emerged with its splendid hide reflecting orange in the late afternoon sunlight, and not a large cat to be seen. I told of my relief but continued nervousness being a defenceless, lone human, dangerously close to the tigers' favourite prey. Out of the forest and across the main track into the park was a hilltop fort. Officially it was outside the reserve and the path leading up was not hindered by jungle. At the top was a crumbling, long and circuitous wall surrounding a vast, rocky, scrubby plateau with a series of pools. I was hot, I was fraught, and the cool, clear waters enticed me in. I was in the middle of the pool, some fifty feet from the water's edge when I perceived movement. A kind of knobbly projectile was moving, ripples of tide being cast from it, exaggerating its rate of progress. It was undoubtedly some kind of creature and it was coming directly at me. And if it was coming at me I assumed it to be dangerous, and the most dangerous water-borne creatures in this area were crocodiles. They lived in the swamps down below in the main part of the park, I knew. I also had enough knowledge from wildlife programmes to understand that these great stealthy monsters hadn't survived since Jurassic times without learning the art of ambush. They conceal their mighty bodies beneath the surface in order to slip quietly unobserved onto their unsuspecting quarry, with only their noses protruding. And that knobbly projectile coming my way meant only one thing to me. In a mad panic I swam frantically for shore, my fear superseding even that of my earlier escapade, expecting at any moment a splash and a clamp of jaws around my legs. But I made it to shore, climbed out, dripping wet, naked, gasping and shaking fearfully. Behind me, not yet having even reached my starting point in the middle of the pool was indeed an amphibious creature, swimming resolutely on. But not a crocodile. A frog (a poisonous frog, I would like to think).

As I finished telling this great personal tale of survival in the wild to my attentive class there were murmurs but no great sense of mirth.

"Any reaction," I asked.

Someone said, "Why you think cocodile nook nike fox? I don't unnerstan'."

"Not fox, frog!"

Rhoda turned up her nose. "Crocodile look like frog! I don't think so."

At such times does the English teacher weary and question his career path.

Later Wendy, who was present in my class at the time of my Indian anecdote, condemned me for not telling her before about the time I was 'chased by tigers and foxes in the jungle'.

COMMUNICATIONAL CROSS-LINES notwithstanding, Wendy and I were getting closer again as a result of her returning to my classroom, after I had succeeded in avoiding her for some weeks in the aftermath of our ill-fated seaside assignation. In class she hadn't really changed and continued to offer moral support to me, even after my enforced move upstairs, offering sympathy when I needed it and advice when I didn't. She seldom telephoned but wrote messages which she would hand me at the end of lessons with instructions of where to meet. Occasionally she just followed me home. And she was over the Christian guilt thing. The randomness of our liaisons and the ever-shifting venues – one day in a karaoke room; then on a hill overlooking the airport; next on the roof of her block of flats; sometimes my place – were a source of regeneration, reviving the spark of excitement each time, where under more settled circumstances it might have faded.

I still welcomed her visits to my class at least as long as no one suspected we had something going. She fitted in confidently despite the comparative poverty of her English, which seldom hindered her willingness to speak up. An example of her high embarrassment threshold was memorably revealed when a young African footballer, who played for one of Hong Kong's semi-professional clubs, visited my class.

He was a tall, muscular centre back, with long dreadlocks dyed blonde. Wendy, sitting opposite him, eyed him with curiosity and without self-consciousness for some time, her gaze excluding all else. I knew she was eager to speak to him. She complimented him on his physique, which he enjoyed, and told him he had beautiful hair like a girl's, which he was less enamoured with. Then, still with that quizzical expression over her face, she asked if his hair colour was natural. There were a few uncomfortable giggles from other students, while the bemused object of Wendy's *faux pas* couldn't decide whether she was ridiculing him or just plain daft. On occasions like this her naivety was endearing, but on others her childish displays were less bearable.

We were in a park one evening when she suddenly started shrieking, then skipping from one foot to another in a hysterical tantrum, all the while maintaining the same level of high-pitched decibels. I was horrified and concerned. She had never reacted this way to being fondled before. The shrieking then gave way to an unpleasant squealing, before mock sobs on my shoulder.

"What is it, my sweet?" I asked, my concern overcoming the embarrassment of the attention her disturbance was now causing.

"A cockroach on my foot."

"A cockroach!... You must be used to them by now – this city has more cockroaches than people." I was beginning to see that, for all Wendy's obvious decency and sincerity, she had quite a taste for high drama.

Another incident in a different park, and Wendy showed a less timid side to her nature. We were again engaged in some kind of petting, when a Tom peeped too far from behind a wall barely two metres away. I instantly rose and collared the little wretch, who started bleating, "No... no... no." I was tempted to thump him or at least dip him in the fountain but found myself deterred by his pathos. I also contended that Wendy, with her Christian virtues, wouldn't approve of violence. I was wrong. For the rest of the evening she was complaining about my lack of valour and indicating she would have liked nothing better than seeing her man knock seven bells out of another.

A WEEKEND IN CANTON with Wendy as a guide was an invitation I couldn't resist, particularly as I had some trepidation at the prospect of travelling alone in China. I had only once crossed the border to Shenzhen, an ultra-new city of five million inhabitants which was built on marshlands in a mere ten years and close enough to be a suburb of Hong Kong.

Canton was something different: its very name was redolent of romance and mystery, a place with history and distinction, the economic and cultural engine of Guangdong province and South China. I'd heard of the Pearl River and Shamian Island; I'd viewed the paintings of Canton docks in a Hong Kong gallery, featuring scores of junks and other vessels with teams of coolies unloading their wares, all effectively portraying the city's life and industry. Now I would see it for myself.

Wendy and I took the Kowloon-Canton Railway, which in fact only goes as far as the border at Lo Wu. There was a mass of people stretching from the station towards the immigration checkpoint like a colony of ants, milling and pressing relentlessly forward. Wendy was a good worker ant, while I was more of an obstacle, and before I knew it she was some fifty yards in advance of me. I had found myself constrained by a British respect for an ordered queue. Everyone else, free of such a social handicap, seemed to be progressing at twice my speed, which they accomplished with a technique no doubt honed over the years of existing in confined spaces. It was more of a 'shove and jostle' than 'push and shove', and worked thus: First apply consistent nagging pressure to the person in front. As he is gently propelled forward, you, the pusher, are in position to sneak in front of the person who was beside the person you have just shoved. This is done by a skilful and cunning ducking motion and assertive use of elbow and shoulder.

The most adept practitioners, such as Wendy, can thus zig-zag their way to the front in virtually half the time of timid old lags like me. And she wasn't the only one. I was frustrated as one after another slipped past me and disappeared into the distance. With their shoulders and elbows nudging my ribs and waist it was no competition. I had no way of countering these little thrusts, particularly when they came, as they invariably did, from short, middle-aged women. If anyone was vertically-challenged around here it wasn't them. By the time I exited, Mainland-side, over an hour had passed.

Having spent twenty minutes looking for me, Wendy was concerned that I had got lost or kidnapped or something. On discovering I hadn't, she was relieved and then annoyed that I didn't have such an excuse for keeping her waiting. "Why you not follow me? Why you stand there? You mus' move, move, move... push, push, push. This is Chinese way, you know!"

We walked the short distance to Shenzhen's mainline station. The scenery glistened, boldly proclaiming its modernity: stupendous skyscrapers, five-star hotels, new shopping plazas. But the people seemed out of place, out of time. Officials in archaic uniforms blew whistles, waving and pointing dementedly at the oblivious human traffic. Out-of-town hawkers – recognisable by their tatty, formal attire and dark weather-worn faces with rosy cheeks – spread their wares on the pavement. Everywhere were women with baskets of every imaginable fruit and vegetable. Along the elevated pathway, crippled beggars on all fours made a beeline for me, tugging determinedly at my trouser leg. Below, a hundred taxis, whose touts approached us every ten seconds, honked for attention and vied for space. If this scene was Hong Kong with added attitude, poverty and anarchy, the railway station hall was pure China: a free-for-all bustle to the ticket kiosks, with loudspeakers incessantly blaring, and spittle and cigarette butts carpeting the floor of an austere, dimly-lit concrete shell of a structure.

The train was something of an improvement. It was punctual, it was quick, and it was relatively clean despite the best efforts of certain passengers. An old man chomping on grapes repeatedly spat pips on the floor; and a woman – with lacquered hair styled bizarrely, and not untypically, into a crisp uniform shape – was merrily clipping her finger and toenails just opposite me.

As we approached Canton, nearly two hours out of Shenzhen, we passed rough, brick-built shanties with smoke billowing from the kitchens within. Already the blue sky was being veiled by a cinereous vapour, gradually reducing the sun to an impotent blur. Outside, just before we pulled into the terminus, was a sight that made me shudder. A man was lying on the ground between two tracks, huddling defensively against successive blows from a man standing above him with a large stick. A similarly armed thug was on his way to join the onslaught. Both were wearing some kind of uniform. I felt sickened to my pits. Other passengers seemed momentarily concerned, while two young men observed with voyeuristic smiles of pleasure as if watching a violent film. We were some distance from the criminal activity by the time the train came to rest. I presumed the passengers at the back of the train would have been near enough to go and help. Wendy, however, told me it was unthinkable that anyone would go to the stricken man's assistance and unlikely that anyone would have called the police. Why? Because they *were* the police.

Beyond the station was a level of air pollution and traffic congestion that was comparable with the largest cities in Asia. The bus terminus, where we headed, was at the centre of a gigantic roundabout, with the bulk of traffic to-ing and fro-ing, fifteen abreast, in an anti-clockwise gyration, while many cyclists and motorcyclists preferred to travel in the opposite direction around the inner and outer perimeters. There were no traffic lights, no footbridges and no order. To catch one of the buses you needed to edge across that maddening maelstrom, dodging a perilous path through the flow of traffic.

We thought taking a taxi would be a safer option. But our driver, who fancied himself as something of an Oriental Ayrton Senna, had other ideas, tailgating large, slow-moving vehicles, pulling out and overtaking with abandon, shimmying around and between other taxis at terrifying speed, nearly hitting several pedestrians and cyclists in the process. His only salvation, and that of other bad drivers in China, is that they are not alone and every other driver is attuned to and prepared for the erratic digressions of others.

Shamian Island, the former European trading post, on the Pearl River, was our destination. Crossing the bridge from the city was like entering a new land, leaving behind the hustle of traffic and the blight of the brutal modern for a tranquil enclave of classic architecture, avenues and riverscapes. Many of the French and British buildings may have lost some of their old self-importance – through neglect and decay – but were scarcely less impressive for it. Unsurprisingly, the Chinese don't value this place: this place from which they were once excluded. It represents a time and a historical situation that is still referred to as a national humiliation. Who can blame them for not flocking to visit or rushing to restore these relics of imperialism? That they didn't bulldoze the lot is at least something to be thankful for. We were booked into the only outstandingly ugly building on the whole island: the White Swan Hotel. If ever there were an example of a structure built out of proportion and out of sympathy with its surroundings it was this gigantic white concrete block, whose unsightliness was mitigated only by the views from within. These encompassed the entire island – revealing just how small it is and the vast city expanses beyond.

Nearby – just over a dirty canal that marks one of the island's boundaries – was Ching Ping Market, an area that brought to mind London's Brick Lane, only even more dilapidated. Terraces of crumbling brickwork – many supporting unplanted shoots of shrubbery and wild rooftop gardens – with unlit, timber-clad interiors, were the backdrop to one of Asia's most exotically displeasing bazaars. Animals of all kinds, from scorpions to donkeys were here. I watched a rabbit being decapitated and gutted before a customer; skinned cats and dogs hung from market shelters. These were the lucky ones. Puppies, cats and rabbits were packed into cages with barely enough room to breathe, never mind move. Aquaria squirmed and teemed with reptiles. Most popular were turtles, which were picked and despatched by a man with a cleaver, on the first step to becoming a jellied soup. The worst sight for me, though, was that of a blind, emaciated mongrel throwing up a piece of biscuit I had fed it. Its body had given up the fight, its life almost spent (although 'life' is hardly a defining term for what this wretched creature had endured). I had seen enough and my companion was equally disgusted, I was glad to note.

Although it was evening in early December the weather was still mild enough to sit at an open-air café, where we enjoyed an unusual but edible local interpretation of chili con carne. Nearby was a large group of American couples, apparently in celebratory mood. Each couple was in possession of at least one baby. I didn't show much interest until Wendy told me to take a closer look. The one on the next table had darker than average hair, I noticed, and stronger than average vocal cords. Other than that it didn't distinguish itself to me.

"Well?"

"Well, what?"

"It is Chinese baby."

"What, with two *gwailo* parents?"

"It is Chinese baby, I make sure." She squinted her eyes, looking over my shoulder. "Behind people have Chinese baby, also."

I looked behind, and sure enough, they did. And the couple beside them. Looking around I realised that all these tots being held and cherished by white Americans appeared to be Oriental.

"I fink they come here adop' babies," said Wendy.

"You don't think they're kidnappers, then?"

This is the kind of silly humour that often tickles the Cantonese, and Wendy was no exception. "You foolish boy!"

"Looks like they've had a successful Christmas shopping trip, then."

She laughed again. "You nike go Christmas shopping?"

I gave it some thought and spoke of my misgivings about rich Westerners coming over, viewing babies in orphanages as if it were some kind of beauty contest and taking home the winners. Wendy pointed out (quite literally in her own clumsy fashion) a baby with a club foot being doted over by an adoring couple. She also told how she admired these people for coming so far to 'save' these unwanted Chinese babies.

"But they're doing it for their own benefit first, surely?"

She said it didn't matter; most Chinese people would be

impressed that these people could love babies that were not their own, and not even their own kind. Nobody would want them here. The children would have no chance of good lives if they stayed in China with no family support and no opportunities. It was wonderful that they could go to a Western country to make a new future.

I told her there were thousands upon thousands of unwanted black American children up for adoption.

She said in that matter-of-fact Cantonese way that of course they would prefer Chinese babies.

CHRISTMAS IN HONG KONG is a fairly low-key affair. Expats and anyone else who can afford to get away usually does so.

I couldn't. So it was a turkey dinner at the Salvation Army – "Spaghetti or rice with the turkey, sir?" – and a boat trip to Lantau Island on a warm, sunny afternoon. It could have been worse, but then Wendy started whining about missing Christmas night mass – and what would her friends think? – and saying she felt pressured into going with me and would have much preferred to go the next morning, and I thought: not much worse.

We got to a hill overlooking the guest house, near Pui O, in time to see the sun set. Except proper sunsets in Hong Kong are a rarity. Usually the sun just slips down the western sky, a blood-orange globule gradually eclipsed and consumed by a sulphurous haze before it reaches the horizon's edge. And, being the tropics, darkness always falls quickly.

A path wound down through forest and over swamp, past banana trees and tall reeds that in daytime conceal a legion of mosquitoes. Now, in the cool of dusk, they were out and about and doing their worst. Wendy was stopping, then hopping, and whimpering as the hungry insects set about her bare, fleshy calves. Wearing denims and walking boots, I for once was spared in comparison. She was all irritable animation, frantically trying to brush them off her legs, when a large black snake slid swiftly and silently across her path. I braced myself for her reaction, but fortunately she was so preoccupied with mosquitoes that it was gone by the time she looked up. She wasn't done with me, though. As we neared the guesthouse, I was blamed for her bites because I had insisted that we went today, and as it was late in the afternoon I should have known about the mosquitoes and I should have advised her to wear trousers, and, oh, mass would be starting in one hour, and she repeated she would really rather be there than here. It reinforced my idea that for most Hong Kongers the countryside is really a place to be avoided. Any appreciation in the Western mind of tranquillity, fresh air, mountain views and nature is outweighed by the more negative symbolism of poverty, lack of civilisation and danger. Only a generation earlier, in Mao's China, hundreds of millions of the bourgeois and other 'class traitors' were expelled from the cities to the countryside for 're-education' and forced to scratch a living on infertile lands frozen by harsh interior winters and scorched to dust by summer sun and droughts, with the cycles of disease and famine as predictable as the seasons. And I suspect it is an ancestral memory that still runs deep.

One advantage of this mindset is that the Hong Kong countryside is still remarkably undeveloped and unspoilt, and it is possible, particularly on weekdays, to walk for an hour or two without seeing another soul. To find yourself alone on a beach in a wooded bay on an island less than forty-five minutes from one of the busiest, noisiest and most congested metropolitan centres in the world is one of the wonders of Hong Kong and indeed Asia. Nonetheless at this particular time I didn't greatly fancy being alone on an island with Wendy in her present mood and was glad to find several Westerners sitting on the beachside patio at the back of the guesthouse. The setting was convivial, with the smell of incense overpowering fumes from a mosquito coil. The furniture was all bamboo, as was a rustic patio shelter – young palm trees at each corner – and a sandy beach in front, with the aural backdrop of breaking surf.

"Wow... hard to believe this is Hong Kong, right?" I remarked.

Wendy only produced a stoutly unimpressed "Huh" in response.

Having introduced ourselves, we were offered a blow of a joint that someone had just lit up. If I turned it down it would be harder to socially integrate; if I took it I knew I would earn Wendy's disapprobation. But I already had that in spades. I took the thickly-packed roll-up and as I inhaled I caught Wendy's glance. Her nose was wrinkled, her eyes almost invisible in an unmistakable display of angry, disgusted disillusionment. She got up in a rush, shoved me on the shoulder and retired to the room. And at that moment I didn't much care. The immature attitude towards cannabis, which Wendy presented, was one I had encountered in my classroom several times. To many Hong Kong people it is a drug, it is illegal, it is indistinguishable from cocaine or heroin, and I hardly met a local person that admitted to having taken any. As far as Wendy was concerned, I was already on the slide to addiction.

A couple of my new 'friends' looked at me with resigned regret, as if to say: 'What did you expect?' while Jennifer, the Australian manager, gestured for me to follow Wendy.

Instead, while Wendy sulked in the room, I enjoyed an hour's release. I mentioned Wendy's close call with the snake, which started a conversation on the nature of Hong Kong. Jennifer was a part-time naturalist and I learned from her that there were pythons and cobras aplenty in the forests and scrubs of Hong Kong, and that her neighbours had killed one recently which had ventured into their kitchen. Another snake had bitten her friend who was returning home along one of the lonely paths in the darkness. He was picked up by a helicopter ambulance and ferried to Kowloon before it was ascertained that the bite was not poisonous.

I was a little high by now and eager to make up and share my new knowledge with Wendy. But she didn't appreciate being woken to discuss the reptilian fauna of Hong Kong, even after being apprised of her narrow escape at the fangs of such. Instead, she said, "You are drunk."

"I am not. I haven't drunk a thing."

"You are drunk with drugs, stupid."

"No, I am not drunk, I am stoned. There's a new word for your vocabulary."

She slapped me hard and even in the state I was in I knew it was deserved.

Next day, after I had apologised for the night before, we took a bus up to the giant Buddha, halfway up Lantau Peak. It is the largest seated bronze Buddha in the world, according to the literature. Which, when you think about it, means there could be several larger standing Buddhas or reclining Buddhas and probably a fair few seated Buddhas made of alternative materials.

But it was still worth the visit, not least for the views, natural surroundings and more.

Wendy and I wandered down the hillside away from onlookers and found a quiet spot to picnic. I was on my best behaviour, tenderly trying to make amends for yesterday's insensitivity, and was starting to win her over. She still didn't appreciate my Western decadence, likewise I her Eastern conservatism, but once we kissed, it didn't matter. After the tension of the night before, the allure of make-up sex was too great for both of us to resist. But the short-term orgasmic pleasure would come at a cost, reviving the illusion of a relationship when it seemed we could bear each other no more, particularly since it was one of the few times we'd had full sexual relations since our original tryst. Post-coital, I pondered this ruefully, while Wendy, seemingly now reconciled with her sins, laid back like a pampered princess requesting I drop grapes into her mouth.

PRIVATE TUITION was the best way to boost our low pay, but I had never had the opportunity until a chance meeting with an ex-colleague led to a twice-weekly assignment which, following a rescheduling of my KEC classes, would earn me more for an hour's work than my normal four-hour stint.

It was the first week of the Chinese New Year and the venue was the clubhouse of a plush new apartment development. The lobby was a grand, high-ceilinged marble hall, the theme of which was classic Rome, with mock columns, fountains and cherubic sculptures, resulting in possibly the most incongruous and tasteless entrance to a skyscraper this side of Las Vegas.

Not that I really noticed on my first visit. I was walking into the unknown, and had other things on my mind. What kind of people lived here? …What would I teach? …How would the students respond? …Would I be intimidated by the environment? The butterflies were multiplying as I climbed the lavishly decorous staircase to the first floor. Here at least the surroundings were more modest. According to the agency employing me, I would be teaching infants, which I took as the British school definition of children five to eight years old. It would be a formidable task for someone who had never taught children before, but it was time for a new challenge and time to start earning real money. I was mentally prepared, with nursery rhymes in mind and armed with picture cards. It wouldn't be easy but I felt I could handle it.

As I entered the classroom, a Chinese woman was singing and clapping her hands, while a dozen or more toddlers with their minders were sat around the table. I waited patiently for over five minutes with an uncommunicative young classroom assistant. Then I wondered aloud when my students would be turning up.

"But, sir, these are your students."

I nearly choked. Half of them were wearing nappies.

"Are you ready?" she asked, as my warm-up act stepped to one side after enthusiastically introducing me to the assembled audience.

"You are going to help me, aren't you?" I enquired desperately, but my 'assistant' merely shook her head and handed me an ABC book.

I stepped nervously to the front of the table, where I was greeted by mild applause from the Filipina helper contingent. They were darlings, with their warm smiles of encouragement, gentle cajoling of their young charges, and active responses to my initiatives. I needed them as I struggled over *Old McDonald* and *If you're happy and you know it.* I was awkward, flushed and uneasy, a feeling only partially assuaged by the enthusiasm of the childminders. The toddlers were less predisposed to my methods, with attention spans of seconds and regular bouts of crying and squirming. And one, who had not even begun to speak his mother tongue, never mind English, threw up over the table. I managed to stretch the lesson to forty-five minutes, which seemed more like two hours, before the rest of the tots' patience ran out. It was an initiation far more harrowing than my first day at the English Club. I wondered how I could cope with two sessions like this a week. It was more nerve-rending and almost as wearying as my usual four hours. Already I was anticipating my next appointment with dread.

The lessons came and went over the next few weeks, but didn't get much easier, and the dreadful feelings prior to lessons scarcely abated. And while I was gaining experience I was losing inspiration. It was hard to come up with original ideas each time, so I tended to drag out the same material, ABC…123, colours, shapes, parts of the body, but using different props, which I would trawl the toy shops at weekends for. But relating to a class full of toddlers just wasn't my thing. I felt like a failure, and with my lack of confidence, spontaneity and enterprise it was becoming hard to maintain the lesson much over half an hour.

I expected the class attendance to diminish, but in fact there were few dropouts and numbers actually began to rise. My self-criticism of lacking ideas and teaching material was paradoxically considered a strength. I was told that I was patient, my teaching method was thorough, and I earned appreciation for not changing the subject too often like other teachers.

The response was some consolation, but not enough to delay

my resignation from nursery duties after two months. I left with an improved bank balance, a commitment never to teach at a kindergarten again, and a new romantic interest.

PAM was her name (or at least an Anglicised abbreviation of her real name, Supamiati) and she was one of the childminders in the classroom. Distinct from most of the others, her hair, make-up and clothes were always impeccable, suggestive more of a successful young businesswoman than a domestic helper. After a session teaching, I wondered aloud if she was the child's mother. It seemed unlikely due to their differing shades of complexion, but I was interested to discover more about her. She laughed, and face to face with her for the first time, I was quite smitten. Her eyes gleamed brilliantly and she wore an expression that combined innocent beauty with an enigmatic worldliness.

When I asked her for coffee she smiled mischievously and not discouragingly but replied, "If you ask me again maybe I say yes!"

I tried again next time and then she replied, "I don't like coffee… you have to do better than that." Then she walked off, with a coquettish glance over her shoulder, before I had the chance to improve upon the offer.

I was left feeling slightly deflated but all the more resolved to secure a date. She was cool and cute and she knew it, but she also knew how to flirt to ensure lasting interest without selling herself cheaply.

When I tried again, she replied once more in the negative. This time I showed a little impatience. "What is it this time?" I asked.

"I am busy this week," she replied firmly. "Write down your

number here and I will call you later." She was both affirming control of the situation and teasing as she rolled up her sleeve and offered her delicate wrist for me to write on. I held her hand as I did, while she looked up at me with those irresistible eyes.

Two more lessons and eight long days passed before Pam finally called me. "Where will you take me then?" she asked cheerily.

I suggested a Filipino restaurant someone had recommended. I thought she could scarcely turn her nose up at that, but all she said was okay in a dubious tone of voice. That enigma again.

I half-expected to be stood up, but she turned up only five minutes late at Causeway Bay MTR station looking even lovelier and glamorous than usual. It was only after I asked her what she recommended on the menu that I realised my faux pas: she was from Indonesia, not the Philippines. It wasn't a good start. I apologised humbly and explained that I'd made the assumption on the strength of her English and the fact that she spoke so quickly in the style of many Filipinos rather than any other stereotypes. I was glad to note she took no offence, only a cheeky amusement at my discomfort.

She remained easygoing and chatty throughout the evening, during which time I discovered she was a Muslim, although she conformed to virtually none of my preconceptions of that religion and how its adherents were supposed to behave. Islam was not an issue for her, she said, at least as long as she was in Hong Kong. She used to have a rich Chinese boyfriend, hence the designer clothes and jewellery, and she didn't have to work too hard as she had a decent employer. She also had a boyfriend in Indonesia but hadn't seen him for over a year and rarely heard from him.

As I got to know her it was obvious that she was far more Westernised and liberal, confident and experienced than most similarly-aged Hong Kong girls. She was perfectly at ease in my company from the start, whether teasing me over the choice of venue, or flirting skilfully and subtly, or kissing without a hint of awkwardness at the end of our first date.

On her first visit to my place she put on a pretence of virginal demureness before revealing her true colours. From then on we usually met two or three times a week but scarcely ever on nights or weekends. She said she had a part-time job as a technician at a film studio, the boss of which was also her domestic employer. My offers to meet her after work there were always beaten away by excuses about overtime or meetings. I tried not to be bothered, but as we got closer my frustration grew. Sunday was my only full day of holiday and I wanted to spend it with her. There may have been the consolation of her company on weekday afternoons at my place, but without complete freedom, with half an eye on the clock and returning for the evening shift. These stolen hours were only a reminder of what I was missing at weekends, and although meeting Wendy had become less habitual I found myself resorting to her on occasional lonely Sundays, before guilt impelled me to tell her about Pam.

I realised I felt something with Pam I had never felt with Wendy. Not only on account of her beauty and femininity, but there was something about her enigmatic self-confidence. She gave the impression that she wanted me but didn't really need me. She had other things in her life – what those were exactly remained unclear – and I would have to fit in around her. Consequently I felt less secure in her company but all the more resolved to win her unconditionally. Wendy, on the other hand, was an open book, vivacious, loving, generous, all of which had attracted me to her at the outset. But these virtues were now being outweighed by childishness, neediness and at times cloying sentimentality. And the communicational and cultural lack of compatibility, which had always been apparent, was now for me becoming unbearable. Although I knew this was less of an issue for Wendy, I expected some understanding and hoped for a mature response in view of her earlier liberal pronouncements about staying together ('friends +' as we called it) until either of us found someone more suitable. Instead she responded with an impassioned fury, leaving in me in no doubt as to the depth of hurt and betrayal she was feeling. I reflected once more on how much neater it would have been had we parted ways on Lantau before that reckless shag on the hill, and that I was reaping what I had sown.

The next week she was in my class every day, mostly staring disdainfully, then casting comments in a disparaging tone for Cantonese ears only. She was determined to rile and provoke me into losing my temper, and preferably demean and humiliate me on the way. But by now I was well-practised at coping with disaffected students, and though I felt pity for her and was disturbed by her tactics, I was confident it wouldn't last and she would be over me soon enough.

Instead I would find the rawness of her emotions unrelenting and her grudge, already sore and festering, become more toxic by the day. On one such occasion, the class discussion was on education in which I asked students to tell me the qualities of a good teacher and the flaws of a bad one, then about their experiences with their best and worst tutors at school. Rhoda told a long-winded tale about a teacher who always picked on her, and I found myself sympathising with him, while wondering why only one teacher had had it in for her. Then Wendy cleared her throat and looked at me with her cold, black-pearl eyes penetrating deep into mine. I took a deep breath.

"When I younger I have affair wiv teacher," she started. There were a few murmurs from other students. "He handsome and I love him very much. But he don't love me!"

For a moment I thought she was going to break down, but thankfully she had the resilience to control her emotion. Nonetheless I was deeply uncomfortable, a feeling only slightly assuaged by my expectation that she would not reveal my identity – not unless she had given up all hope of getting me back. I wanted to maintain normality, so refrained from changing the subject, which I immediately regretted when someone asked her which school it was and inadvertently gave her the opportunity to point the finger when perhaps she may not have done otherwise.

My composure was melting as she looked down, delaying her reply, before at last simply saying, "It is private school."

I looked around at everyone but Wendy. "Anyone else had a romance with a teacher? …No? …Good. It's not a good idea."

"My teacher…" Shit! It was Wendy again. "…my teacher… all the other girls in the class dey nike him very much. Dey talk about him. Other girls want to date him. But he choose me. I so proud and happy be wiv him. I never tell other girls I wiv him. I want… erm… I want protec' him, you know? I always help him, nook after him, but he don't care about that… don't care about me. He find new pretty, slim girl and he finish me. He is bastard!"

This time I couldn't even look at the other faces, and nor could I retreat to the gents' or the coffee machine. That would be too obvious. The best I could think of to earn respite was to give Rhoda a subject and let her talk. But when I did she just glanced at Wendy then back at me and said, "I think *you* need to talk."

WENDY'S OBSESSION was not sated by her classroom antics. She had succeeded in shaming me, scarring me even, and deterring some female students from returning to my class. But it wasn't enough.

I hadn't seen her for nearly two weeks when I got wind of her latest tactic. I was with Pam, meeting her for lunch after my morning session of teaching, when I saw Wendy as we sat down by the window of a Western-style restaurant. It could have been a coincidence except she was walking in the same direction as we had been, over a mile from her office, and looking searchingly through the window.

When we left I looked anxiously around, but there was no sign of her. After a couple of minutes I swung a glance over my shoulder before crossing the road, and there, a short distance behind, was Wendy. Our eyes met briefly, hers focused purposefully. She was challenging me to challenge her, seeking another scornful showdown, this time in front of Pam. To avoid such a scene, I took Pam's arm and slipped down an adjacent street, in through the side entrance of a shop, then back out the front of the main entrance. Wendy was given the slip and Pam accepted my explanation that I had just wanted to avoid a boring student. But the incident played on my mind. How many times had she trailed us before and how many more would I be looking over my shoulder?

I felt I couldn't share my concerns with Pam even as Wendy's campaign continued apace. She followed me home a few times, even going as far as watching me into the lift. When I stopped to confront her she just stopped and stared, blanking my requests for reason. She came to the class at least once a week, where she would sit in the most prominent position available and fix me with that stare from the time she arrived until she left. Her expression never changed: cold eyes and pursed lips, even when everyone else in the class was laughing. Fun was in diminishing supply by now, though. How could I remain spontaneous and amusing under such a spotlight? On the few occasions that I found any sparkle under Wendy's scrutiny, she would strategically get up and leave with a rustle of papers and a banging of books in an attempt to disrupt my flow. If I spoke of anything vaguely personal she would respond with a knowing 'huh'. What the other students made of her behaviour I didn't know and dared not ask, but I was becoming increasingly unnerved. Even when she wasn't in class I found myself glancing warily down the corridor every time I heard someone approach.

Wendy had become a different person and I was starting to wonder if, in her current state of mind, she might just be capable of something more sinister. I tried to make sense of her apparent psychosis. It was true I had taken her for granted and dispensed with her when it suited me. I recalled her calling me a selfish *gwailo*. She was half right. I had been caught up in the hedonistic Hong Kong expat lifestyle of living for the day and fuck tomorrow as much as anyone, but I understood that had left her feeling betrayed and humiliated. I also knew how it felt. But whereas I had rationalised past disappointments with the thought that an unrequited love was a wasted love, Wendy seemed unable to move on. She was unaccustomed to being in a romantic, sexual relationship and therefore emotionally ill-equipped to let go. Although I had always tried to stress that ours was a casual relationship, she had clearly harboured bigger aspirations. I remembered her talk of mixed-race Eurasian babies and how beautiful they usually were, and that I would make a good father one day. I had paid lip service, but did nothing to encourage the sentiment. Now, as I was mulling over the cultural difference in attitude towards relationships, love and sex, I was starting to wish I had borne these local factors more in mind on starting things with Wendy. This was firstly because of the pain I had caused her, but now increasingly due to the effect she was having on me: one night I awoke from a nightmare in which I was watching powerlessly as she pummelled Pam unconscious in my bedroom. It confirmed, if there was any doubt, that she was getting to me.

It was surely a coincidence, but when I came home tired and slightly spaced on a Friday, after a week's teaching, and found Wendy waiting in my room, I felt cast back into that nightmare. As I walked in, the door was slammed violently behind me and there she was, arms folded in grim resolve. I was shocked and angered more than afraid.

"What the fuck are you doing here? What if I'd come in with Pam? …How did you get in anyway?"

"Shut up you questions. Sit down, you bastard!"

"Don't talk to me like…"

She shoved me hard on the chest, making me lose balance and fall backwards onto the bed, then looked down on me with eyes ablaze. She appeared as I had never seen her before, heavily made up with mascara and scarlet lipstick, wearing a black leather mini, fishnets and low cut top.

I protested again, but she wasn't listening, her countenance fixed with sly intransigence. She was reading me, looking for signs… Then she smiled, thin and cold, a smile that I didn't recognise as hers. Then she was kneeling on the bed, legs either side of me with her pelvis pressed heavily against mine and her arms placed around my neck. She was bigger, stronger, less feminine, uglier, more sluttish than Pam. I didn't need her or want her. As I tried to pull back, feeling disgusted by her looks and conduct, I could feel her rubbing against my groin and somewhere in the midst of my personal repulsion something was stirring. It was the Helen Syndrome again: that symbiotic physical attraction, exclusive of gentleness and devotion. Still I struggled and tried to spurn her advances, but she was wrapping herself around me like a python. To extricate myself now would have taken a degree of force that I was reluctant to inflict on Wendy. For, in spite of her actions, I couldn't find it in myself to hurt her in any way. And in her present state, had I thrown her out, there was no knowing how the shame compounded by existing pain would manifest itself in her response. But in not doing so, I was demeaning myself, betraying Pam and giving Wendy the green light to continue her pursuit, perhaps even providing grounds for blackmail. I knew I would feel grubby and used, empty and guilty as a result. I knew it would be a compulsive but ultimately degrading thrill, like being with a whore, but without the luxury of being able to pay her off and forget all about it afterwards. And I knew none of that would count for anything in determining my lack of resistance.

Once it was done, Wendy left with few words spoken. I went downstairs to remonstrate with Akram – who was looking after Mr Mohammed's properties – for letting her into my room, telling him that my relationship with Wendy was finished and imploring him to refuse her entry next time. He said he would, but it didn't matter. She had other plans.

A week or more had passed when she phoned, telling me she had urgent news for me. "Just tell me!" But she refused unless I agreed a rendezvous at a Tsim Sha Tsui noodle shop we used to frequent.

This time she didn't look like a vamp, but something more akin to a career woman. She ordered a couple of bowls of wun-tun with noodles and a plate of spinach with oyster sauce. Then she informed me that she knew of Pam's secret.

"What is it?"

"She have rich boyfen'. You know dis fing?"

"No, I didn't," I replied wearily.

"I see dem many times together…"

"Don't tell me you're stalking her now!"

"No, she live near me, I see dem when I go home."

"Okay, why do you think he is her boyfriend? Were they kissing or holding hands?"

"No but dey very close, I know. Sometime dey stop and argue, nike me and you before," she laughed.

"He is just her boss. They have many things to discuss, you know."

I said it as convincingly as I could but secretly I had always had doubts. So much of Pam's behaviour was enigmatic and secretive. She changed arrangements frequently; she was aggressively defensive whenever I quizzed her about her life, her job and her boss. Wendy's allegation made sense, but I didn't want her to know I believed it. I concentrated on her tactics instead, berating her for interfering in my life, and telling her to keep away from Pam.

"When you see her next time?"

"I don't know. She's going away for a couple of weeks."

"Wiv him?"

"No, she's going back to Indonesia to see her sister. She's very ill."

"You believe her? …Huh! You are stupid… stupid… stupid."

"What does this man look like?" I enquired.

"He is quite old man, but very rich, I fink. He wear expensive clothes; he have Porsche car. She love him for the money and use you for the sex. *Lei chun gwailo!*"

"What?"

"It mean you stupid foreigner man."

I laughed and she affectionately pinched my cheek, just like she always used to, reminding me of those happier, easier times together; reminding me that, despite her intensity, she had qualities that Pam lacked. She was loyal and loving, she was passionate, frank and honest. Pam, on the other hand, was delicate, pretty, charming, and subtle: all virtues that Wendy did not possess. If I could have found a woman with the combination of the two…

"What you fing-king?"

"Oh, just about me and Pam." I was also thinking about Wendy's observation that she loved him for his money. Pam certainly had a materialistic nature and several times she had aired her frustration about my lack of earning power and ambition, telling me I should do business or get a job in a proper school.

"You need fink about you and Pam and Pam's other boyfen. You believe me about this?"

I sighed. "Yes, I suppose I do. It would explain a lot."

"You not upset? You still want see her?"

I looked at her and she sensed my doubt.

"Maybe you can have two girlfens, if she have two boyfens."

She smiled and pinched my cheek again.

PART THREE

Ain't No Glamour in Grammar

PRIVATE LESSON

Most of the long-term KEC teachers had at least one or two private lessons a week. Some even gained enough to quit the daily grind and work freelance full-time. I envied them. I had no students of my own and I felt less of a teacher for it. The few enquiries I had received had come to nothing, and six months in, I had virtually given up looking.

Then one evening after class I was asked by Carmen, a girl who had only recently started coming to my class, if I would like to come and teach her and her friends on Sunday morning at her flat in Sham Shui Po. They would pay me double my normal rate for the two-hour lesson, which sounded good, although was actually well below the going rate for 'privates', and I would have to spend some time planning and would lose my one chance of a lie-in for the entire week. I wasn't going to shut the door on this opportunity, though, if it meant broadening my teaching horizons.

The first lesson passed quickly, with the usual introductory topics of favourite foods, countries you've visited, what you like or dislike about Hong Kong and inviting them to ask me questions. At the end of the lesson they suggested going for *yam cha*, the traditional Hong Kong brunch of *dim sum* – delectable prawn dumplings, spring rolls, pork buns and the not-so-delectable jellyfish, chickens' feet, and baby pigeons.

Yam cha literally means 'drink tea', but it is much more than that, more indeed than just a meal; it is a social event, a family occasion, a ritual, a Hong Kong institution. It is the one time and place where the Cantonese can really be seen to relax: gabbing, shouting, laughing, smoking. The noise is a shock to the uninitiated, but not everyone is talking. At almost every large family table there are men, leaning back in their chairs perusing the morning papers oblivious to all, but contented just the same.

People look at me – the only non-Chinese out of hundreds of people – as I walk past the tables on entering the restaurant. It doesn't bother me: I love the food, the atmosphere, and the friendly service from the old trolley ladies, but I'm with a group of Chinese who are unused to dining with foreigners. My chopsticks technique is about to be scrutinised, discussed and judged while I will be required to pass opinion on every item put in front of me. But, in the cause of a delicious free meal, I accept with good grace.

We sit down and I commit my first *faux pas* by failing to follow the crockery/cutlery hygiene code which requires diners to use the tea to cleanse chopsticks, bowl and cup before consumption. In times when cholera was rife it was a wise precaution. Now it is a superfluous ritual and a waste of good tea, in my opinion. But it is not for me to question. We drink the remaining dregs of tea from the pot, then wait some time for a refill. Service is not a premium in these vast, crowded dining halls. When the food arrives I notice that the earlier obsession with hygiene is abandoned for a free-for-all dip into shared sauces and dishes with the same chopsticks that deliver the food to the mouth. When I can't reach my favourite fried beancurd and vegetable roll, one of my dining companions 'kindly' uses her chopsticks to deliver it to my plate. I'm not complaining (I've been to India and my stomach has put up with far greater hazards), merely noting contradictory habits. The allusion is that you won't be infected by someone you share a table with but watch out for everyone else.

Usually the conversation is ninety per cent Cantonese on these occasions. I don't let it trouble me, although it sometimes makes me wonder why I have been invited along. After any lesson the temptation to revert to the native tongue is for them quite overwhelming. There can be few peoples around the world so attached to their language as the Cantonese-speakers are to theirs. Ask any native of Hong Kong what he most misses when he is away and the likely answer will be – aside from the food – speaking and listening to that distinctive South China dialect. Communicating in English, many of my students are nervous and shy, but in a local setting, spluttering hesitancy and diffidence are replaced by clear, loud voices and spontaneous actions. There is something in the character of this language (officially Cantonese is termed a Chinese dialect, but it is as distinct from Mandarin Chinese as Spanish is from French) with its hard consonants which almost demand to be barked, and its bizarre-sounding vowels, crude guttural stops, yet subtle intonations that allow native speakers to expand with a vocal clarity and confidence that few other tongues can match. Nobody mumbles in Hong Kong and stammering is almost non-existent as a result of their boisterous communication methods, which are learned young, when hollering kids are rarely discouraged. But obscure and exclusive to the outsider, rich in idiom and slang, it is a language that unites only the initiated. It is not meant to be learned by foreigners. It is not expected and it is not encouraged, evidenced by the dearth of language-learning books or tapes available on the subject. The idea of a Westerner communicating well in Cantonese is almost as preposterous to them as a Chinese talking Cockney rhyming slang would be to a Londoner. I wished to learn it, especially on occasions like this, but more important was the need to teach properly. And I still wasn't fluent in this language.

The third lesson with Carmen and her friends was more arduous than the first two. Lazily I hadn't brought any material, thinking I could once again get away with conversation. But two hours is a long time to occupy, especially with students like these. There was Melanie, an albino with flashing ephemeral smiles and blinking eyes, competent at English but nervously uninvolved. Her friend, Angela, was pretty and pleasant but hardly understood a word I said. Then there was Queenie, a plump, jolly girl, unafraid to speak but reluctant to think. Finally Janet, an assertive Taiwanese woman, who was charm one minute and abrasiveness the next. She was older than the others and she was also their boss, which meant they never fully relaxed in her presence.

Just before leaving, Janet told me that the others wanted to learn grammar next time, although she herself preferred conversation. I was relieved and daunted: glad to be free of the strained artifice of 'free talk' but apprehensive about my lack of grammar teaching experience. Most of the teachers at the Club were reluctant to teach grammar, by perpetuating the myth that it was an unnecessary formality. The usual refrain to students enquiring about grammar was: 'I never learned grammar, so you don't need to', which conveniently overlooked the fact that learning a second language is a conscious discipline compared to the instinctual process of acquiring one's mother tongue. I had met too many students who applied the rules of Chinese grammar to English, and no amount of conversation practice (children excepted) was going to eradicate their errors without some knowledge of tenses and awareness of the different forms – verb, noun, adjective, adverb – of the same word. If I wanted to consider myself a real teacher grammar would have to be taught.

I immersed myself in text books whenever I had the time, trying to revise my unstudied knowledge of language rules and then reconnect them in a conscious context. I knew, for example, when to use the present continuous tense, but how do you explain that? And when should you use the present perfect instead of the past tense? What about the 'ing' and 'ed' forms of an adjective? I considered teaching the noun-verbs known as gerunds, but decided that the 'passive voice' would be a less complicated item to teach in the first lesson. I would give an example of the active voice, for example: "A mosquito bit me." They would be asked to give the passive equivalent: "I was bitten by a mosquito." Easy to teach equals easy to learn.

I wanted to teach properly and felt it beat the idle repetitive chat I was used to. I was challenging myself as well as my students, and striving to impress them with my new-found knowledge. I started to see myself as something of a failure in lessons if I only indulged in frivolous conversation. I was tired of discussing the same old topics, eager instead to inform. If grammar was the key to learning, I would be the gatekeeper. Except I was in danger of becoming an obsessive bore to all but the most committed of students, and my inquisitive enthusiasm for the intricacies of the

English language was seldom shared by those who paid for my services.

When I decided to do a two-hour period of grammar at the beginning of my evening session at the language club the bemused faces gave picture to sentiments only dear old Rhoda was brave enough to articulate: "Why are you teaching this, sir?"

At least they had the excuse that they hadn't requested this form of tuition. Unnoticed by me, the Sham Shui Po quartet were also stirring with discontent. Certainly the lessons were more orthodox than the previous ones, with laughter replaced by concentrated frowns. Even so I was shocked to be told after only the fourth lesson of the new regime that my services were no longer required. I was going to ask why, but Janet saved me the bother, with words that blew my confidence: "You need to make your teaching more fun. These last few weeks are so boring."

I wondered silently what she had expected from grammar lessons. And I hated the way she said so. Although the Taiwanese, in common with the Cantonese, are known for their frankness, I couldn't help resenting her comments.

Recounting my private teaching experiences to Robert, an experienced English tutor, he told me it was pretty much to be expected, and that it was better to stick to individuals if possible. "You will never be able to satisfy more than one or two students for more than a couple of months, particularly when they have different abilities and aspirations. And when one loses interest the others soon follow. Teaching privately is the most insecure job in Hong Kong."

SHAM SHUI PO

I didn't miss my private Sunday lessons greatly, but working in different areas and getting the opportunity to discover new areas such as Sham Shui Po, where Carmen lived, was something else. I enjoyed wandering these thronged market passages and roughened neighbourhoods, observing a section of life quite distinct from anywhere else in Hong Kong.

Crouched and compact below the steep escarpment of the Kowloon hills, Sham Shui Po is the essence of old, working class Hong Kong – probably the grubbiest, cheapest, poorest district in the entire territory, with the highest ratio of mainland immigrants, and brothels on every other street. There is a quarter given over to computer and electrical retail, which at night becomes a flea market of televisions, computers and hi-fi; several other streets are exclusively wholesale lower-end fashion and accessories. There are also extensive markets, tatty and tacky, with ramshackle stalls and open-fronted shops, where old-world practices hold sway and the sophisticated shopping of Central and Causeway Bay seems a million miles away.

I used to watch with amusement as women – young and old – poked at butchers' offal with their fingers or weighed it up in their hands, checking for tenderness or firmness or whatever other criteria they deem desirable in a pig's heart. In places, blood stains the pavement from deliveries to butchers' shops. You need a strong stomach as you pass the displays of hanging intestines, twelve-inch cow tongues, sheep brains and organs of various other livestock. The customers are not squeamish, though, which is just as well when butchers chop at carcasses, oblivious to the speckles of blood or shards of bone being spattered over passers-by. At the end of the day, all the inedible slop and grisly offcuts are chucked into wicker baskets and left on the street for rats, stray dogs and, finally, next morning, street cleaners to attend to. It may not be Ching Ping Market in Canton, but I have seen snakes plucked writhing from cages, despatched and skinned in the gutter; while lizards, turtles and aquaria of seafood await a similar fate. Freshness is paramount and if it's not alive it's not fresh. Pigs are also slaughtered in the area, then conveyed to the stores and restaurants, cooked or uncooked, in the back of old lorries or sometimes by other means, which I discovered – almost to my cost – one overcast Sunday afternoon:

Crossing any road in Hong Kong, one-way or not, it is wise to look both ways. In Sham Shui Po it is imperative. Aside from the legions of coolies and refuse collectors (municipal and private) pushing their trolleys against the flow of traffic there is another hazard peculiar to Hong Kong, and as I stepped onto the road only the ringing of a bell prevented me being run over by it. As I swung around, the surreal and nightmarish vision of a giant pig on a bicycle was bearing down on me. With a speed/weight combination of deadly potential I had no time to appreciate the bizarreness of the spectacle. I hopped back onto the kerb, from where I was able to ascertain that the bike was in fact being piloted by a small human male hunched behind his porcine front-seat passenger which was hanging over the handlebars. The bike was a rattling old contraption and the rider, nonchalant to a fault and entirely unconcerned by our near-collision, was equally unyielding to modernity. He wore a Chairman Mao cap, string vest, grey flannel shorts and Wellington boots, roll-up cigarette dangling from his mouth. I watched as he turned left onto the busy three-lane highway of Cheung Sha Wan Road and headed straight for the fast outside lane. Buses were forced to slow down and give way, but nobody tooted their horns. It would have made no difference. Everyone knew that characters like him, in a place where anyone on a bike is considered not wholly sane, were as likely to give way to a twenty-ton Dennis double-decker as to a cockroach.

And that is how it is in Sham Shui Po, the nearest Hong Kong offers to an authentic mainland experience without crossing the border, where the markets are interesting but less interesting than the people, and the produce less impressive than the industry. It is a place of glaring poverty and neglect but with none of the menace you might feel in the deprived urban districts of Europe or North America. Pollution is a much bigger issue than crime, and the next time I returned it was just to catch a bus bound for the brighter scenery and fresher air of those nearby hills.

MONKEY HILL

Overlooking the Kowloon peninsula is a forested highland area that supports a surprising array of wildlife, including a colony of rhesus macaques. These were introduced early in the twentieth century on completion of the Kowloon Reservoirs to consume harmful weeds that might otherwise have contaminated the water. Now, through inter-breeding and increased competition, they have virtually wiped out the native species of monkey. Nearing overpopulation, hundreds of the invasive species roam freely without fear of humans or any natural predators, their behaviour encouraged by irresponsible day-trippers feeding them.

On alighting from the No. 81 bus I could see a troop already waiting in anticipation of hand-outs and, as it was the end of the week, they were hungry. The appearance of a woman of some seniority and eccentricity (she had brought dozens of bottles of water to distribute to her beloved monkeys, despite their living by a series of streams and reservoirs) immediately gained their attention. After a couple of tentative forays by lone raiders the old woman was mobbed, and her trolley, which also bore several loaves of sliced bread, ransacked. Half her stock was gone in ten seconds of mayhem, as she first fought to free herself from a junior macaque caught up in her hair and then, without any sign of panic, restored order with a few vigorous swipes of her walking stick. The largest may have been less than half the size of a man, but with potentially infective nails and fangs of Transylvanian proportions it could have been serious. I vowed to be on my guard, particularly since I was hungry and unprepared to share any of the nosh in my daypack. But clearly it wouldn't be safe to eat it here.

I hiked for half an hour – away from the reservoir where young monkeys were jumping from high in the trees into the cooling water – and into the forest. Here I came across a family of macaques, large in number and physique, which perhaps explained why they were unwilling to give way. They looked unconcerned, at least, nonchalantly scratching themselves and nit-picking each other as if I were invisible. Still, I was nervous as I edged my way around and between them on the narrow pathway, eyes fixed on them. So fixed, in fact, that I missed a large root in front of me, tripped and nearly fell headlong into a mother grooming a couple of babies. As I staggered, desperately flailing to remain upright, the whole family bolted *en masse* for the cover of the forest without the merest sign of dissent. I continued with renewed confidence, my place at the top of the food chain confirmed.

I reflected that less than a hundred years ago, monkeys would have been the last thing to worry about when tigers were still on the prowl. Now, dangerous creatures are restricted to reptiles. Other exotic species include the armadillo-like Chinese pangolin and the porcupine, evidence of which I found in a black-and-white quill along the way.

Ten minutes after disturbing the monkeys' party I stopped at a picnic area, at last satisfied that I could rest and refuel in comfort. But no sooner had I opened my bag of nuts than a macaque, attracted by the rustling, dropped from a tree in front of me. This time it was my turn to be blasé – I had just witnessed the true mettle of the species after all – and I carried on munching. But there is something unnerving about a monkey on a post fixated on your nuts, so I decided to move on, deposited my snack and stood up. With just a quick glance away and my bag momentarily unguarded on the table, the creature saw its chance and made a dash for it. I responded quickly and fearlessly and for the briefest of moments we were almost head to head, locked in a struggle, man against macaque, each of our hands on one of the straps. I pulled it back, my weight advantage prevailing, and swiped hard, while the wretched animal retreated, albeit only about ten feet, where it sat on a table, legs apart, teeth out, in a despicable display of bravado and defiance. With my bag in one hand and the porcupine quill clenched in the other I walked away, with one last vigilant glance over my shoulder, feeling a good deal more stressed than my adversary appeared. I may have won the physical confrontation but the psychological battle was his.

It was a strenuous hike to Lion Rock – so called due to the shape of the rock rather than any local fauna – from Monkey Hill, the route taking me up and down a steep, forested trail, passing only a *gwailo* mountain runner, before emerging into sunlight near the summit. Most of Kowloon and all of Hong Kong Island's dramatic north side were visible. Best of all was the view of Kai Tak Airport and the sight of airliners approaching. From an elevation of about 2,000 feet the full sweep of the flight path and the difficulty of the pilots' task could really be appreciated. As I watched the planes skirting the slopes below me, it appeared that on the aircrafts' final bank the runway would be invisible from the cockpit. No wonder every landing varied. The differences in angles of approach were even perceptible from my range. Sometimes I sensed one was going off course, but always, just as in my landing, it would straighten late, before the reassuring puff of smoke and dust as rubber hit tarmac.

Going in the other direction from Monkey Hill takes you away from Kowloon and towards the Shing Mun Reservoir. In 1942 this was where invading Japanese troops overwhelmed British defenders in the decisive battle for Hong Kong. A series of defensive tunnels known as the Shing Mun Redoubt still stand, in many places hidden by shrubbery, nothing on the outside indicating any historical significance. At first it looks like some kind of disused water channel to the reservoir. But as you crouch into the darkness you notice shafts of light ahead. These were the air and light holes and possible escape routes in case of emergency. One use tragically overlooked by their designers, however, was their ready convenience for the dropping of Japanese grenades. Inside are two London Underground signs, with an arrow one way to 'Charing Cross' and the other to 'Piccadilly'. It is a poignant testament to the humour of those trying to make light of homesickness and adversity. And for most of the men stationed here, it was the nearest they would ever get to seeing home again.

THE FALL OF FRASER

Few of the long-term teachers at the English Club could be said to radiate joy, but compared with poor old Fraser they were positively charged with good humour. The first time I met him he ignored my morning greeting and strolled past me like I was invisible. Next time he just grunted. I immediately disliked him. He had an upper-class accent and I marked him down as some kind of arrogant elitist. Over the next few weeks, however, I began to revise that judgement as I discovered his indifference to others wasn't born of any conceptions of superiority but something deeper and more excusable: Fraser was a profoundly dejected individual struggling through the bleakest winter of his working life.

I started to sympathise when on passing his room I saw him sitting lonely in the corner, staring out of the tiny window or at a wall. On the occasions when he had one or two students his entire being would be transformed from lethargy to animated eagerness. This was clearly a man who wanted to teach. And yet he had become unpopular, ignored by the students, left feeling rejected and stigmatised.

Other teachers, like Duncan, didn't give a toss when they were in this situation. He was happy to sit reading his newspaper – "Still get paid the same, after all" – and even got away with telling students to go to another teacher when he wasn't in the mood. Fraser wasn't like that. He took pride in his professional duties and wanted to teach properly, using textbooks, concentrating particularly on grammar, of which he had a comprehensive understanding. He was much more highly educated than any other member of staff, backed up by a professional life in journalism, the diplomatic service, and as a lecturer at university. He had all the experience and qualifications, yet here he was teaching for a pittance in a tatty old tuition centre on the rough side of town. Despite that, he took his duties seriously and was methodical and painstaking in his planning, organisation and prosecution of lessons. It wasn't his style to indulge in idle, frivolous chatter. He didn't see himself as an entertainer, raconteur, chat show host, agony uncle or sex instructor, unlike some of his colleagues. He was a teacher and teaching was what he wanted to do. If only he had someone to teach. But his old-fashioned style and ponderous delivery didn't go down well with students who had been fed to the gills with conventional teaching methods and just wanted the chance to practise conversation or to learn in an unchallenging environment. The few swots who did require extra grammar tuition were generally put off by Fraser's appearance. This is an image-conscious society and an ageist one, despite the traditionally elevated status the old are supposed to enjoy. I heard several students say things to the effect of "He's a good teacher but he's too old" – the perceived negativity of one inexplicably outweighing the benefit of the other.

His age was far from the only barrier, however. He was a huge man, both vertically and laterally, with receding grey curly hair crowning a massive red face, adorned by a boisterous set of side-whiskers. He probably didn't know it, but the conservatism of his nature and his sheer size and unconventional appearance were a daunting prospect to the clean-cut and relatively diminutive students. Fraser's dress sense was also quite a deterrent to image-conscious young Hong Kongers. His shirt always seemed to be tucked half in, half out, while his grey, stained flannels were held under his grotesquely bulging waistline by a safety pin. Usually he wore a tie, too short in length, too wide, and thick in the knot. It epitomised his look of stuffy, untidy formality.

Then there was his drink problem. How long he'd had it I couldn't say, but it likely accounted for his former careers. However bad it had been I had no doubt that in the few weeks I knew him it was becoming chronic. At first I hadn't noticed, but it soon became normal to see him swigging from a flask, then slouching on the bench, arms stretched wide, eyes unfocused. His lifeblood seemed to be ebbing.

In a rare moment of sober lucidity he poured out his grief and grievances to me. Although a Scot, he spoke in English public school tones, with the stentorian timbre of a tragic Shakespearian – so apt, considering the lofty early chronicle of his life and its subsequent descent.

"All was well until I took my annual sojourn in Thailand," he began. "Prior to that I had a loyal band of schoolgirls in regular attendance, following the HKCC syllabus. They were so bright, eager and inquisitive. I miss them." He paused, his eyes glistening somewhat. "Now they are gone – I know not where – and I… I am left on the shelf. Nobody wants to study any more… I mean really study. The death of teaching is nigh, the death of the teacher is nigh."

Later these words would come back to me, but then they just seemed like the sad ramblings of an eccentric old man disturbed by self-doubt. I tried to lift him.

"It'll pick up, it always does. There are always ups and downs."

"I've had nothing but downs since I came back, I can assure you."

"Don't worry. It doesn't really matter how many students you've got. If I were you I would just relax and enjoy it."

He chuckled, mirthlessly. "Change seats with me, young man, feel what I feel, experience what I experience, the stigma and humiliation. How can you possibly relax and enjoy it, sitting in solitary confinement waiting for students to come and alleviate the misery and isolation of your state; and when they do, they take one look at you then turn and flee? Then there's the staff with their clipboards looking in on my room in vain to count the customers, always with a disapproving frown and hint of disgust. How would you feel?"

For a moment I struggled for a suitable response, but all I could find was the defeatist and only vaguely optimistic: "At least you're still in work."

"Ughhh! For how much longer, can you tell me that?"

"What are you talking about?"

"The writing's on the wall for me, I fear. I'm being undermined by that damnable witch Maxine and her coven. They're determined to force me out."

"Surely not."

"You doubt it? You doubt Maxine's capable of such treachery? Beware your naivety, dear boy. It will get you nowhere, particularly in this place. Just don't allow yourself to become bogged down here. You're too good, and you're young enough to do better; I'm too good, but I have nowhere else to go. I would get out now if I were you. This place is a haven for chancers, perverts and incompetents... and that's just the teachers! What's more, the staff and management know it."

"No wonder Maxine doesn't like us."

"That's the problem, she doesn't discriminate. To her we're all expendable *gwailo* trash. But some of us do actually care. Some of us are actually conscientious. But who does she pick on? With all that other dross of humanity corrupting innocent minds with their kinky humour and depraved filth, who does she pick on? They are the lowest of the low, but I'm lower still, in her mind, and worse than that, in the minds of the students. That's the hardest thing of all to take."

"They wouldn't get rid of you, though," I ventured. "Not after all the years you've been here."

"What did I say about naivety? They'll never mind that I've been here the last seven years, never mind that I produced an advanced-level syllabus for free, never mind that I'm the only damned teacher who knows how to teach... never mind... never mind. I'm past my use-by date. Time to be discarded, thrown on the scrap heap, sent to the knackers. That's the fate that awaits this old horse." There was a painful pause, during which I feared he might break down. That wasn't him, though, and despondency quickly gave way to defiance. "But I won't give them the satisfaction. They'll have to physically remove me. Can you imagine?" He cracked another hollow, joyless laugh, but I couldn't even raise a smile. Under other circumstances it might have been a comical picture to conjure with, but this was too real. This was a man with an illustrious background, approaching retirement age, now facing a future of indignity and uncertainty. For someone who had risen to the top in Fleet Street, then carved out a career in the diplomatic corps over the Indo-China region, before becoming a lecturer at Singapore University, now reduced to this state of pitiful bathos, scratching a living at the Kowloon English Club and holed up in the squalor of Chungking Mansions, it really was no laughing matter.

Once again I struggled for anything that could genuinely console or give cause for optimism, but such eloquence eluded me. The only thing I could think of was, well, at least he's had a full, eventful and adventurous life, which is more than most people ever manage. I wasn't tactless enough to utter these sentiments of misplaced optimism and implied finality. We both knew that 'most people' were in a familiar place, secure in their jobs and homes with their families and home-cooked dinners. They had all the things in life Fraser lacked and, no doubt, yearned for more than anything else. The next time we met I got the feeling he was thinking along these lines when he asked if he would be eligible for unemployment benefit if he returned to the UK. That he was considering returning to live in a country he would scarcely recognise after an interval of over twenty years was the measure of his desperation.

The last seven of those years, during which Fraser had been employed by the KEC, had seen his time split between Hong Kong and Thailand. It was a comfortable arrangement that I'm sure Fraser would have gladly maintained to the grave. But now his job insecurity threatened that lifestyle, resulting in this mood of hopelessness: "Let's face it, I'm an over-the-hill, unemployable old man. Who's going to take me on now? I won't last long on my savings, that's for sure. I think the UK is my only viable option. But the winters... the shame of signing on... the loneliness... I don't know if I could endure, truly I don't."

He would be leaving a job he once loved in Hong Kong and a woman he perhaps still loved in Thailand. ("I wouldn't expect her to put up with me if I arrived with empty pockets, though.") He would be leaving the best part of his life in Asia. But, critically for so proud a man, his departure would be infected by despair, tainted by failure. Despite the good times professionally and personally – or perhaps because of them – Fraser would never get over this abject overturn of fortune. Particularly so if he returned to the British Isles with nothing but the dole cheque and the bottle for comfort.

I tried to cheer him by mentioning an advert I'd seen in the *South China Morning Post*, asking for a 'lived-in driver with fluent English' (I used to scan the papers for such teaching material). There was no flicker of a smile as he said he could certainly meet the first and last criteria, but the only thing he'd driven in the last twenty years was his friends up the wall, and himself mad.

"No, seriously," I wondered. "Why don't you look for another job?" This seemed the only thing that could possibly salvage his pride and living quality. I knew it wouldn't be easy with his confidence dislocated and a raging drink problem to contend with, but anything else would be to surrender. Of course he was far too stubborn a mule to be swayed by what he called my 'sentimental and unrealistic outlook'.

"Look, I'm already in the darkest depths of the English teaching world, which I may have mentioned before. There is nothing below these wages and working conditions, believe me. And yet... and yet... I'm still dispensable, not deemed suitable. That being the case, who else would have me? Any suggestions? ...You, young man, you're the one who should be looking elsewhere for job opportunities. You don't need this place at all, but for me it's the final resort... The final resort."

I watched him totter towards the gents', having just spoken his final words to me, the impact and moment of which would again not be fully realised until later.

That evening, travelling home, we happened to be on the

same MTR train. I could see him from the other end of the
carriage, bobbing his head and muttering away. When he got off
he stretched his arms in a breaststroke motion as if swimming
through the floods of humanity below him. He cursed and
spluttered his way past everyone who got in his way. In the throes
of drunken derangement his demise was nigh.

Back at the centre the knives were being sharpened, and when
the thrust came it wasn't from Maxine but one of her sidekicks,
who had clearly been instructed to do the dirty work. Fraser had
still shown up at work, somewhat surprisingly considering his
sunken mood and erratic behaviour the day before, but it was
another lonesome evening session for him with only his hip
flask for company. I was photocopying some material when he
came down the stairs humming tunelessly to sign the register
in reception. Perhaps Miss Lee, Maxine's assistant, took the
humming to be a sign of good temper on Fraser's part. Just the
time to confront him, she might incorrectly have supposed.

"Fraser, sit down, please," she said, calmly.

"No, I'm more comfortable standing, thank you very much.
I've been on my fat arse the last four hours, you know."

She looked up at the giant figure before her. "I want to ask you,
what are you teaching?"

"Beg your pardon!"

"What do you teach? Because you have no student at all on
Monday, two on Tuesday, only one on Wednesday, nobody
yesterday, and nobody today. Why the students don't like your
teaching?"

"What! You call them students?"

"I don't understan'."

"That's your problem. You don't understand. You don't

understand anything about communication or respect or common courtesy. And you obviously understand nothing of teaching and learning, Miss Lee. Give me students who want to learn and I'll damn well teach, but what do I get? …Bloody kids who treat this like a social club. Whose fault is that, eh?"

"You mus' give… er… students what they want. They pay us, we can pay you. But now, Mr Fraser, we pay you for do nothing. This cannot continue."

"You really know how to kick a man when he's down, don't you… treating me like a dog even after seven years of honest toil. You should be ashamed of yourself."

"Why I feel shame? I just do my job."

"For God in heaven's sake, woman! That's the point: it's not your job! You're just an employee, like me, so why do you feel it necessary to talk to me in this way?"

"Because you must change your teaching methods or your style, you know. You mus'… er… attrac' more students."

"But why do you care? Why not leave it to Maxine? I could take it from her, understand it even. But you! What are you thinking? What is your motive? Your attitude… frankly I find… disappointing."

"We are disappointed of you," she barked back.

"We?! We?! What do you mean *we*. You're not damned management. *We* should be inclusive. *We* should be you, me and the other staff against Maxine. But I suppose when you say *we* you are referring to all the Chinese staff? I always had the feeling you looked down on us teachers."

"We do not look down on you."

"You don't bloody well respect us, do you?"

"You have very easy job, just chatting to students all day. You are lucky but always the teachers complain... complain... complain. Never satisfy. Maybe you don'... erm... deserve respect."

Fraser's eyes narrowed and his forehead creased. "Do you have any experience of teaching a foreign language? Have you ever stood in front of a row of blank, uncomprehending faces and tried to make conversation, never mind teaching? Have you ever tried speaking for four or five hours without a break, with a hoarse, dry throat? Any idea what that feels like? Any idea of the wearisome drudgery of being locked in classrooms like dungeons, with people whose knowledge and experience of the world is about as limited as your emotional quotient? ...No, I didn't think so."

I remembered during one of our brief chats Fraser had made a broad generalisation about the women in Hong Kong, saying they tended to be either sweet, charmingly feminine but often given to immaturity, or they were coarse-tongued, aggressive and lacking in refinement and grace. Into this latter group undoubtedly fell Miss Lee. She appeared only mildly flustered by the altercation and was certainly not prepared to give in. Arguing in a foreign tongue must be one of the hardest of all linguistic challenges, but she seemed to be relishing the opportunity not just to have a dig at Fraser but at all of us teachers. It was difficult to imagine that her comments were not borne of feelings deeper than merely a grudge against Fraser.

She rejoined the fray with: "Now I hear you don't respec' your students and I think you don't respec' me also."

"How can I respect people who come into my class, refuse to study, demand 'free talk' – whatever the hell that is – and then sit in silence while I'm labouring to introduce suitable topics? As for you, Miss Lee, you exude contempt and spite, so what do you expect in return? Respect isn't free, you know. But I think with my seniority, experience and knowledge I'm due a little. I thought these things were important in your culture."

"No, not if you are not respect*able*." She really stressed the *able* part of the word, smiling, smug at her own cleverness.

Fraser was not taken with it. "What did you say!? Are you saying that I am not respectable, is that it?"

"I say respect is for respectable people. You are British, I think you know about these things. We also respect people who have smart appearance and who are productive."

"Are you familiar with the terms 'adding insult to injury' and 'pouring salt in the wound'? …No? …But you're certainly familiar with the practice, you vicious… vicious…"

He paused, staring with a vehemence that would have paralysed a lesser character. The back of his thick neck was crimson, and I detected a slight tremor… or was it a rumble? He was about to blow: the pain, the angst and the shame simmering for so long were at last ready to overflow in a boiling rage. For the first time, Miss Lee also seemed to recognise the signals. She was becoming aware of the depth of his feeling and no doubt braced for the backlash as he leaned on her desk, lowering his face so they were eye-to-eye at uncomfortably close proximity. "…You damnable, disrespectful fire-breathing dragon you, how dare you question my professionalism?"

She looked startled and chastened, her eyes flicking in all directions but Fraser's, as her self-assurance melted with the realisation that she was no longer in control of the situation. Moments earlier she would have cut him with another close-to-the bone comment, but now she was starting to look vulnerable. Too late to earn mercy from Fraser.

"I've seen you applying make-up, plucking your eyebrows,

reading fashion magazines at your desk. And yet you sit in judgement on me!"

A few onlookers had gathered, teachers and students drawn to the brouhaha. Fraser didn't notice them but Miss Lee was starting to sweat and fluster under the spotlight. Still, he didn't let up. "And another thing, you are utterly heartless. God knows how the blood gets pumped around your body."

Miss Lee, with a look of disgust, leaned back in her chair. "You are drunk. You don't know what you say."

"Damn you, I am as sober as a lord!" he bellowed.

"I can smell you are drunk."

"Maybe I am... maybe I am, but better to be full of drink than poison." With that, he made a show of producing his hip flask from his pocket and took one last swig. "And Miss Lee, to paraphrase our great wartime leader: in the morning I'll be sober while you will still be ugly."

"Mr Fraser!"

"Miss Lee, I have said enough. I can resist no more. I'm tired and spent. You win. You win."

Miss Lee, evidently unnerved by his performance: "Get out you crazy man, get out!"

"But, my dear, I am already out. Down and out... Over and out."

"Time for you to leave. Please."

Fraser looked exhausted. "Miss Lee, for once I am inclined to agree with you. I hope you can sleep well." With that he turned and left.

It had been a flamboyant last stand, a melodramatic but tragic climax to his teaching career. I could have wept for him as he wobbled down the stairs singing *We'll Meet Again* at the top of his voice. But we would not meet again and, for him, his days were almost done.

FUNERAL

Everyone – Maxine, Miss Lee, the students and the teachers – was evidently shocked at the news. I felt a nauseous current of emotions but shock was pretty low on that scale. In the days following Fraser's drunken overdose, sorrow took over; a sorrow aggravated by a powerful sense of anger and injustice, which I wanted to take out on Miss Lee and Maxine. Only my own sense of guilt dissuaded me from such a course. If they had pushed him towards the edge I could have pulled him back. I had let him walk out of the door – just stood and watched – knowing his emotional state and depth of anguish. In some ways I was as culpable as they were, for he had confided in me, but when he needed empathy and support most it was wanting.

So now he was dead and I had to reconcile that I had seen it coming but had done nothing. Hindsight may be a fickle judge, but it was still a burden to bear. I hoped Fraser's tormentors would also be struggling with their consciences. I may have neglected him in his hour of despair but I hadn't put the boot in as they had. Seeing their wan faces on Monday morning seemed to confirm that they were at least in some state of grief. But Fraser's death would not be recorded as suicide, so there would be no soul-searching on their part. This I regarded as a travesty, but to confront them now would have been inappropriate and no catharsis for me.

Within a day or two, however, the colour had returned to their cheeks, the volume to their voices. There was laughter and good humour among the staff. And even the other teachers, once over the initial shock, didn't seem unduly affected. It disturbed me to witness such indifference and prompt resumption of normality within the halls of the Kowloon English Club. Life must go on, of course, and everyone has different ways of coping with bereavement, but I found it less easy. Until the funeral service my thoughts were never far from Fraser. With teachers and students I only wanted to talk about him; to find out more about his life, his death and how he was driven to it. I asked fellow teachers how someone with such personality defects as Fraser's could have been a diplomat.

"That was at least fifteen years ago," Robert replied. "He's been on the way down since then. Even in the five years I knew him he became increasingly detached from reality, increasingly bitter. I suppose none of us in Hong Kong ever saw the real Fraser."

I asked if he had any memories of Fraser in Hong Kong.

He pondered a moment. "I remember seeing him one winter's day up on Signal Hill with a portable stove, boiling water for his instant noodles. He was warming his hands with all the eagerness of a kid on his first camping expedition. He was all alone on this cool, grey afternoon, but you could see the anticipation mounting as he poured the boiling water over his noodles. It was the highlight of his day. Saddest thing, just the saddest thing."

"He was a really lonely old boy," said Gerry. "But he didn't exactly help himself. I heard he went out with a group of students for dinner, a couple of years back, and walked out halfway through dinner because he got pissed off with everyone using Cantonese instead of English. Maybe if he'd shown a bit more tolerance and respect for the ways of the people he might not have been so unpopular."

In class, my students were stunned and I think genuinely moved by his final plight as I described it, while I was eager to glean any insights into this eccentric man and his extraordinary life, times and downfall. But, in common with the teachers, there were but a few who knew him, and fewer still who knew him well. This I found one of the saddest aspects of his passing. To think that I, who had spoken to him on just a handful of occasions, could be one of the few people to seriously lament his passing.

On the morning of the funeral I was in a state of concern. I wanted to see him given a fitting send-off, but feared only a few teachers plus Maxine and Miss Lee would turn up, with no family and no friends in attendance. There would be no tears… no affectionate farewell speeches… no emotionally-charged hymns… no post-service get-together to reminisce fondly over the old boy's foibles. Nothing to celebrate his unique life and ways. Instead I expected it to be something perfunctory and hollow: formality without respect, farewell without feeling. Which, if it came to pass, would represent something almost as tragic as death itself.

I didn't know if I could face going under such circumstances, but I knew I must. If there was truly nobody who cared for him I would get up and perhaps deliver a few home truths on his last days. Fraser deserved that much at least.

The day came. Anxious to avoid any small-talk fraternisation with Maxine or Miss Lee at the church, it was a couple of minutes past the scheduled time when I turned up. The organ was playing, the service was commencing, and to my astonishment the church was virtually full. With relief in my heart I slid onto one of the few remaining vacant pews. The congregation included mostly friends and colleagues, past and present, and no sign of Miss Lee I was glad to note. Also in attendance were Fraser's brother and sister, who had come all the way from Scotland.

Between the hymns, a number of former flatmates, ex-teachers and drinking partners got up to give their reflections of Fraser. They painted a portrait not of the sullen, moody man I knew, but of a carefree character – albeit one that didn't suffer fools – with a wicked, dry sense of humour. It wasn't actually so difficult for me to visualise him in the happier times they knew as they told hilarious tales of his domestic arrangements, disputes, and recollections of his classic one-line put-downs. All the speeches caught the man and the moment, and the laughter that rang out in response was the greatest tribute to him and the finest tonic for us.

Fraser's brother was the last to take the floor. He was noticeably overwhelmed by what he had seen and heard. "If you judge a man by his friends," he started, "my brother was obviously a very special man indeed, because you… you are just… wonderful." His voice was cracking and his demeanour projected the loss he was feeling. He didn't need to go on. Everyone knew what he was feeling. He had listened to the anecdotes about this wry, bluff, sardonic but much-loved old sod who, perhaps, he didn't even recognise. He was surrounded by people who knew his brother better than he did. We all had shared some part of Fraser's recent life, while he had only seen him once in nearly three decades. We knew this was what was biting the hardest. This was his sense of loss: not for the future but the past. No recent happy memories of the man for him to fall back on; no recalling of shared experiences to console. I wondered if Fraser had been written off by his family and best left in distant, foreign climes. But now was the realisation that he had been something special, appreciated, cherished and known more in this faraway place than in the family home. This was clearly hard for him to accept. We could see it all over his face taut with tension, and hear it in his voice breaking with emotion.

The rest of the speech was unmemorable in content since he had so few memories of Fraser's adult life to fall back on. But its melancholic tone, replete with layers of pride and regret, punctuated by head-bowed pauses and long deep breaths, was truly moving. I felt for him and his sister, but it would have been far worse for them had it gone according to my worst expectations. As it stood, there was at least a certain glory along with the grief, and comfort in the pride to offset the remorse. I strolled from the church into the bright late morning sunlight, feeling rejuvenated by the occasion. I could look forward to a restful night's sleep once more, and dear old Fraser, God bless him, could rest in peace.

JEEVES

Harold was one of the teachers most affected by Fraser's demise. Until then he tended to keep his own counsel. He had always appeared aloof and straight-laced, but with the loss of his only real friend he shed some of his inhibitions. After the funeral he told me he had appreciated Fraser's company and that he was one of the few people in Hong Kong to whom he could relate. I was curious – Fraser was some thirty years his senior and, whatever his virtues, being young at heart was not among them. This scarcely mattered to Harold, though, for whom fashion, pop music and all vestiges of modern culture had somehow passed him by.

Being different came as second nature to him. He wore silk cravats in winter and a straw hat in summer. He was a genuine eccentric borne of Anglo-Indian ancestry and burdened by issues of identity and belonging. He confided in me that he didn't belong in Hong Kong, was not accepted as Indian in India, and didn't know England, although India under the Raj just might have suited him. This devout but frustrated Anglophile, who had never been within four thousand miles of England, sourced much of his knowledge of that far-flung land and its language from Victorian novels. Hence when you heard students use words like *toodle-pip, thrice, swoon* (without any romantic connotation) and Anglo-Indian expressions such as *tiffin, nullah*, and speaking of ten *lakhs* (one million) you knew where they had been studying.

Harold was obsessed with the English language and intimated more than once that his ambition, more than anything else, was to speak like a public-school educated Englishman. I believed he would miss Fraser for his eloquence and enunciation as much as any personal reasons. They had a mutual loathing of sloppy English, bad grammar, slang, and above all, Americanisms. Another of their shared hang-ups was a disapproval of nearly all post-war additions to the English lexicon. He would utter archaic phrases with ponderous deliberation and just a trace of an Indian lilt. Fortunately most of his students accepted him as English, owing to his fairish complexion, and rarely questioned his unconventional vocabulary or accent. Choosing to teach only elementary classes was also a wise move on his part as it meant he could avoid any embarrassing questions from students on sex, swearing and slang, allowing him instead to concentrate on the intricacies of grammar and comprehension. Like Fraser he could dissect the English language down to its bones and reconstruct it in a logical format, enabling him to appreciate the mental process of learning the language as a foreigner. He tried not to bore them with too many labels but provided examples and situations in which such-and-such a tense could be used. And this he did without reference to textbooks. Sometimes if I arrived early for work I would sit discreetly in a nearby room pretending to read when instead I was listening carefully, picking his brains and mentally taking note of the style and content of his teaching.

His fixations with usage didn't end at the classroom door, though. I recall him once, during a post-class curry, taking Robert the American to task for saying 'did you ever…', insisting it should be 'have you ever'.

Pedantic didn't come close. Asked to adjudicate, I said Robert's version was fine in spoken English.

"What about written English then?" Harold asked firmly.

"Not quite sure."

"Come come. The past simple is referring to a definite or aforementioned time in the past, which must be cancelled out by the use of 'ever'. You must know that, you are English teachers, are you not?"

"You may be right in theory, but the thing is, if it don't sound wrong it ain't wrong, right Robert?"

Robert was smiling, while Harold looked nonplussed.

I told him he would be disappointed if he visited England expecting everyone to talk in the manner of Victorian gentlemen.

"I know that time has gone. It is hard enough to find any young people who know how to put an apostrophe in the correct place, not to mention the chronic standards of spelling. And I believe Americans are even worse."

Robert was not impressed with Harold, but I never shied from his company. The analytical workings of his mind fascinated me. He didn't think or talk or behave like anyone I knew. He never loosened up, always focusing on what was being said and how it was being said. Others found it difficult to warm to him when he communicated in such a cold and purely logical fashion, but I liked the challenge of selecting diction meticulously to avoid his naïve queries and disapproving looks, and on rare occasions, trying to impress him with my eloquence.

For such a supposedly – albeit self-taught – linguistic scholar who spoke with such painstaking formality, he was not especially articulate himself. To him, English was less an art than a science, and I occasionally found myself wanting to offer modern alternatives to his stilted terms or to correct his phonetic pronunciation. You were better to accept what Harold said, though, to avoid long drawn-out debates. And to avoid being made to look foolish. He was a man with the knowledge of an oracle: politics, world affairs, geography, science, history, as well as more practical matters concerning law, banking, insurance. If you had a question or a problem, chances were, Harold could answer it or solve it. That was where his nickname Jeeves came from, which he was content to accept.

We reminisced a bit about Calcutta, Delhi, Darjeeling, chai stalls, Indian railways, the Hindu ceremony of Holi, and more besides. But he was always more dismissive and derogatory about Indians and Indian ways than I ever felt. Then I remembered the Anglo-Indians I had known in Calcutta and how contemptuous many of them were of their countrymen and I knew it was in his upbringing. Many Anglo-Indians were successful but others felt like they didn't belong and only coped by taking alcohol or drugs, or, as in Harold's case, by leaving.

He wasn't alone.

PART FOUR

Expat Trash

MY COLLEAGUES, aside from the fact that they were all men (female teachers had the pick of the lucrative junior market so never hung around here for long), were about as varied a bunch of people as you could expect to meet in one workplace. They were old and young, educated and uneducated, worldly and unworldly, moral and amoral. Some had been there so long they were immovable fixtures. Then there were transients – mostly young, free and self-centred – working their way across Asia with their rucksacks. This latter group were generally too shallow or callow to be of any interest here. They were just starting to make their personal histories, while the more permanent teachers were steeped in the stuff – and more often than not burdened by it.

Take Gerry, for example. He'd been seven years in the Orient – mostly Hong Kong – after splitting from his wife and then fleeing to avoid what he called 'alimony and acrimony'. This he told me without a shred of shame, but a residue of bitterness towards his ex still all too apparent.

"What about your daughter?" I asked him.

He answered me with a shrug and a deep sigh.

"Do you think you'll ever go back?"

"I like to go back in summer but I spent a winter there a few years ago, only it reminded me what a bloody depressing place England can be: miserable weather, traffic jams, public transport doesn't work, even the food made me sick. No, this is home now. I'm settled for good. I'm used to the climate, food, pace of life, and work here. Couldn't return even if I wanted to, though, what with all the legal and personal problems. No going back now, son."

Modestly he didn't mention that he had mastered the Cantonese tongue – one of the very few Westerners I met to do so – and even the bewildering written form, which is more complex than the simplified mainland version. He was tutored by his Cantonese girlfriend, who was slim and poised, with a fine tanned complexion on a pretty face. Gerry, with his permanently unkempt demeanour, distended waistline, pasty skin and big nose, looked almost double the age of his youthful-looking girlfriend, although the gap was in fact a mere six years. They were the physical antithesis of each other, typifying the (Eastern) Beauty and the (Western) Beast syndrome, which is a common arrangement in countries such as Thailand and the Philippines but not so in Hong Kong. I remember discussing this topic with a group of lads one Saturday evening in class. It wasn't long before Gerry was cited, which spawned speculation as to how he could have acquired such a choice partner. Under normal circumstances I would not have encouraged gossip about the private life of another teacher, but when you are low on inspiration and preparation, with four hours to kill, virtually nothing is off-limits.

"So what's the attraction for his girlfriend, do you think?" I asked.

"Personality," someone offered. "Maybe he has a good personality."

"Yes… yes, I suppose he has." Although in reality I was thinking he was a curmudgeonly old goat. "Give me some examples of good personality."

"Funny. He is funny."

"Yes… yes, I suppose he is. He has a dry sense of humour." (I then spent some moments trying to explain what that meant).

"He can speak good Cantonese. He is very clever."

"Anything else?"

After a pause, someone said, "Maybe she likes big nose. Some girls like this."

"Maybe she likes big something else. All girls like this!" The speaker was a Canadian-educated Chinese, who hardly needed lessons but enjoyed showing off his English.

I interrupted the laughter. "Hold on, hold on. Let's change the subject." I felt somewhat diminished as a teacher with the shabby level of discourse I was encouraging. Without the moderating influence of the 'Innocents' I was in danger of following the same sleazy path as many of the 'old hands'.

These 'old hands' included Duncan, a friend of Gerry's with a similar personal background, who seemed to believe that Hong Kong's young people needed to improve their sex education more than their English. I didn't necessarily shy away from such themes but certainly never started a lesson, as he did, with the question, 'What is a blow job?' He was also fond of explaining and comparing different sexual positions to his small band of students – a clique of impressionable lads and the odd broad-minded female – and proving his manhood with tales of old flames and new conquests. He tended to avoid mentioning his wife and child.

And if he was explicit, then Curt, a Texan hulk of a man, was positively indecent. He was dismissed before I started but his place in the annals of KEC teachers was secure. Months later, stories still abounded from students and teachers of his antics. In his cleaner moments he would eye a pretty girl and exclaim, "Have ah gaht the hahts for you!" before glancing down at his bulging crotch. To a girl who introduced herself as Fanny (Curt had been surrounded by Brits for long enough to know the non-American definition): "Hey Fanny! Whadda beautiful name! It's so warm and soft and moist, ain't it?"

To another girl he was purported to have asked: "What do you like to do with your middle finger?"

Other times he apparently played the father figure – for he was in his late forties – to good effect, and managed to get a few dates on a platonic pretext with young ladies who wouldn't find out his true intention until halfway through dinner when a fat, sweaty paw would land on their thigh.

He survived these and other indiscretions, and would probably have continued to do so had he confined his lewd comments to the more worldly female members of his class. But when he started picking on the vulnerable and the youthful he was nearing the edge. He would ask them about their 'first time' and then, after the inevitable nervous silence, follow up with his killer: "Are you still a virgin?"

On one such occasion a Christian teacher named Jonathan overheard from an adjacent classroom and marched in boldly to challenge Curt. He gave a brief lecture on the impropriety of his comments and reminded him that he was a teacher and should therefore exercise greater moral responsibility and sensitivity.

This was countered by a volley of expletives from Curt and a warning that if he ever again stepped inside his class he would be squashed, which, given his size and temper, was no idle threat. As Jonathan returned to his own classroom, Curt shouted, "You're a Kiwi, right? You're in danger of extinction, man."

There was no further altercation between the two men, and no action was taken by the management, despite news of the uproar reaching their apathetic ears.

The next time – indeed it could have been several times later – Curt was less fortunate. The recipient on this occasion was of a more sensitive disposition than previous prey and, furthermore, still a schoolgirl. Subjected to his usual 'virgin' routine and suggestive stare, she stormed out, humiliated and tearful. Perhaps she didn't intend to complain, but the girl at reception, seeing her state, comforted her and made sure she got all the details. This time, when word reached Maxine, she was not so lenient and Curt's downfall was assured.

On hearing news of his enforced departure Curt went out with a typical blaze of fury – anything else would not have been him at all – "Ah've sweaded tears in there for you bastards and this is the graditood Ah get, you fuckin li'll narrow-minded losers. Ahm talkin 'bout social innercourse an' you think ahm talkin' 'bout sexual innercourse. Now who's prahblem is that, eh? Who's the sick one?... Ahm tryna keep those bastards in there ennertained for hours on end. You any ahdea what that's like? You have no fuckin' clue. We cover ground, man, free talk on any topics, ain't no taboos in mah class, you know what Ahm sayin? Ah admit Ah ain't no prude. Ahm an open-minded guy but that don't make me no pervert. You run this five-dime show butcha know nothin'. Nothin' 'bout teachin'... nothin' 'bout howda run a company. Ya know nothin' an' you could care less. Yer doomed, all of ya, you bunch of incompetent cowshit losers. You see if Ah ain't right. Ahm bedder oudda this fuckin' sixty dollar an hour sweatshop. Thanks and damn good riddance to y'all."

Robert, the only other American colleague, was a similar age to Curt but cheese to his chalk. He was a small, shy man, in complete contrast to Curt, and only talkative when he got going, but with a habit of saying the same thing over and over. For example (in his characteristically breathless monotone): "Curt's a redneck. Do you know what that means? …Blue collar… ignorant as hell… but red, white and blue to the core. Really. We have nothing in common aside from our nationality, but he's from the Deep South and I'm from New England. He's a right-wing conservative, I'm a liberal; he drinks, I don't. And he's racist. Really. He complains to his students about Mexicans flocking to the States and taking American jobs. Of course he never mentions Chinese immigrants and fails to see the contradiction between his living and working overseas while trying to prevent others enjoying the same right."

"But I thought you two were mates."

"Nah, he wants us to be buddies, and he contacts me from time to time. I think it's cos I'm the only other American and we both have Chinese wives who know each other. Aside from that we have nothing in common. Really."

"There's one other thing maybe."

"Really?"

"How can I put this?... I heard a rumour you both like to dabble in the Manila market?"

"On occasions, Joe, but I do it for the company as much as anything. I've got serious marital problems, you know. We only stay together for the sake of our daughter. I'm afraid if we split I'll never see her again, so I work my socks off six days a week to support them, but all I get from her and her damned family is criticism, demanding that I get a better-paid job. On Sunday I need a release, which I can find in the Wan Chai bars. I'm lonely, the girls are lonely, that's the deal. There's nothing physical, no exploitation."

Robert was one of the few men I knew who could make such a statement without provoking cynicism. And yet despite his patent sincerity and tolerance he couldn't stand New Zealander Jonathan: "I hate those sanctimonious Christians, they make me sick. Peace and goodwill to all men?… Caring and sharing?… He's the meanest son-of-a-gun I ever did meet."

Behind the animosity was a history of competing for students at a time when they were both teaching elementary classes in adjoining rooms during the evening. Robert was proud of his usually full attendance, while Jonathan was desperate to match his performance. There was no financial incentive for having more students but many teachers felt under pressure to fill their classes. This was encouraged by the company policy of counting students in all the classes every hour or so, and then publishing the figures every evening for all to see. Inevitably it resulted in rivalry, which was probably considered healthy for motivation, but in reality was a morale sapper, especially to the likes of Jonathan. He tried to catch up by luring Robert's students to his class with promises of homework, which he would review individually in his own time after the next lesson. It seemed nothing more than a pitiable gesture from a lonely and somewhat desperate ageing teacher, but to Robert it was akin to a declaration of war.

When he caught Jonathan one evening in the act of approaching one of his favourite students he blew up. "You call yourself a

Christian? It's immoral what you're doing, do you know that? You damned hypocrite, trying to bribe *my* students."

There were no further outbreaks of hostility, only a bitter stand-off between two gentlemen who should have known better. But that was the atmosphere of the place and the strain they were under. I could understand it well, this battle of the egos. A full class was an endorsement of your teaching, your style and your character. A regular complement of students and familiar faces meant you were popular, and it felt good. This was important to all the teachers with any personal pride and professional integrity about them, but to one in particular it meant more.

It was easy to see how and why this obsession had built up. He was Hong Kong born and bred, of English parents, and this was the only job he had ever known. Now in his late twenties, Toby was a consummate performer in front of the students. Benefiting from his years of experience and knowledge of all things Hong Kong, he had the technique and the topics to hold any class in his thrall. Sometimes there would be standing room only and the overflow would be taken by my class and others, but still he wasn't satisfied. He didn't just want the most students, he didn't just want the best and the brightest; most of all, he wanted the most attractive. He loved to impress and amuse the girls, and when the feedback of laughter and approval came he was on a high. How else could his ten years of service be explained, when a man of his talent and experience could easily have walked into any other teaching job and tripled his salary?

I would have relished the opportunity to ask him about his experiences and aspirations over a pint or two, but in common with most of the other 'old hands', he kept his distance from us newcomers. I could understand this; it must have been tiresome seeing all these new faces come and go. Why should he bother to befriend us when he had his own reliable group of old friends? In any case he had more in common with Hong Kong people than he did with us and I had the impression that he was ill at ease in the company of me and other native Brits, particularly those of working-class origins. He was cordial enough but the only times he ever asked me anything were regarding students he had noticed in my class. And for some reason they always happened to be feminine and pretty.

I tended to socialise with the 'transient' teachers for post-lesson drinks. They reckoned Toby was more inscrutable than the Chinese. "He's gone native," said one. "He is native," corrected another. Discussing the reasons for Toby's longevity, they inferred that he had the pick of all the best-looking available girls and was obviously taking advantage of the situation. "Well, wouldn't you?" I would, but somehow I doubted that he would get the opportunities in such a packed classroom. "Do you think that after ten years on the job he hasn't found ways and means?" Again I conceded it was a possibility but still I maintained that popularity was his primary motivation. That was stimulation enough for him.

My theory was confirmed one evening after class, while I was waiting for a few of my new friends. Looking unobserved from outside, I saw Toby approach the noticeboard and scrutinise all the facts and figures on that evening's published attendance record (something I had never seen any other teacher do). He was like a complacently successful football manager perusing the league tables after yet another victory. I could see the smirk of satisfaction spread, spoiling the innocence of his baby face. It spoke volumes about his priorities and insecurities. I allayed my contempt with the thought that my class generally had a greater ratio of females than his (even if, overall, I couldn't match his attendance levels), and the knowledge that it bothered him. With no doors on any of the classrooms, Toby could never resist nosing his way in to check on my class and greet any pretty young refugees from his class while completely ignoring me. This I regarded as an intrusion, particularly when he engaged them in pathetically childish small talk. *Bugger off and take care of your own students,* I thought. But, since he was generally unsuccessful in luring back his most prized students, I began instead to gain a certain cheer from his shows of insecurity, and determined not to let it develop into some kind of Robert versus Jonathan feud. The tragic and untimely demise of Fraser had in any case put such petty concerns into perspective.

FINDING NEW DIGS became a priority soon after the nocturnal incident involving Annie and Abdul. That had been one disturbance too many and now I was in Mohammed's main hostel, three floors down, holed up in a 10'x12' cockroach-ridden dormitory with five strangers. The chances of living contentedly in such accommodation for the best part of six months appeared remote, but my ordeals upstairs had desensitised me to such a degree that it was an easy transition. I managed to get into a rhythm and routine: up at eight, quick shower, walk the short distance to work, a cup of tea and a bun, then a nine o'clock start and a four-hour stint. Home thereafter for a couple of hours' siesta in an empty dorm, revived for an evening session that would also pass in a blur, before finally heading home with a meal and a couple of drinks inside me. Then I would sleep like a child.

Before bedtime my room-mates would usually come in. There

was a hardcore of three or four permanent residents, while the couple of spare beds were in turn taken by Japanese and German backpackers, a Dutch escort girl and an English electrician amongst others.

Matt, with two years under his belt, was one of the long-stayers. He had a bottom bunk, with a hanging sheet his one concession to privacy. When he emerged he usually had little to say, apart from passing racist comments about local people or moaning about his job or boss, or the crowded streets.

"Why don't you go home?" (to East Anglia) I once asked him.

"What! You must be fuckin' jokin. What'd I wanna go back there for?"

"Well, you're obviously not satisfied with your life here."

"No chance. Nothin' for me to go back for."

"At least you could communicate with the people, walk down the street without bumping into people and wouldn't be sweating your nuts off at work and have to live in a hovel like this."

"I like it 'ere. "It's cheap, it's got a telly, air-con, okay people…" (This was a rare positive utterance from him, but not one he could maintain for a whole sentence) "…apart from that bitch Clare."

Maybe he found contentment and solace in negativity, or perhaps he had settled into his daily schedule, and with money in his pocket that was enough. I doubted it, though, seeing how, after a ten-hour day toiling on a nearby railway station construction site, usually in sweltering conditions, followed by an evening in the Base downing large vodkas, he returned home every night inebriated but still as lugubrious as ever, only more vocal in his cheerlessness.

The 'bitch Clare' Matt had referred to was one of our roommates. Later, when she had returned and Matt had gone out, I tried to find out what lay behind the enmity.

From her bed on the bunk below me, she answered, "He's in a rut and probably needs a good shag."

"Not tempted?" I teased.

Clare made a curious snorting sound. "He did try it on at first, but no, I just find him so miserable and charmless."

I could see why Matt was attracted to her. She was a barmaid with a barmaid's attributes. And I could see why the attraction was not reciprocated even if, looks-wise at least, they might not have been a bad match.

"Is that why you two always ignore each other?"

"Ask him, he's the one with the attitude problem."

Clare was seeing a black American singer at that time, who performed in her bar. She said Matt had refused to talk to her since he found out, but neither of them seemed unduly bothered by the bad air, which was nothing unusual in a place where everyone seemed to live quite easily with grudges and bitterness.

And it was an unhealthy atmosphere in a literal sense too.

THE KITCHEN, for example, was host to bugs and germs and other ills symptomatic of our retrograde living environs. Stepping into this neglected quarter, amid the unwashed pots and pans in the sink, grease, grime and crumbs everywhere, with cockroaches scurrying for the cover of crevices and sinkholes, reminded you that you were in a place scarcely fit for human habitation. The air was worse than stuffy, but the window remained fixed shut – not that opening it would provide relief, for outside was a blackened chute, typical of these 1960s blocks, polluted by discarded newspapers, plastic bags, rags and condoms. I wondered at the design concept of these grim shafts with windows facing onto them, which in the event of fire would surely be transformed into chimneys, with rubbish-filled bases providing a ready supply of fuel.

Some fellow residents had found a function for this otherwise decrepit and unused vertical corridor, however. For rodents it provided safe, well-sheltered access from the guts of the building to the rooftop. The kitchen window had to stay fastened or they would stream in overnight and take over the place, which according to Clare, happened on at least one occasion.

Although I tended to avoid this stinking galley, necessity sometimes overcame my natural reluctance. One evening I went in to boil some water for a pot of noodles, but finding, as usual, the constant-boil kettle empty and disconnected I resorted to the microwave. As I closed its door I happened to notice a couple of little cockroaches inside. Nothing unusual in that, except they aroused in me a certain scientific curiosity. How long could one of these repellent but hardy creatures survive a dose of microwave radiation? I shut the door and turned the power on full. A minute elapsed and both were still strolling around quite jauntily. Two minutes up, and with the water simmering, there were still no adverse reactions from within. Once or twice they appeared to wander to each other, perhaps commenting that it was a warm one today, before departing to opposite corners. The water was boiling over after two-and-a-half minutes, but no sign of panic from the resilient invertebrates within. When I opened the door, one dashed out, but the other stayed for more. Another ninety seconds of full-powered microwaves would account for it, surely. Or not. I gave up, full of grudging respect for these great ecological survivors. The old claim that the cockroach was one of the few creatures that could survive a nuclear holocaust seemed ever more credible. The other, if memory serves, was the common rat. But what chance a rodent surviving four minutes in a microwave? And how does the humble roach do it when a similar-sized broad bean would be desiccated in half the time?

Despite marvelling at their toughness and indestructibility, it is hard to deny that these are amongst the most obnoxious of all creatures. Particularly so the large ebony-coloured species that sport a thick yellow stripe across their backs. They wait motionless and stealthy, with only their antennae waving and protruding eerily from their hiding places, then dash and disappear on discovery with great haste. Bombard them with insecticide and watch them shrug it off; swat one with a newspaper and, more often than not, it will limp away to safety, leaving a nasty, viscous, poisonous mess of pus. Finding them lurking around the toilet rim also does little for their reputation. But what I hate most is just their supreme, miniature-monster ugliness.

As I was pouring the hot water over my noodles, trying to banish all thoughts of cockroaches and uncleanliness, a giant Geordie builder from along the corridor entered the kitchen and looked in the fridge. There was a brief rustling of plastic bags before the fridge door was violently slammed shut. "Uh don't fookin' believe it. Not a-fookin-gain! Some coont has been an' swiped me fookin' bacon. Hey you! You seen anyone eatin' bacon, have you?"

"No."

"Well, who the fook's had it? When Uh find the coont who's filched it he's goin'a fookin pay, Uh'm tellin' ya." Still steaming he went out to the reception, where young Akram was stationed as normal behind the counter. "Someone's been and took me fooking bacon. D'ya kna who it was? Uh hop' for your sake it wasn't you, Akram."

Akram looked bewildered, hardly understanding a word but wisely denying it all the same.

"What about your mates? They're always hangin' around the kitchen. Did one of them nick it, eh?"

"Muslims don't eat bacon," said I, bravely coming to the aid of the beleaguered Akram.

"Who asked you? When Uh find out who took it Uh'm goin'a kill the bastard. That includes you, oonderstand?"

I ignored the threat, reasoning that any further dialogue with such a psychopath, particularly one as large and irate as this, may not be beneficial to my health. Instead I was hoping he would have a go at either of two athletic-looking Africans sitting by the reception desk. They might not have been so reticent and perhaps would have taught him some manners, regardless of his size.

I looked in the fridge, wondering how anyone could even consider cooking in this germ-zone. Inside was a surprising amount of produce, all of it well wrapped in plastic bags to disguise its identity and deter sticky fingers. Perhaps that was his mistake.

With nowhere to sit down to eat, I had to perch on the bottom bunk hunched over my pot of noodles. The Hong Kong variety are scarcely more satisfying and flavoursome than the British ones – noodles and dried bits of veg floating in an insipid, watery soup. Is this what I worked for? I was almost nostalgic for the sandwich delivery days when I could at least rely on something fresh and edible.

Matt came in. I apologised and removed my arse smartly from his bed. "Wasn't expecting you back so soon."

"Obviously not."

He would have been apoplectic if he had caught anyone else sitting on his bed but he seemed to tolerate me. Perhaps he appreciated my efforts to cheer him up, while everyone else did their best to ignore him. It wasn't only for his sake, though; I found a perverse pleasure in coaxing out the irritable, laconic side of his nature, and being alone with him was when his humour was at its dry, dark best.

"Matt, do you know what, if there was a nuclear war, the only creatures to survive would be?"

"We would for a start. Anyone who can put up with this place could survive anything."

I laughed at his trademark deadpan. "No, seriously, do you know?"

"I've got a feelin' you're goin' to tell me."

"The rat and the cockroach."

"That makes sense. We've all got a lot in common, 'aven't we? After all, we share our fuckin 'ome with enough of 'em. No other creatures could stand the squalor."

"Were you here when the rats took over?" I asked him.

"Yeah, of course, I've been 'ere longer than anyone else. One got in 'ere, yer know. I chased it out with a fuckin broom." He chuckled at the memory, and I felt strangely privileged.

I suppose his equanimity was quite typical of the prevailing attitude amongst the backpacker trash. We were accustomed to dealing with all manner of squalor: Insects, vermin? ...All part of the experience. Unhygienic, cluttered kitchens? ...Who cares? Noisy neighbours and telephone messages that never get passed on? ...Trivial concerns. Damp, mouldy bathrooms with toilets that frequently overflow? ...Nothing we couldn't handle.

Infestation and insanitation along with agitation. We could take it all, scarcely questioning conditions that would never be tolerated even in prisons at home. But this is how we lived, and how we made light of how we lived.

"How did they get rid of them?" I wondered.

"Well, Akram went out and got a cat, while Mohammed laid some poisonous bait. The result? …One dead cat and a dozen or so rats still at large." He laughed again. It was becoming a riot.

"The poison didn't work on the rats?"

"Killed a few, I think, but often they're immune to it now. Either that or they're too cute to touch it."

"They're impossible to wipe out, just like the cockroaches. Do you know, I just spent the best part of five minutes trying to kill a cockroach in the microwave?"

"No, I didn't know that… and…?"

"It didn't die."

"My God, you've got too much time on your hands."

"Come on, you've got to admit, it's pretty bloody incredible."

"D'you see the white ones?"

"What, you mean like albino cockroaches?"

"No, I don't think so. I think it's because they live in the fridge. Seems like they've changed colour to accommodate the different environment."

"What, they survive living in a temperature of only about three degrees?"

"They're adaptable, like the rats. Short life cycles and high reproduction rates means evolutionary design modifications kick in quick."

I was impressed. "Sound like a bit of a scientist on the quiet, Matt."

"I have a bit of an interest in genetics and evolutionary development, but yeah, I tend to keep it under me hat. Don't pay to let the bastards round 'ere know too much about yourself."

That he was ashamed to reveal his intellectual interest was the greater shame, and perhaps symptomatic of the attitude that many working-class Brits have towards education.

"Maybe the cockroaches in the fridge ate the Geordie geezer's bacon." I was laughing to myself but Matt, true to form, was indifferent. Not dark enough for him.

"Impossible," he answered.

"The Africans maybe?"

"Equally impossible."

"How do you know?"

"Because," he paused, looking unusually pleased with himself. "Because… I had it."

"What!"

"Last time someone stole his bacon I was innocent but the wanker accused me. I bit me lip and bided me time, checkin' the fridge every day, waitin' for me chance. Now, listenin' to 'im rantin' and ravin' out there, makes it all worthwhile." He laughed loud and unrestrained as a blue moon rose in the eastern sky.

ANDY was the one other permanent resident of our dormitory. Despite being of average stature and equable temperament, he worked as a doorman at a Wan Chai club. His unsocial schedule meant we rarely saw him in daylight hours, but in the early evening this prolific womaniser was usually there to regale anyone, male or female, with tales of his latest international conquests. He even recorded his latest 'scores' by colouring in countries on an

A3 photocopy of a world map, which was hung proudly on the wall over his bed. This was his own personal British Empire, with pink more widespread than on the original, taking in the land masses of China and Russia as well as the more familiar territory of Southeast Asia, Australia, North America and much of Europe. He still hadn't made inroads into the Indian sub-continent, Africa and South America but said he was working on it.

Being chirpy to Matt's chippy it was no surprise that they hardly related to each other. Matt seemed to resent Andy's style and looks, his confidence and success with women: "He acts like he owns fuckin' Hong Kong Island, the flash bastard, just because 'e's pulled a few. I bet 'e's never done a hard day's graft in 'is life… never got 'is 'ands dirty, the soft northern lad. Makes 'is livin' 'angin' around outside fuckin' clubs lookin' out for tarts like a bleedin' pimp. And another thing, 'e's into drugs. 'Ave you seen 'is eyes lately? He was up all last night, just like starin', he was, like in a trance… the bleedin' junky."

Clare, who had been listening with rising irritation, hit back: "Give him a break, you're not exactly a clean living guy."

"Fuck off, I ain't no smack'ead."

"No, but you're a cynical old alcky git."

"I'm no fuckin' alcky, girl."

"So you admit to being a cynical old git, then?"

"Well, it ain't difficult in this place."

Clare laughed bitterly. "Why are you so uptight and full of such negative energy all the time? Why can't you lighten up, like Andy?"

"Course he can lighten up with all that stuff in his veins."

"Well, maybe you ought to try some. What have you got to lose after all? You might even get yourself a life."

"And to think I used to like you!"

I let them get on with it, wryly reflecting that at least they were talking again, and went downstairs in search of company more convivial.

THE BASE BAR, being the local pub of choice for much of the hostel community in Tsim Sha Tsui, was a place I could usually rely on for finding familiar faces. This subterranean enclave below Nathan Road, of *gwailo* tradesmen, labourers, squaddies and miscellaneous itinerant workers, was a very different venue from the cosmopolitan Hong Kong-side nightspots, where expat businessmen and bankers on low-tax, all-expenses contracts happily paid double for their drinks. Here in unfashionable Kowloon there were no Armani suits and nothing more sophisticated than untucked button-downs. Most of the Brits tended to stand or sit on stools around the long bar, while most in the sitting areas were tourists or other foreign residents, with few Chinese faces to be seen. Locals were understandably deterred by the boisterous foreign crowd and their occasional punch-ups, drunken songs, chanting and cheering during the regular 'live' English football screenings. Not that the guvnor had cause to complain. He told me that business had never been better and he gladly put up with a bit of rowdiness in exchange for his multiplied takings (according to him, a pub full of British drinkers would drink four or five times the volume of locals). A flourishing economy, full employment and a large local contingent of foreigners determined to live up every night like a Friday night. Everyone knew that this time next year all would have changed, with the Chinese in charge and a British passport would no longer be a guarantee of a year's visa-free access and promise of work. This was a unique period – 'Pre-handover Fever', as he put it – and nowhere was the feeling more tangible than here.

As I waited at the bar I saw Marco – the bloke Helen scored from prior to the ill-fated assignation with Rajiv – perched on a stool occupying his customary place in the corner. He wasn't a friend, barely even an acquaintance. The few times I'd spoken to him he was pissed, and in sober times never seemed to recognise me. He was a squat, balding and garrulous Londoner – more Bob Hoskins than Bob Hoskins, albeit a young (and still alive) Bob Hoskins. He held sway over a clique of half a dozen backslappers who clustered around him laughing at his gags and buying him drinks. He was in his element, with his status as a minor celebrity assured partly because of his personal charisma but more to do with his 'occupation' as a dealer. "If you wannit I can get it," he regularly boasted. "It's not what you know, it's 'oo you know."

His connections included traffickers, cigarette smugglers and bootleggers of various designer products and other fake luxury goods; he also flogged a range of 'stock' fresh from the backs of lorries. But he remained small-time, refusing to sell hard drugs for instance and seemingly content to make enough to subsidise his daily drinking binges and preclude the need to get a proper job. More importantly, his 'business' put him in the spotlight and gave him the kudos he craved. He was known by virtually everyone in the *gwailo* quarter of Tsim Sha Tsui and Marco wouldn't have had it any other way. To his 'hangers-on' he was a demigod, spewing nuggets of cockney wisdom and humour, and in his darker moments, railing against the 'injustice' of Britain handing Hong Kong back to the 'treacherous' Chinese. They flattered his ego, helping to shape the smug little monster he was in danger of becoming.

Standing some twenty feet down the bar I could still hear every word he said: "We built this fuckin' city. We made it what it is… and what fanks do we get? This was nuffink but a jungle an' a pile o' rocks before we arrived. Now it's the fuckin' 'igh-tech, international, financial centre of Asia. While just over the border they're livin' in huts and eatin' bleedin' dog meat. Now we're givin' it all back to those Commie bastards to ruin."

The thought occurred to me that this was precisely the reason why nobody in the territory was likely to thank the British: we fattened the Hong Kong goose only to feed it to the Dragon. (Of course none of the apostles, nodding in agreement with the messiah, pointed out this flaw in his argument). I could also mention that millions of those hut-dwellers who came to Hong Kong had at least as much, if not more, influence on the development of this great city, first with manufacturing and then trading; and prior to colonisation the Chinese of Canton were customers of Britain's lucrative opium business (trading rights courtesy of Royal Navy guns), which would fund Hong Kong's successful establishment. This after gaining the island in 1841 from the Chinese in the wake of their Opium Wars defeats.

Marco was probably not even aware of this shabby little episode of colonial history but would surely be proud of those pioneers and glad to follow in their footsteps. I didn't suppose the irony would be lost on him either: where once the British sold drugs to the Cantonese, he now bought most of his stuff from local Chinese sources to sell to young Britons.

There was a tap on my shoulder and someone said, "Hey Joe." Failing to recognise the voice, I looked around and found my colleague Damon standing behind. I didn't know him that well but was aware, if not wary, of him due to a forceful and opinionated streak in his personal make-up that belied his years. I was acquainted with his arrogance from his occasional visits to my class during lessons. At such times he would usually come in with a technical question on grammar, spelling or definition, although he always gave the impression that he didn't actually want me to know the answer. Generally I did, but once he came in and asked me how to spell 'idiosyncrasy'. I think I was supposed to be impressed that he was teaching such a word. I said I wasn't a hundred per cent sure but I thought it ended 'cy'. The next day he couldn't contain himself from interrupting my class to announce that my spelling had been wrong. Another time I recall him berating students for listening to Canto-pop instead of Oasis, then deriding Hong Kong as a 'cultural desert' after someone asked who the Beatles were. Mainly for these reasons I rarely tried to engage him in any friendly conversation and, considering he had such an air of cultural superiority, I was surprised to find him with Gerry, the Cantonese-speaking Englishman who had gone native, and Robert, the 'Metrognome'.

It was good to be in the company of some big opinionated characters and it wasn't long before the conversation focused on another man with a big personality (Fraser): I wondered aloud if anyone could explain why there were so few Chinese at his funeral. As both Gerry and Robert had been resident for several years in this part of the world and were in relationships with Chinese women I thought they might have some insight.

"The Chinese have a major taboo where death is concerned," said Robert. "They wouldn't come to a funeral unless they were absolutely obligated. You know, apartments in Hong Kong that face cemeteries sell for twenty-five or thirty per cent less than the apartments on the other side of the same building. These are very superstitious people. Really. They have tons of fears and hang-ups and prejudices."

I was reminded of Fraser's allegations of Chinese racism, which in turn brought to mind Curt's. I had never been on the receiving end of such discrimination – not overtly, at least – but it made me think. "Prejudices against us?"

"I get some grief from my wife's family, but it's cultural more than racial," Robert answered. "In general, you're as likely to receive positive discrimination as negative."

"Well, that's just as objectionable, really, isn't it?" Damon spouted. "I don't want people saying 'hello' just because I'm a foreigner, or 'excuse me' when they pass with plenty of space available. Sometimes I think they have to say something just to prove how modern and cosmopolitan they are."

Six eyebrows were raised.

"How about you, Gerry? How do you get on with your girlfriend's family?" I enquired.

"They didn't accept me at first. I think they wanted her to find a nice Chinese boy. But now I'm speaking the lingo they're not so bad. Other than that, racism against us in everyday life is so insignificant it's hardly worth mentioning."

"Oh yeah?" piped Damon with customary aggression. "What about the word, *gwailo*. You can't tell me that's not a racist term. It means white devil, for god's sake."

"Well, it means ghost, really," said Gerry, wearily dismissive.

"Ghost… white devil… who cares? It's derogatory and offensive."

"Relax, man. It's only offensive if the intention is to offend, but I've hardly ever heard it used in that context. It's an everyday word used in conversation by almost everyone without a second thought."

"Well, that makes it worse, doesn't it, when racist terms are taken for granted. I mean the 'n' word used to be commonly spoken."

Gerry scoffed. "Bloody hell, there is a difference. I don't see too many *gwailos* in chains, do you? Anyway you're applying your nice, cosy, politically correct Western ideals to a place that has no concept of these things. Whatsoever."

Damon butted in: "Maybe it's time they got themselves a concept."

"Why? There's actually more real freedom of speech here than back home. Everyone just speaks their mind regardless of who they might offend, and long may it continue, I say. At least you know where you stand with these people, in contrast to complex foreigners who want to control our thoughts and speech, or the hypocrites who smile at your face and scowl at your back."

"I think I'd rather have people scowling at my back instead of my face... I'm fed up with being ignored by surly waitresses; I'm fed up with people pushing to get on the train or in the lift while I'm trying to get out; I'm pissed off with people walking into me down the street; I'm sick of..."

An exasperated Gerry didn't let Damon finish. "Well, they're hardly picking on you! That's how they treat each other. Difference is people here just tolerate it as a way of life and get on with it, which is what you should be doing, you know, when in Rome and all that."

"Sorry but I just can't tolerate the intolerable," Damon replied confidently.

"It's not for us to tolerate but to be tolerated, we're the bloody outsiders! Nobody asked us to come over here. I mean we're taking up valuable living space and seats on buses, generally adding to Hong Kong's overcrowdedness and pollution, while our contribution to society here is pretty negligible."

"Bollocks, I provide a service that there's a demand for, and even if I don't belong doesn't mean I'm not allowed an opinion, does it? All I'm trying to say is that a lot of people here are racist as well as rude, and I still can't get my head around this word, *gwailo*."

"Shouldn't that be the 'g' word?" I teased.

Damon wasn't listening. "I mean *gwailo* is purely a racial term. It's not generic for foreigner, or anything like that because Filipinos aren't *gwailos* and nor are black British or Chinese Americans."

"Come on! What do you expect, when the word in question means ghost?" asked Gerry.

"That's neither here nor there. They're up in arms if anyone uses the word chinky and yet *gwailo* has a far more negative connotation."

"Well, hypocrisy's a universal currency, but I'm not sure as many people in Hong Kong would get as worked up about being called chinky as you do over *gwailo*."

"When you've been here as long as we have," said Robert, "you won't even give it a second thought. We even use the word amongst ourselves. There's no stigma, just let it go."

"Well I get the feeling people here don't respect us. You agree don't you, Joe?"

"I don't know, but I suspect Fraser and Curt would."

Gerry was chuckling. "Well of course they would. People that don't take responsibility for their own inadequacies always blame racism."

I didn't agree with the sentiment, but as a way of putting Damon on the back foot it worked. He was outraged of course, screwing up his face indignantly, while his cheeks reddened slightly. He bit his tongue, trying to give the impression that he had not taken it personally, before replying: "Sounds like you've been here so long the local habits are starting to rub off on you."

Gerry glared back. "How long have you been in Hong Kong… a few months? Yet you see fit to judge all things Hong Kong and condemn it all. I don't understand why you don't have more respect for Chinese people and culture."

"Hang on, who said I don't have any respect for Chinese culture? I spent two months teaching in China before I came here. What a difference! The people there are so much friendlier…"

"But their manners can leave a lot to be desired," interrupted Robert.

"What do you mean?"

"They never stand in line, they spit, they stare at foreigners."

Damon glared at Robert dismissively. "But there's no malice, you know. Of course they have different habits, but when they spit or snort on the ground they just see it as ridding their bodies of toxins. When they see Westerners blowing their noses and then replacing their snotty hankies in their pockets *they* are disgusted. And when they stare it's only curiosity."

Gerry looked on in disbelief. "Are you telling me that you have no objections to people in China staring at you while you go to the toilet, as long as they're curious, but if someone in Hong Kong says 'excuse me' at the wrong time it's unacceptable?"

"You're using my words in a completely different context. I'm just trying to contrast the two attitudes, that's all. In China the people are completely genuine and natural. They have no airs and graces, no pretensions. I really admire their simplicity and honesty. And another thing, they're more good-humoured: you can have a laugh with strangers; people working in the restaurants and shops actually smile and even say thank you. One country, two systems?" said Damon, citing a China government reunification slogan. "…One country, two worlds, more like."

I was beginning to read Damon. He had obviously enjoyed being an attraction in China, where foreigners are a rarity. Doubtless he had been flattered by the attention, but here in Hong Kong he was just another *gwailo*. Generally I found him disagreeable, not so much for his opinions but for the way he presented them. There was never any doubt as to the veracity and importance of everything he said, and he always seemed to make the most mundane issues contentious. His cocksure attitude, alternating between brashness and belligerence, might have been easier to accept had he been older, wiser and more experienced. But he wasn't. Gerry, on the other hand…

"It's a great pity that people don't smile at you enough, and don't say 'hello' when they should, and do when they shouldn't. It's a shame that people don't always say 'thank you', and I feel sorry that you get ignored and nobody pampers you in the way you've become accustomed. A shame really, but when you think about it, a small price to pay for living in a cohesive, safe, peaceful society, with a very decent economy and efficient public services."

Damon rolled his eyes and shook his head.

"I know when you first come here," said Robert, "everybody seems cold and mean, but really they just have a cautious, defensive nature. Once you break down these barriers and really relate to the people you'll be surprised. Friendships are genuine and they last."

"Well, I made more friends in China in one week than I have here in four months," said Damon, grouchily, with a touch of defeatism. "And surely you can't deny," his defiance returning as he found more ammunition for his anti-Hong Kong offensive, "the attitude of local people towards mainlanders is absolutely appalling."

"He's got a point there," I had to concede, as I had often heard disparaging comments from students regarding mainland immigrants. "It is amazing, considering nearly everyone has parents or grandparents who arrived from the mainland. I don't really understand how they can be so hostile toward their own people."

Robert was nodding, but Gerry wasn't swayed. "People from Hong Kong go to the mainland and they generally don't like what they see: the habits, the lack of hygiene and the squalor. I think they worry it will spread."

"But the people who come here always integrate within one generation," Robert remarked. "Apart from a handful of Tanka tribes nobody is indigenous to Hong Kong. Remember this was only a handful of fishing and farming communities. The immigrants have made it and they are of precisely the same stock, region and culture as those they wanna keep out."

"I appreciate that, but the people just want to preserve their way of life..."

"But their way of life isn't under threat!" cried Damon.

"Isn't it?" asked a rhetorical Gerry. "I think you'll find overcrowding is one of the biggest impediments to quality of life anywhere in the world, but particularly in the world's most densely populated city. And another thing, in case it escaped your attention, this great, unique city-state is about to be subsumed by the People's Republic of China."

"Not before time."

Gerry shot back at Damon: "What are you talking about?"

"I'm talking about self-determination, national self-respect, and ending the indignity of colonial rule."

"You sound like a Communist Party propagandist. Virtually no one on this side of the border sees it like that. Why don't you try listening to them for once?"

"I'm just trying to look at the wider picture. Hong Kong, geographically, historically and culturally belongs to China. Deep down, the Hong Kong people know that and have to accept it."

Gerry looked more disgusted than at any time during the debate.

"You've got no understanding and respect for these people. If you did you'd know the apprehension they're feeling in the run-up to the handover. The rule of law, free press, financial independence – all the things that make Hong Kong unique from the mainland – are under threat like never before. You might not get it but six-and-a-half million people in Hong Kong certainly do. And remember in China there are well over a billion people, most of whom would give their right arm to get into this tiny, crowded space; while every year, Hong's population and pollution increase, the few remaining tracts of workable land get bulldozed to make way for yet more high-rises to fill with newcomers, and the harbour looks more like a river every year as more of it gets filled in. No wonder they're developing a siege mentality."

"That's no excuse for the way newcomers get abused... I've seen it and heard it in my own classes, and everyone knows that school kids from China get routinely bullied." Damon screwed up his face, as he always did when he was getting to a pertinent point. It made him look ten years older and twice as unattractive, which unfortunately made it harder to agree with him even when, as in this case, he had a valid argument. "I think it's an absolute disgrace, the way they look down on these people... absolutely shameful."

"Well, you might have a point," said Gerry in a conciliatory voice. "One thing I can tell you, though" – conciliation evaporating – "nobody's as negative about mainlanders as you are about Hong Kongers."

Damon looked as if he was wearying of being constantly challenged by Gerry, even if it was a ploy that he had used often enough against others. "Perhaps you could educate me with their virtues."

"They're self-reliant; they're generally trustworthy and hardworking; they seldom resort to violence; and they're more tolerant than the foreigners that live here: you don't hear Hong Kong people whingeing and complaining all the time. No, they just get on with their lives without bothering anyone and they expect others to do the same."

Damon responded, after a long sigh, "What about the way they look down on Filipina maids, or the way they discriminate against Indians by refusing to let them flats? Where's the tolerance there, man? There's not even any legislation to protect them against this kind of thing."

"There are labour laws and minimum wages to protect the Filipinas, unlike in most of the wealthy Middle Eastern countries they work in. And another thing, at least they can walk down the street here without any fear of being abused or attacked, unlike a lot of other places I could mention."

"I wonder what Fraser would make of you guys squabbling like this," interrupted Robert, dowsing the sparks that were threatening to inflame.

"Oh, he'd approve, believe me," laughed Gerry.

"Whose side do you think he'd be on?" I asked.

"Knowing Fraser, he'd find a way of disagreeing with both of us," said Gerry.

Damon smiled, which signalled an end to hostilities.

VICTORIA PEAK, or The Peak as it is more commonly known, is the number one tourist sight in Hong Kong. The best way to reach it is via one of the world's steepest and most exhilarating tram rides, in old carriages that have been trundling their way up since 1888. At that time the only competition was the sedan chair; now buses ply a circuitous route, but there is still nothing to compare with this four-minute ride, pinned back in your seat, with glimpses of skyscrapers emerging through the trees, then rooftops, before the harbour and Kowloon are revealed beyond.

You disembark into a commercialised zone outside the Peak Tram terminus and the blight of a giant metallic mushroom (the Peak Tower) and a modern shopping mall across the road. Assuming this is the summit – when in fact it is a plateau some three hundred-odd feet below the two summits – most visitors are content to hang around the arcades or take a leisurely stroll around the Harlech Road loop, which on clear days is taken over by a procession of camera-wielding day-trippers and tourists. The route offers fine views overlooking the harbour, with Kowloon and Lion Rock in the distance and a forest of tower blocks to the fore, stretching in a narrow swathe west to east. The tallest of these are barely below the line of vision, giving an impression of encroachment, with slender apartment blocks creeping up the hillsides and giant new office developments conspiring to obscure the view with their escalating heights.

A twenty-minute climb from here, however, takes you away from the throng, past some of the world's most expensive real estate, through fragrant forest and parkland gardens, onto a true vantage with one of the great panoramas at your feet, taking in outlying islands, the range of Hong Kong hills, as well as the more familiar cityscapes. Looking down on even the tallest buildings you feel complete detachment from the clang and the clatter of the city far below, with only the faintest hum of urban life to be heard. Freshness and coolness pervade the air and the unfamiliar sight of birds and flowers and even that rarest of commodities in Hong Kong, grass, can be found.

The British, in early colonial times, also sought refuge from the heat, noise and pollution, making these highlands the most desirable residential location, which they continue to be today. The native Chinese weren't even allowed to live in the Peak environs then, while today it is home to the wealthiest businessmen and most famous stars of Hong Kong. I remember seeing the up-and-coming Taiwanese actress Siu Kei coming out of the Peak Café looking more glamorous and sensuous than anyone I had ever seen.

A less pleasing – and certainly less stylish – sight that greeted me while wandering along a woodland path on the plateau was that of my old flame Jan and the Scottish room-mate of hers. I was some distance behind, but still recognised Jan's shape, gait and crumpled, khaki cargo pants. I felt very little emotionally and I realised I was over her. There was some tension, as I wondered whether to approach her, but that was all. If Jan had been alone, there would have been less of a dilemma, but there was something about that other girl. And, as I looked more closely, there was something about the pair of them: they were holding hands. I followed at a safe distance, wondering if their apparent intimacy was platonic, while beginning to harbour serious doubts. After a couple of minutes they stopped in the middle of the path. They seemed to embrace but, by trying to obscure myself behind the nearest bush, I couldn't be sure. Peering through the leaves I saw them sit down on a bench. The Scottish girl was ruffling Jan's hair playfully before stretching her arm over her shoulder. Then they kissed. I felt a range of emotions, finally settling on reprieve. I thought back to our trysts. She had never been the most responsive of lovers, it was true; and then she had apparently shunned my attempts at a reunion, which was something of a blow to my confidence. I had felt devalued by being unable to satisfy her or maintain her interest. But now it seemed that perhaps no man could have. And that was the reprieve I felt as I turned back and walked out of the woods into the sunshine.

That should have been enough excitement and drama for one day. But in these fag-end days of British Hong Kong, it just wasn't working out like that for me. I had made acquaintance with too many dodgy characters who all seemed to be moving in the same small circles as me, with potential for trouble around every corner.

It was near the tram terminal that I saw them: an apparently loving couple, with a small daughter holding hands between them. The woman was wearing a plain Islamic gown and black headscarf while her husband was dressed like a Westerner. As they got closer, however, I could see this was no ordinary couple, or at least no ordinary husband. It was Abdul, the dysfunctional, brutal Lothario and would-be rapist, looking relaxed and casual, despite a lack of any communication between the three of them. Again I had a bewildering array of reactions to wrestle with. My first instinct was to do nothing, second to go to the police. And third…

I kept my eyes on him as we approached each other, hoping he would look up and see me. I wanted him to receive the knowing stare of my eyes into his, and feel the prospect of justice shadowing, haunting him. Instead his attention was taken by a man flying a kite, which he pointed out to his daughter. He wasn't going to see me.

I cleared my throat loudly. "Excuse me, have you got the time?"

He turned to face me, wearing a momentary look of blankness before the startling recognition set in, transforming his features to stone. His eyes dilated and he was suddenly drawn, as if he had seen a ghost, which in some respects he had. Except I was more dangerous than that.

He seemed to lose some control of his senses for a moment. His wife nudged him. "Oh… oh," he gasped. "It's um… nearly six o'clock."

"Oh, it's Abdul, isn't it?" I cried with forced enthusiasm. "How are you doing? Oh, I see you've got a new watch. That's a pity 'cause I found your old one." I paused, awaiting his response, but he remained mute. "I handed it in to South Kowloon Police Station, so if you go along there you'll be able to pick it up. The police will be very glad to see you, I'm quite sure."

Abdul sounded unconvincing and breathless as he replied: "I'm sorry, I think you are mistaken."

I might have left it at that had he not spoken. Instead I said, "No, it was definitely you. You left it in the room opposite mine. Do you remember a couple of months ago, when you left in a hurry?"

Abdul was edging away quite frantically, almost hauling his wife and daughter behind him.

"Thank you, thank you," was all he could mutter.

I had more power in those moments than I'd ever had in my life. I was holding the keys to Abdul's very liberty, and with it the future of this small family. There was a police station just a few hundred yards away. All I had to do was walk in and blow the whistle and their lives would have been destroyed. It wouldn't have been an easy decision regardless, but without Annie's permission, impossible. I had tormented him and got my taste of schadenfreude at his expense, while he had been reminded of the consequences of his actions and the prospect of detection. It wasn't justice, but it was something.

I made for home, wondering why such things kept happening to me when all I wanted was a quiet life. I had no appetite for any more such disturbing incidents and hopefully assumed my life would settle into some kind of normality soon enough. "What a day!" I muttered to myself as I approached the minibus stand for Central. "What a fucking day!" Alas, this would be the mantra of more days to come.

DUNCAN was one of the middle-aged sleaze pedlars from my place of work, you may recall. Despite this and his washed out expat demeanour, I welcomed his invitation to join him on one of his frequent nocturnal expeditions. If nothing else, it had to be more relaxing than a night out with Gerry, Robert and Damon.

Sitting in his local in Tsim Sha Tsui he told me how much he missed England, in particular the cricket and the pubs, the fresh air and even the weather. But he knew there were few opportunities at home for middle-aged men without relevant experience or qualifications.

He wasn't alone. I could think of a score or more people like him – nearly all male – who had stayed so long in Asia simply because they had run out of other options. We had more in common in terms of qualifications, career and indeed direction in life than I cared to admit. One notable difference was that I hadn't yet committed myself to an incompatible, inextricable relationship. The longer you stayed in this place, though, the more likely it was to happen.

Duncan admitted to being in a rut, tied down by his own personal circumstances and lack of ambition. He had a wife from Suzhou, near Shanghai, and a four-year-old son. In an effort to bring some cheer, I mentioned that my students had said Suzhou girls were renowned as the most beautiful in China.

"Yeah, they're supposed to have the best attributes of the northern and southern Chinese... you know, slightly taller than the Cantonese, paler complexion, higher cheekbones, but without the very narrow northern eyes. She has a typical Suzhou outlook."

His choice of *outlook* instead of *appearance* made me smile. This is a common error made by Hong Kong students and one

Duncan obviously had heard so much he'd adopted himself. I remember another teacher who reported having heard him say 'it not is' instead of 'it isn't' and I'd heard him several times addressing students in pidgin English, which seems to defeat the purpose of a native-tongue teacher. If an English teacher's English is deteriorating to the level of his students, it is probably time to quit and head home, I reflected, but instead said, "Sounds wonderful, what are you complaining about?"

"Well, she was an angel when we met. I thought I'd hit the jackpot. But everything was against us from the start. Her family didn't approve of her marrying a foreigner, at least not an impoverished, middle-aged foreigner. They suspected she was pregnant, and when she admitted it they cut her out of their lives. So we had all that stress and pressure from the start and then we had Callum. On top of that you have all the cultural and language issues to deal with. At first the communicational misunderstandings are tolerable, even fun, but they quickly become wearing, believe me, especially when you've spent all day with a class full of English novices."

I could understand where he was coming from and told him I couldn't imagine living with someone like Wendy.

"Right, first and foremost you need someone you can communicate with. If you don't have that, then you lose the freedom to be yourself. I always used to take care over choosing my vocabulary, mentally deleting slang, and that sort of thing, just to be understood. Gradually it became second nature, but at some expense. My brother telephoned last year and said I sounded odd – I'd lost my old accent and was speaking much more slowly than I used to. I suppose I have lost something of my old identity, but what can I do?"

I commented, "You lose something and you gain something when you move to another country, but you're just adapting like good immigrants do."

"But I didn't choose to immigrate to Hong Kong. I'm only here through unhappy circumstances. Still, I've tried to settle and belong as best I can."

"Have you learned the language?"

"I've picked up some Mandarin from the missus and Cantonese from the students. But Mandarin is no use in Hong Kong and she obviously can't teach me Cantonese. So it was hard, although, to be fair, her English has improved greatly. But when you just don't have the same background, cultural reference points, sense of humour to fall back on it really is not easy."

"There are still plenty of happy mixed couples around."

"I suppose if you're like Gerry and you love the culture and learn the language thoroughly, then become a part of the family, you can make the relationship work; or when the girl is very westernised it's easier. Other than that you get the marriages of convenience which are a sham, or the happy young couples who haven't reached that awkward stage and don't yet know what they've let themselves in for."

"Sounds like you don't recommend such relationships?"

"All born of experience and observation. I've lived it and seen it, and I'd just advise you not to make the same mistakes, that's all. You should know what I'm talking about anyway after your experiences with that Indonesian girl. Have you heard anything from her, by the way?"

"She's back in Indonesia at the moment now, and I'm wondering if we have a future."

"Missing her?"

I nodded. "But not as much as I did. For a while she had such a hold on me I thought I couldn't live without her. Yet we had little in common except chemistry and it was still the nearest thing to love I've ever felt. Hard to explain really."

"When you're far from home and lonely you fall in love easier and the breaking up is harder because you need a companion more. And it's easier to confuse those feelings and lust with love under such circumstances."

"No, it wasn't that primitive. There was something deeper, even if the connection was more physical and emotional than intellectual. I missed her like mad when she was away and felt more protective of her than anyone I've ever met. She was so small and delicate and pretty, and when she looked at me with those misty eyes I would have done anything for her. It hardly bothered me that our conversation was a bit limited."

"But the physical attraction and appeal of the exotic are the driving forces. Jane and I were exactly the same. But, once the stardust has worn off and the novelty has gone – although the beauty remains – it's not enough, believe me, it's not enough. When your relationship is built on something so fragile and fleeting you've got no chance. The one thing you *have* got is eroded by familiarity and suddenly you realise you've got nothing else and you're wondering why the hell you didn't see this coming. When you look at a beautiful face or body you delude yourself that this is a beautiful person, and when you're having the best sex of your life you think this is truly love and it will never end. But you're wrong on both counts and by the time you realise it you're condemned, one way or another, to live with the consequences of the biggest misjudgement of your life."

I knew there was sense in his words. Equally I knew such advice would be quickly and quietly disregarded if I found myself in a similar situation again with such a woman. I would probably make all the same decisions and errors of judgement, and no doubt so would he. The 'weaker sex' label is not without foundation.

I mentioned I had been impressed by his articulacy and surprised, considering his occasional lapses.

"Well, it's wasted on the students and the missus so I save it for the bar. The alcohol helps bring out my old self too."

"What does your wife think of you going out on the town?"

"That's what she thinks." He showed me a bruise on the back of his hand, evidence, he said, of a frying pan attack. "She also had a go at me with a meat cleaver but missed, thank God."

"Why?"

"She suspected I was having an affair."

"Were you?"

"Good God, no. More of a fling than an affair."

"I expect the distinction was lost on her."

He smiled thinly. "She drives me to it. You'd do the same in my situation, I promise you. It's all I can do to maintain my sanity."

"Are you not attracted to her any more?"

He paused. "Yes, but it isn't mutual. After the birth of our son, she withdrew favours."

His use of the word 'favours' was quaintly anachronistic and perhaps revealed something of his ideas around sexual dynamics, but I let it go.

"Maybe it was post-natal depression."

Duncan snorted, "No, that was me," and then laughed a hollow laugh.

"How did you cope?"

"Fuck, with more difficulty than you would imagine. I was like a dog on heat, following her around the flat, virtually begging her for it. I didn't love her or even like her by this stage, but physically I wanted her more than ever. Weird. It was torture."

I could sympathise to an extent, but I could see from his wife's point of view that his desperation and lack of sexual charm must have been a turn-off. But I wasn't here to judge.

"Why do you stay together?"

"If we could afford to live apart we would."

"What about your son?"

Duncan leaned on the bar and motioned towards me and I knew he was about to impart something exclusive. "I know this sounds callous, and I hate myself for feeling it, but when I see him I see her... in his features and his aggressive, hyper-active behaviour. I sometimes almost feel that he belongs to her alone. I'm sorry... I shouldn't say that, I shouldn't." His eyes were watery and downcast.

"But he's still yours as much as hers."

"I know, I know... if we all lived back in England and he was brought up in our culture and spoke English like me that would be a different story and I'm sure I'd have more of a connection."

It was all getting too morose and I was thinking of home when Duncan suggested a change of scenery. I wasn't planning on a late night but he was persuasive and in need of the company. "Come on, maybe I can introduce you to a couple of nice little friends," he said with a wink.

On the way I asked him about work and why he'd stayed so long at the English Club.

"Keeps the wolf from the door and the dragon from my back."

"You must get some satisfaction to stay all that time?"

"Look, Joe, I've been working there for the best part of a decade. I've met literally thousands of students. None of them remotely interests me any more. I've seen them all and heard them all several times over – hardly an original thought inside any of them. I don't listen anyway now, don't retain anything from the lessons. I'm on auto-pilot. It's just a routine, spoon-fed platitudes and repetitive chit-chat, then home to bed. You think I want to relive all that, on my night off? ...That's why I don't normally go out with new teachers. That's all they ever want to talk about."

We crossed the harbour by MTR train and then descended into a typically lair-ish Wan Chai disco, whose door policy allowed free entry for Westerners while Indian and Chinese men and even Filipina girls were charged. Chinese men don't complain because they scarcely patronise these places anyway and Indian or Filipina protestations don't carry much clout in this part of the world. It seemed that the management's thinking was that the Filipina women, who greatly outnumber other foreigners in Hong Kong, are drawn to such places by Western men, who generally spend a lot more on drinks, and therefore should not be deterred by admission fees. The girls who may share one Coke all night are considered expendable. Damon was right about one thing: discrimination was rife and legal in 1990s Hong Kong.

I was uncomfortable about frequenting such an establishment: a feeling not alleviated by the manner of our entrance. We were approached by a pair of Asian girls, in skimpy outfits and extravagantly made up, who grabbed us each by the arm before planting kisses on our respective cheeks and leading us towards the bar. I'd heard it was easy to pull here but this was ridiculous. I obediently followed my attractive companion, caught between flattery and suspicion. No such dilemmas for Duncan, however, who had already extricated himself and was now observing from the other side of the bar with remote amusement.

"Don't trust them," he told me as I joined him. "They'll cost you a fortune if you're not careful. They work for the bar."

I noticed Duncan scanning the place as if he were looking for someone. "Shit!" he suddenly cried. "That's a friend of Jane's over there. Let's go."

We went up and down into a similar venue and likewise through a routine of side-stepping hostesses, with Duncan then scrutinising those in attendance for faces to avoid or approach.

"Come on, let's go over the other side. I had a bit with that one a few months back." I followed his line of vision to a petite girl in a black turtle-neck, with long scarlet varnished nails and impeccable, shiny, waist-length hair. "Nice bit of stuff, but too possessive, best avoided."

I had to shout to be heard over the booming stereo. "My God, man, how do you live with all this stress? I'd be a nervous wreck."

"No, you've got it the wrong way round. Coming here keeps me sane. This is my leisure, my playground, if you will. This is what keeps me going through the week… stops me going to the wall."

"What about all the faces you're trying to avoid?"

"I admit Hong Kong is not the best place in the world to have an affair. Too bloody small and everyone you know goes to the same places, so you're always bumping into people you know. That's the worst thing, but it's usually safe enough here. I actually feel free to express myself here, be young again, do what I want."

"With who you want," I added.

He winked. "You've got it. We're kings and this is our palace."

I didn't see it that way, but again, fast forward fifteen or twenty years and you never knew.

He continued in similarly unashamed fashion. "We've got the pick here. See, look over there in the corner. Where else but Asia would you see that?" His gaze led to a huge, fat, red-faced, white-haired geezer with his arms wrapped around the puny shoulders of a pair of dark, Oriental babes, whose combined weight was probably not much more than half of his. He was smoking a large cigar that one of the girls would take from his lips between puffs.

"I know him," announced Duncan. "I'll introduce you to him later when his hands aren't so full."

"Rather you didn't."

"Why?"

"Grotesque comes to mind."

"So you wouldn't swap places? …Now take a look around, Joe. What do you fancy?"

I wasn't impressed. "Don't you find this whole scene a bit sordid?"

"What are you on about?"

"I just find it quite sad that these poor, desperate girls are reduced to products to be picked up and pawed then discarded by all these charmless, middle-aged foreigners with beer bellies… present company excepted of course. And… what are you looking like that for?"

"You sound like a fucking feminist. It's quite condescending, anyway, to assume they're not capable of deciding for themselves what they want and who they want to spend time with. And another thing, I bet you a pound to a penny your principles would be out the window if you had the chance of getting your leg over with that one on the dance floor."

That one was rhythmically swaying in a one-piece outfit she wore like skin, every contour highlighted to perfection, and the smooth, dark gold of her complexion standing out against its brilliant whiteness. I couldn't see her face clearly, but it hardly mattered.

"But what's in it for these girls?"

"Look, there are up to two hundred thousand Filipinas in Hong Kong and several thousand more Indonesians. They've all got menial jobs; they're bored; they're lonely; they're far from home. Pretty much the same as us. So they like to let their hair down once in a while, have a drink and a dance, meet someone. Again, just like us. Only difference is the numbers are in our favour, but you can't complain about that, can you? Might as well just make the most of it."

Duncan had a glance around. "A-ha, there they are." He led me down to a table and introduced me to his two friends, Serena and Angela.

Serena was clearly the one Duncan had marked. She wasn't particularly outstanding, but the way she dressed – short red vinyl skirt, stilettos and scarlet lips – was more important to someone like Duncan. Her image was matched by a lively, extroverted personality, full of laughter and tactile expressions, completely at ease with the environment and company. She was a tonic to him, it was obvious. And when he agreed to join her on the dance floor I could see the feeling was entirely mutual.

I was left with Angela, who was pleasant, cheerful and natural as all Filipinas seem to be. But we had little in common, and I didn't want to come across as condescending by asking about her job or background. Maybe I was being overly sensitive. I could have asked about her family or hobbies or taste in music but I wasn't in the mood and she wasn't making much effort herself. Instead she was singing along to the music, quite unaffected by my presence. Then she joined a conversation with a separate bunch of girls on an adjacent table. I was left in isolated contemplation. So much for Duncan's comment about being kings…

Actually I was quite glad to see the girls had more dignity and less desperation than he had implied. From a personal point of view I also welcomed the lack of attention, not just because Angela wasn't for me, but because I hadn't yet reached the stage where I needed the boost of such flattery and artificial stimulation.

I watched Duncan and Serena moving on the dance floor, she all animation and poise, he trying gamely to keep up: each trying to impress and outdo the other and regaling in their efforts. It wasn't simply about sex on his part and money on hers. It was plain to see, undeniable that they were genuinely enjoying each other's company and I couldn't begrudge them that. But the feeling wasn't universal, and with the appearance of Duncan's ex-girlfriend, the sense of fun evaporated in an instant. Tired and humiliated by their provocative routine, the girl in the black turtleneck and scarlet nails marched over, abused him and threw her drink all over his front. Serena acted like she hadn't noticed and Duncan was too high on adrenalin and drink to worry. The jilted girl made a lonely exit while her tormentors twirled on into the night, careless to the world.

An hour or so later Serena and Angela had to leave to be ready for their early morning routine. And when Duncan came back I was also ready to turn in.

"No, don't go," he protested. "It's still early and I haven't introduced you to my old American friend yet."

"Some other time, perhaps."

"Don't you know who that is? Don't you want to meet your famous predecessor?"

"Who is it… not Curt?"

"The very man."

"Why didn't you say?" This I couldn't turn down. The legendary Curt, original *hum sup gwailo*, tyrant teacher, gob-almighty, and the man who put Maxine in her place. This was someone who had to be met.

I followed Duncan to the weighty Casanova in the corner, now sitting alone.

"Hey Dunc, how you goin', man?"

"Hiya Curt, this is my friend Joe."

Curt acknowledged me by compressing my hand in the huge, sweaty palms of his. "Curt J. Schnitzenburger's the name but friends call me C.J."

"Okay, I'll call you Curt."

He looked a little non-plussed and then: "Ha… ha… ha… Bridish humour, right? That's Bridish humour, uh Dunc?"

Duncan nodded and smiled. "What happened to the girls?"

"I gave 'em the rest o' the night off. I'll catch up with 'em later. Nice pair o' li'll sparrows, uh?"

"How do you do it?" I asked with a smile.

Curt looked mildly disgusted. "Say, whadda you gettin' at, boy?"

"Well… one I can understand, but two…?"

He looked away, nostrils flaring slightly, and without any perceptible irony, said, "You better ask them next time you run into them. Ya might learn somethun, my friend." Then, relaxing somewhat, he continued, "So, you're a workmate of my ole buddy, Dunc, are you?"

"Certainly am."

"Betcha got those l'il Chinese chicks eatin' oudda your hands, don'tcha?"

"Don't know about that," I replied coyly.

"Well you sure ain't workin' there for the money, so you might just as well take advan'age of the only perk goin', son."

"Admit it, your class is full of totty every night," said Duncan.

"I knew it! That's the trouble with you Brits, you're all so damned modest. But let me tell ya, you'll never be a winner with an additood like that. Take it from me, humility don't getcha nowhere."

"So it might get me somewhere then?"

Curt glared at me with a mixture of animosity and bemusement, unsure as to whether I was too clever or too stupid.

He continued nonetheless: "All I'm sayin' is, you want somethun, you go the hell out an' geddit. You wanna say somethun, you go the fuck out an' say it. Don't give a shit what anyone else thinks, that's my advice to you."

I looked at Duncan. "I don't remember asking for any advice, do you?"

"Where I come from, we don't stand on ceremony, know what I'm sayin'? We don't need no invitation to speak. You oughtta be grateful for a bit of paternal advice, boy."

He was amusing and annoying in equal measure. "Where's that then?"

"Lone Star State, boy."

"Never heard of it," I fibbed.

"Try Texas – biggest and best state in the greatest nation on earth."

"That's some claim, big boy."

"Well, in my humble opinion, it cannot be denied."

I chuckled slightly. "Humble?" *Was that humble as in the loud, brash and overbearing respect of the word?* I wondered to myself.

There was no acknowledgement of the slight. "Guess you Brits were the same when you ruled the world not so long ago, right."

"Maybe so."

"Hey, while we're on the subject, what has happened to the once-so-Great-not-so-Great-anymore-Britain? Back in the States I was always comin' across Brits disillusioned with the ole country who couldn't get enough of the Stateside life."

"Well I don't think it's for me, Curt."

"Hey, don't take this personal, Joe fella, but you probably wouldn't get in anyway. We only cherry-pick your most intelligent, highly-qualified, skilled people. What makes 'em desert li'l ole England, though? I wonder."

He chuckled gently to himself, but there was nothing gentle about this giant Texan redneck, insuperably self-assured in disproportion to his wisdom.

"Money," I replied.

He taunted me with his laughter again. "Oh, it's like that, is it? Like Saudi Arabia, you mean? Get in, make some dough, then cut and run?... Don't see many folks a runnin' away from Uncle Sam, sonny."

"What about you?"

"I'll be back, don't you worry yourself about that. But right now I've got family commitments here. When the time's right I'll be back in the land of the free."

"Freedom isn't unique to the USA, you know."

"That may be the case but ours is enshrined legally in the Bill o'

Rights, Constitootion, the Second Amendment, and culturally in the American Dream. You don't have the same freedoms."

I have nothing against America normally, but I'd had a few drinks and Curt needed to be brought down. "Does that include freedom of access to deadly firearms; freedom to pollute the global environment; freedom to talk at the top of your voices regardless of where you are and who you're with, whilst wearing Hawaiian shirts and Bermuda shorts?"

"Man, that was some diatribe. Gotta say, Robert was right about you Brits. You gotta be the most negative sons-of-bastards on God's earth. You ain't buying this bullshit, are ya Dunc?"

Duncan had been sitting conspicuously quietly while Curt and I were busy scoring points off each other.

He opened his account with: "I suppose Joe's trying to point out the contradiction between America's claims of freedom and the reality." But when he continued – "and what about all those poor bastards on Death Row who get wrongly executed?" – he'd handed Curt, whose red neck had been getting progressively redder, just the opportunity he'd been looking for to strike back.

"Glad you brought that up, Dunc. You know I was talkin' to one o' your compadres and d'you know what he told me? He tol' me that seven'y per cen' of Bridishers are in favour of capital punishment. Seven'y per cent, I tell ya! But your self-servin' government won't approve it. Is that your idea of freedom and democracy? ...Well, is it?"

I was waiting for Duncan to deliver a swift and succinct rebuttal since he'd brought up the subject, but he seemed overawed by Curt's offensive. Eventually he muttered, without conviction, "If it's wrong, it's wrong, no matter how many people agree with it."

Curt was waiting. "Sorry buddy, but it ain't for you to define right and wrong, that's why we have democracy and you either believe in it or you don't. It means that much more to us than it does to you, clearly; that's another reason why we're the Land of the Free. Your European governments, on the other hand, don't trust their own people to decide for 'emselves, uh? …like they've got some kinda moral authority over the rest of you. And it don't say much for the rest of youse that you let them get away with it. Far as I'm concerned you're all just a bunch of pussyfootin', bed-wettin' lily-livered liberals. Absolutely gutless when it comes to defending your rights and freedoms."

"How come America is one of the most violent, lawless countries on earth?" I countered.

He hardly drew breath. "At least we're doin' somethun 'bout reducin' it – and succeedin', I might add – while you people just quietly disapprove as crime and violence keep rising. If as a society you only concern with the human rights of the criminal, pretty soon you won't have any human rights yourself. Follow America's example and one day you too might have a nation with a sense of pride and order, with a decent standard of life. Think on, guys, think on." He rose and condescendingly patted me on the head and playfully slapped Duncan on the cheek before heading for the gents'.

Duncan and I looked at each other and simultaneously exclaimed, "Bastard!"

"You let him get away with murder," I said.

He looked a little hurt at my suggestion. But there was also a flash of resolve in his eyes. "Well, now's our chance."

"Chance of what?"

"To get away with murder." With that he pulled out a tiny transparent bag containing some white powder, eyes shifting suspiciously all the while, and gestured as if he was going to pour some into Curt's glass.

"What the hell is that?" I demanded to know.

"Just coke."

I had drunk enough, and didn't appreciate being lectured by the fat American abroad any more than he did, but I couldn't let him get away with that. "Don't even think of it!"

"You're right, Joe. My need is greater anyway." Once Curt had returned he headed for the toilets himself.

A few minutes later Duncan was back and it didn't take Curt long to recognise his change in mood.

"You've lightened up a bit, I'm glad to see. If I was of a suspicious nature I'd swear you was up to somethun."

With that, Duncan was in hysterics, and it was infectious.

"Whadda you guys on? A lot o' you Brits are really into substance abuse, right? Seems to me you ain't got the confidence to cope without it, uh? ...huh huh huh?"

For once, Duncan, with his blood chemically altered, didn't appear intimidated by Curt. "I'm confident, man, don't worry about that. I'm just not as arrogant as you. In fact I don't think I've ever met anyone with so much arrogance but with so little substance to back it up. To me, you're just an oversized, overbearing bully-boy, fat-full of bluster, bullshit and ignorance."

Curt sat back beaming. "Wow, that must be good stuff, man! But sorry, can't compete with you no more, not this time of night. I'm wasted." He downed the remainder of his drink in one gulp and slammed it down, before shaking Duncan's hand.

After shaking mine, he spoke quietly, out of Duncan's range. "Hey, Joe, I like you. You're a spirited fella, but don't spend too much time with this guy. He's seriously bad noos."

It wasn't supposed to end like this. Curt was the bad boy, but clearly he hadn't taken any of the insults against him or his nation personally, and now he was giving me fatherly advice. And for that, I had to concede, he was a bigger man than either of us.

He was right about Duncan too, and I had also spent enough time in his company. As I left, moments after Curt, Duncan took to the dance floor where he started spinning his stuff in front of a group of Filipinas, no doubt amused by this unattractive, ill-dressed and beer-bellied white man who, drug-aided notwithstanding, was moving with a fluidity and rhythm that belied his appearance.

A STORM WAS GATHERING in the South China Sea. By the time it hit Hong Kong I found myself in the middle of an unscheduled social gathering in the dormitory, which included roommates Clare and Andy, Helen – the American I had the sex-hate relationship with – and Tom, a Welshman from next door. Normally most of them would have been working, but with a maximum No. 8 typhoon warning, everything in Hong Kong was shuttered up and battened down.

The dormitory television was on – it was always on – and for the first time it took my attention. I heard the familiar jingle of the Late News Bulletin, which usually heralded fifteen minutes of parochialism, concerning falling masonry in Mong Kok, bus fare rises of fifty cents, or irregularities in students' exam papers. Never mind genocide in the Balkans or the uprising in Chechnya. Tonight, however, they had a potential story to get their teeth into: Typhoon Ethel had hit town. Only problem was, from a news point of view, she had arrived without her typhoon. The word 'typhoon' actually derives from the Cantonese *dai foon* (literally 'big wind'). This *dai foon*, however, amounted to little more than a giant rain cloud. So, in the absence of fallen trees and devastated fishing fleets, all we got were a couple of damp and bedraggled reporters doing their utmost to make something of nothing in a series of painfully prolonged off-the-cuff descriptions like this:

> *Hong Kong is still bracing itself against Typhoon Ethel. We've had few reports so far of damage or casualties, but as you can see it's raining hard and it's quite… quite breezy.* (Cue pictures of palm trees swaying gently). *All ferry and bus services have been suspended this evening.* (A double decker passes behind). *You are advised to stay at home until the number 8 signal is lowered. Don't go outside unless it is absolutely necessary. As you can see the public have heeded this warning and the streets are deserted. Normally in this part of Mong Kok at this time the streets would be packed with night owls going to bars, karaoke clubs and restaurants, and people hurrying to catch buses and trains. But tonight, all is quiet. No buses, no trains, no… people.* (Cue camera following a couple strolling along Nathan Road). *Ah, they'll have to be careful crossing the road as the puddles are… rather deep. I wonder where they are going. Surely everything is closed down tonight.* (We see the valiant couple enter a restaurant). *Well, there you have it, for some in Hong Kong it's business as usual and life goes on, despite the conditions. On that optimistic note, it's back to you in the studio, Henry.*

Another equally laboured reporter appeared, this time by the harbour. She was also impressed by the rain and the lack of people, but with the added excitement of a slightly choppy sea to focus on. The only other items of news I can recall were a quarter per cent rise in interest rates and the recurring theme of Governor Chris Patten being attacked from all sides over the handover.

We were sitting on the floor in a tight little circle, passing round a joint, smug like a group of rebellious schoolchildren. It was a scene I was over-familiar with after months of backpacking on the subcontinent, where it could be a tiresome experience. But not this time: not with company as lively and challenging as this. Tom was recounting his journey through China. None of us had travelled much into the Mainland interior and we were eager to hear of his adventures. He described how he was forced to sleep in the open through lack of funds, keeping his few belongings in a rolled-up sleeping bag. We heard how he used to wake in parks, usually under a pagoda beside the pools and cascades, often at first light to old ladies singing Chinese opera songs. Then, on getting up, he would join in with groups of *tai chi* practitioners. He mentioned the men – always men – who would bring their delicate pet birds in ornate cages to hang from trees, giving the captives at least a hint of freedom. Then there were the huddled groups of retired men, some playing *mahjong* and gambling, but most simply observing in silence. As he said, "All Chinese life can be found in the parks."

In Hong Kong he was getting by doing occasional film 'extra' work, including a recent Jackie Chan movie called *Gorgeous*, and selling second-hand books from his dormitory, which he acquired by exchanging, scrounging and 'finding' before advertising the sale on all the notice boards of local hostels. He said it kept him fed, clothed and sheltered, and that was good enough for him. He recalled working but had no intention of reliving the experience.

"I used to be a tout for one of the Chungking Indian restaurants. I'd hang around at the entrance with all these Indian lads. They would pester any white or Chinese faces that came in, surrounding them and hustling them to get them to their restaurants, pulling them and waving cards under their noses but they repelled as many as they attracted. So when the poor beleaguered punters have fought though the scrum I'm ready to pick up the pieces. I act casual, like, as if I'm just passing, so they think I'm just being considerate as I mention I know of a good restaurant if that's what they're looking for and tell them I'm going that way anyway if they'd like me to show them, and they're usually reassured enough to follow. Most don't even know I'm working: they think I'm just doing a good turn."

"Sounds a bit like you're playing the race card," said Helen.

"But I was employed by a Sikh and it was *his* idea."

"What did the other touts think of you taking their business?" asked Helen.

"Don't know, they never spoke to me. And, tell you the truth, I don't much care."

Helen looked disgusted.

"How much did you earn?" I wondered.

"A hundred dollars an evening, plus board and free grub."

"That's better than you're getting now, isn't?"

"Yeah, I suppose it is, but you can get enough of eating curry for breakfast, lunch and dinner, believe me."

"Why don't you get a bar job? I could put in a word for you, if you like," said Clare.

"Not bloody likely. That has too much in common with hard work, that does. No, this suits me... for now at least."

"Teaching?" I suggested.

"You must be joking. Too much of a commitment. Anyway, I've come to the conclusion that life's too short to spend in an endless, repetitive cycle of drudgery. But if you're assuming my life must be somehow miserable, inadequate or deprived simply because I don't have a proper job, don't. So spare me the job offers and sympathy. Save it for the poor bugger who has to work six days a week down a mine or in a factory to support a wife and family. He's the one I feel for. No light at the end of the tunnel for him, while I'm free as a *jerk jai* – not that Chinese birds have that much freedom. I can do what I want, when, where and how. And if the wolf comes knocking at the door then I'll consider the job offers. But that's the last resort. You of all people should understand that. The poor devils back home, stuck on the same old grindstone, wouldn't have a bloody clue. They'll never experience communal living like I have, or sleep out under the bright stars of the Gobi Desert or walk remote sections of the Great Wall; they'll never feel true peace of mind and contentment because they're all too damned busy vexing themselves over mortgages, unemployment, taxes and God knows what."

No Welsh windbag he, this man from the valleys could talk. In his late thirties, I reckoned, with at least ten years seniority over any of us, he had done more living than the rest of us put together and he held us in his thrall, with the possible exception of Helen.

"What do you do with yourself every day?" prompted Andy.

"I sleep, read, walk, wank, meditate and do yoga, from time to time. That keeps me pretty well occupied. No need of much other entertainment, me. I'm a man of frugal means and simple living. Not interested in booze or nightclubs or…"

"Sex?" ventured Clare.

"Ah, sex! I remember that, yes. I take it when it comes, sure. But when it doesn't, I make do, as already listed in the hobbies and pastimes section."

Helen eyed him suspiciously. "You're weird."

"He's just an old hippie, that's all," Andy said.

"No, fair dos, girls and boys, and less of the 'old' if you don't mind. Granted I lead an alternative lifestyle, but I'm an individualist and a libertarian really. I enjoy a bit of weed as much as the next man but I'm no dopehead – can't afford to be – and I haven't got long hair or dreadlocks, as you can see. I mean hippies are still conforming to a lifestyle that isn't unique or personal. So they're compromising as much as the city businessman with his suit and tie and *Times* under his arm. I don't compromise my identity or my beliefs."

"Which are?"

Again, before Tom had time to reply to Helen's aggressive inquiry, Andy had something to add: "Anarchist, I reckon."

"You shouldn't judge so quickly, my friend." Tom's tone was ever patient and benign. "I've already told you, I don't follow trends, nor am I influenced by dogma. That's the fucking problem with politics: everyone's so stuck in their own narrow little line of thinking, always ready to pigeonhole you. If I believe in wealth distribution, I'm left-wing, if I'm in favour of personal responsibility and self-reliance, I'm right. Why can't I believe in both?"

"Because they contradict each other?"

"Come, come Helen. You can increase the minimum wage to stop exploitation, you can give tax relief to low earners. But don't give money to people for doing nothing, especially when there are jobs available."

I don't know if it was drink, drugs, genuine conviction or –
more likely – a combination of the three, but the bee in Helen's
bonnet was starting to sting. "Hippie?... more like hypocrite! How
can you say that when you don't even work yourself?"

"I may not have worked much, but I've never claimed a penny
from the government. That's the difference. I may be lazy but I'm
no parasite. I don't want to be subsidised by other hardworking
folk."

Helen's face was reddening over a grave expression as she
retorted: "So everyone on unemployment benefit is a parasite, is
that what you're saying?"

"No. Of course a lot of people are legitimately out of work
and deserve assistance. I should know. I come from the Rhondda.
But for every one genuine claimant there's another abusing it
by refusing to look for work, or making big lifestyle choices to
receive free housing and other benefits, while others work the
black economy to supplement their giros. Most of these people
won't change their ways because they have been been systemically
institutionalised. What I'm saying is the government could cut
some of these benefits and use it to give tax breaks to low-earners,
increase the incentive to work, break the cycle of dependency. I've
seen what dependency does to people: removes their self-respect,
promotes inertia and deprives them of ambition and motivation.
They really think the world owes them a living and they become
incapable of getting off their complacent arses. It's an affliction,
really – addiction even – and they're hooked."

I said, "I would have thought that an old loafer like you –
no disrespect – would have had more empathy with the idle
unemployed."

"Look, Joe, I told you, it's the workers I feel for, because I do actually know what it's like to work day in day out. That's why I rejected the exploitative monotony of such an existence. But those that don't, deserve all the help they can get. They're the ones with the rough deal."

"What about the rich?" Helen said. "Do they get a rough deal? What about tax relief for them?"

"In an ideal world you tax the rich and give to the poor, but it's been tried and what happens? They all bail out and take their cash with them. So who benefits? Certainly not the poor, not the government... just some bleedin' Swiss or Bermudan bankers."

"Any country's better off without people like that. Let them go. There's something very sick about a society that values bankers and lawyers and entertainers at twenty or thirty times more than nurses. Surely you can't deny that."

"Granted, there's a flaw in the system, but what would you suggest? ...Revolution?... Sounds nice in theory, but would you really prefer to live somewhere that imposes such restraints like Cuba, North Korea, or the old USSR?"

"Reckon I could handle Cuba, and the old socialist USSR was definitely preferable to the new capitalist Russia, that's for sure. At least there's equality in these countries. The gap between rich and poor in the States is just... obscene."

Tom sighed disparagingly. "Forget about the rich for the moment. They're only relevant to the argument if you want to be rich yourself or you envy the rich. Personally I don't. Instead of comparing the rich and poor in America, you need to compare how the poor live today compared with twenty years ago, or compare the poorest Americans with the poorest Cubans. That's the real litmus test. The point is, do the poor have the opportunity to better themselves or not? Surely they have a better chance of that in America than in Cuba."

"Oh, yeah," said Helen, with typical defiance. "The poor have virtually no healthcare available in the States, except in emergencies. Cuba has a great health service for all. And the education service in the States sucks, man. It really fails the blacks. They have no chance compared with the white, privately-educated, middle class masses. And another thing, the life expectancy is less for African Americans than Cubans. How do you explain that?"

"Lighten up, have another puff and relax your fevered brow. I understand where you're coming from, and when I was an idealistic 21-year-old like you I would have agreed with every word you've uttered." Tom paused a moment. "But the reality is, Helen, if Cuba treats the deprived so much better than your country, you would think that its poorest citizens would be content and settled... but instead there is a constant flow of economic refugees, braving shark-infested seas and tropical storms, desperately trying to reach Florida. And I wonder how many are going in the opposite direction to Castro's communist utopia (which they obviously would if your theory was correct)?... You fill in the blanks. And another thing, for someone with such revolutionary ideals, Helen, I've gotta ask, how come you're in Hong Kong? Because it seems to me that Hong Kong is about as diametrically opposed in ideology to Cuba as it's possible to find on this planet. This is a Thatcherite, or Reaganite in your language, paradise and yet here we all are enjoying all the fruits of opportunity that this capitalist, ultra-low-tax haven can offer... Correction. I should say *you* are, but then I'm a hypocrite – just an old Welsh anarchist, hippie hypocrite – so of course I don't practise what I preach."

Helen was vanquished into a fuming silence.

Clare, perhaps trying to allay the ignominy of her friend, launched into Tom for the first time. "You've got an answer for everything. You ought to be a politician."

Clare's tone of voice was challenging and typically robust, and although she was no intellectual match for Tom, her presence and purpose were irrepressible. And Tom, wisely, had no wish to include her in the argument.

"You're quite right, Clare, old bird, I've said quite enough on this subject and many more besides. I appreciate the forthright manner of your comments and I'll consider the career advice, thanks."

Clare looked disappointed that he had disarmed her instead of biting. "You're a clever bastard, you really are."

"Fuckin' hell you lot. Can't you keep the bloody noise down a bit?" It was Matt, cocooned in his little pod, disturbed by the increase in volume. But if he had expected her to heed his complaint, then he didn't know the girl at all.

"If you want a quiet life, what the hell are you doing in a dorm? Shut up or ship out."

Hysterical giggles greeted Clare's rebuke while all we got from Matt were a few muffled groans.

"If I'm a clever bastard, you're a ruthless bastard," said Tom.

It wasn't that funny, but the hash was doing its best and now we were in convulsions, except Helen, who was reluctant to show any expression of solidarity with Tom.

"Hey, this stuff is right good," said Tom, after inhaling deeply for perhaps the first time all night. "Where did you get it, Andy?"

"Can't remember, to be honest. In my line of work it's not 'ard to come by."

"You've got to be careful out there. I got caught having a blow over in Kowloon Park a couple of months ago. Cops everywhere in this city," said Tom. Then, alluding to the typhoon, "Reckon they've got their hands full tonight, though."

Helen seemed to perk up at the confession. "What happened with the police then?"

"Arrested and charged, appeared in front of the Court of First Instance – magistrates to you and me – got fined a couple of grand and bound over. Wouldn't expect them to be so lenient next time, though."

Tom didn't notice, but a sly smile passed over Helen's face.

I decided to take advantage of her improved demeanour by asking what she had been up to in the months since we had last spoken.

"I'm working nights at Rick's Café and I've just landed a job teaching kids three afternoons a week."

"Enjoying yourself?"

"I'm having the best time, Joe, the best time. I feel like a student again. No, it's better than that 'cause now I can drink."

"How about the teaching?"

"I love it. They're such cute little darlings. Well paid too."

"Why don't you quit your night job and just do the teaching?"

"No way, that's my social life and work in one. I don't wanna give that up. I've met too many great people. I'm smoking, drinking, sleeping around, having the time of my life."

I asked Helen if she was missing Craig.

" …Oh yeah, sure. Well… actually, not so much. To be honest, I'm so into everything here, I've hardly had time to think about him or home. It just seems so parochial now, do you know what

I'm saying? It's like here there is just so much energy and life, so much happening. When I compare it with my life in small-town America… And yet that's where he is right now. That's where he feels safe and comfortable. He couldn't cope with the lifestyle out here, while I'm thriving… That says it all, really."

"Not much in common, then?" said Andy.

"You could say that. He and I were like in different stratospheres. Didn't realise it myself before, but now we're thousands of miles apart in every way."

"Does he write?"

"He's written a few times but I'm afraid I haven't found time to reply. Guess I will have to some time."

I thought back to Craig's sorrowful and ignominious departure, and Helen's effortless lack of concern.

Andy had other things in mind. "So you sleep around, do you?" He paused pensively for exaggerated effect. "Mmm …already it seems we've got something in common – and the most important thing. But tell me, 'ow come you and me 'ave never managed to get it on together? Like I say, I've been around a fair bit meself."

Andy was good-looking in a boyish way and could get away with lines that would earn the average punter a slap in the face. It wasn't just on account of his looks; he had an unworldly front, a certain innocent appeal and uncomplicated humour that put girls like Helen at ease. They wouldn't take him seriously at first and nor would they feel threatened. He had a Mancunian swagger – arrogant but not aggressive – and Helen was not going to resist his charm. When he started badmouthing Tom in hushed tones, I knew he was onto a winner. This was confirmed by Helen's howls of laughter and pretty soon they were whispering in each other's ears and falling into each other's arms.

I didn't resent the fact. I had no further designs on Helen, but still I couldn't help being impressed and a touch envious of Andy's success and tactics. All evening he had listened but never challenged Helen, then supported her during her contretemps with Tom. He had won her confidence, bided his time, picked the moment, then the topic.

Forget Tom. Andy was the clever bastard.

Tom and Clare were quietly finishing off the last spliff of the evening. Andy and Helen had departed to a place more intimate. I was dog tired and relieved the party was breaking up. Jaded after another evening of intense cross-cultural political arguments and recriminations. Jaded from herbal excess on top of teaching with a hangover (quite possibly the hardest of all jobs to manage in such a state).

The idea of going to work the next day never seemed less appealing. I was burning both ends whilst the inspiration and novelty of the job, which had kept me going, were on the wane. Another four hours in class with a groggy, weary head and no preparation was beginning to feel like purgatory.

PART FIVE

Disappearing Acts

I emerge from the English Club, squinting into the bright daylight at one-thirty, looking forward to a rest. But before I have crossed the street my progress is interrupted by an elegant but grave-looking Chinese woman, wearing black sunglasses over her forehead, holding back red-tinted hair, her make-up and nail varnish immaculately applied, and a sleeveless white frock embracing her figure.

"Are you Joe?"

"Yes."

"I am Duncan's wife. Do you know where is he? I heard you were with him two nights ago. Maybe last person to see him."

"You mean he didn't come back home?"

"No, he never come back."

"Has he ever done this before?"

"One time, yes. He been on what you call, I think, a bender. Was it like that then?"

"Well…" I pause, reluctant to tell her about the cocaine. "…he was quite drunk, I must say."

"What was he doing last time you saw him?"

"Just dancing."

Her eyes narrow. "Dancing with who?"

"On his own."

"Really?" She sounds sarcastic. "What was he talking about before he started dancing?"

I sympathise, but I'm not sure she needs to hear the truth that he felt physically and culturally trapped with her and preferred the company of Filipina females. I suspect he is with one of those females right now and, that being the case, she would find out soon enough. But what if his absence was to do with the drugs he was taking? I don't want to put ideas into her head either way, don't want to add to her worry, and most of all I don't want involvement in their personal affairs. I plead ignorance, pretend I have an appointment and make for home, but not before she tells me the police have been informed.

Afternoon sleep doesn't come easily. I remember Wendy is not working today, so decide to give her a call. We have met a few times recently since the revision of our relationship. I feel cheered by the prospect of speaking to her now. The breezy vitality she exudes and the shallow content our discourse usually follows could be just the tonic I need. As I pick up the phone I'm thinking back to our last outing, where we slept under the stars on a beautiful and remote New Territories beach. I'm thinking of asking her if she would care for a repeat performance. I can think of no better way to alleviate the tension. In spite of everything, she is once again my closest confidante in Hong Kong, the one I would turn to in a crisis, the one whose advice I would trust. I know, in this situation, Pam would be less caring.

Wendy tells me I did the right thing; reinforces that I wouldn't necessarily have known about the drugs Duncan took in the toilet and that the details of his conversation were confidential and should stay as such. It's not a big deal, she doesn't say anything I don't know, but just having her confirmation, her compassion is comforting. It almost feels like a watershed. If I am turning to Wendy at times like this, what is the point of Pam? Where Wendy is giving, Pam is wanting, and where Wendy is reliable, Pam is evasive and deceitful.

Pam should have been back from Indonesia by now. On her sporadic calls she tells me she has been detained by family problems but won't expand on that despite my questions; only that she will tell all when she returns. When I ask for her contact details in Indonesia she refuses, saying it would cause problems. Feeling frustrated and left out I tell her I can't take any more of her smokescreens. Only then does Pam give me further details: her sister is seriously ill after a curse was placed by the family of her boyfriend with whom she wanted to end the relationship. It is so outlandish I can't believe what I am hearing. If she is lying why doesn't she come up with something more plausible? But if she is not, the idea of being in a relationship with someone who believes in voodoo is even more disturbing. When I tell her I can't get my head around what she is saying, she just goes quiet. I don't respond and she says she will phone again. The next day she tells me, without emotion, that her sister is dead. I am silenced, shocked beyond words. My heart softens and I apologise fulsomely, but Pam only berates me for doubting her earlier. Compelled by guilt, compassion and confusion, I offer to fly out to comfort her, but am emphatically rebutted by Pam, who insists my presence would not help the situation. I feel a combination of relief, hurt and the return of that niggling, gnawing perception that I am being deceived or at least kept in the dark. And that it can't go on.

I realise I have been seduced by Pam's beauty and femininity for too long. Even after Wendy's revelation about her Sugar Daddy Mr Wong, I still couldn't fully accept it because I didn't want to accept it and didn't want to believe that I would never again get to kiss her elegant neck or feel her perfectly-proportioned breasts against my chest. Now such considerations seem superficial and shallow. I'm pondering whether to express my feelings to Wendy, tell her I'm done with Pam, but first she says she has something to tell me.

"Joe, you remember when we start our relationship, we say stay together until we find someone more suitable?... Well, Henry I work with, he ask me to go out wiv him to cinema and dinner."

"Okay, but you've been out with other male friends before. Maybe this is the same thing?"

"No, no, he say he really nike me and fink about me a lot."

"But you've worked with him for years. Why has it taken him so long?"

"Well he used to have other girlfen' but anyway in Hong Kong these things always take time!"

"Does he know about me and you?"

"Yes I show him pictures of us."

"And that didn't put him off?"

"I fink it will put off many Hong Kong men or maybe I say many Hong Kong boys!" She laughs that wonderful, uninhibited laugh and I feel a pang. "But maybe because he is experience, he don't mind I have experience too. I fink maybe even he nike the idea that I have handsome foreigner man before, make me seem more attractive!" And once again that laugh.

I feel some regret, jealousy and, to a lesser extent, relief. The regret and jealousy are emotions of the moment, selfish and most likely temporary, while the relief, although less powerful, is more telling. The relief is for the future – a future I still could not see with Wendy despite her human qualities. I feel a little sorry for myself, but if Wendy can find happiness with someone else, I am happy for her and happy I won't have the ability to hurt her again.

"Tell him he'd better treat you well or I will pay him a visit."

If I said something like this to Pam she would have taken it literally and wondered why I would like to visit someone who had done something bad, but Wendy, despite her poor standard of spoken English, often picked up on the subtle meanings and humour of my language. And this is no exception. With her laughter once again in my ears, I ring off and prepare myself for the evening shift.

The class is quiet – with the rare luxury of forty-five minutes' solitary before the first of my regulars turn up – and thankfully uneventful.

Back at the hostel, I am just climbing to my top bunk for a pre-sleep read, when Akram comes in and tells me I have a phone call. I assume it is Wendy with an update on her love life. Instead it is the voice of Duncan's wife, and my spirits slump on recognition. She tells me she has suspicions of Duncan's drug-taking. When I plead once more my ignorance, she becomes quite aggressive, saying she knows that I know more than I am admitting. I continue my tactic of evasiveness regardless.

"Come on, I was not born only yesterday, you know! Duncan seldom takes stuff like this. He go out one night with you and this happens. I know what you young British backpack-type people are like."

"Well, this young British backpack-type person is not like that."

I cannot persuade her and the call ends: "Maybe you will have to tell that to the police because I think they will be interested to speak to you."

I hang up, cursing to myself. I know another long restless night stretches ahead of me.

I am up early, as expected. It is one of the first really warm nights of spring and I feel sticky and in need of a cool shower. As I exit the dormitory, the clock shows six o'clock and the only sound is a gentle snoring emanating from the reception where Akram is spread out across the counter. I make my way past him to the shower room. I let the cooling jets of water drive down onto my crown and into my temples for several minutes, gradually soothing the tension in my head. I'm thinking more lucidly. I have done nothing wrong, committed no crime, so why have I allowed Duncan's wife to make me feel so unsettled and guilty?

I turn off the shower and take a few deep breaths, starting to feel better. But my calmness evaporates as a series of heavy footsteps thud in the hall outside, followed by doors being thrown open. It sounds like bedlam. I hear Chinese voices and then Cantonese-accented English. "Wake up… wake up… I.D., passports." My chest tightens, wondering if they are looking for me. I poke my head out of the door and the hall is momentarily vacant, with all the police in the dormitories. I put on my shorts, T-shirt and flip-flops, considering my options.

I start to open the door, but then think better of it: being in the bathroom would hardly arouse suspicion and if they leave without speaking to me, all the better. I re-lock the door and stand looking in the mirror, listening carefully for any clues from outside. I hear consultations in Urdu, and in the background somebody, perhaps Tom, swearing in English. I wonder if the police have mistaken him for me, as it sounds like they are giving him a good going over, and Tom is responding with indignation. Of course, he is indignant because he is innocent.

Assertive Cantonese voices sound ominously close. Surely they cannot ignore the bathroom any longer. Then I hear Akram speaking and they are temporarily distracted from their duty.

"Why you come here at this early time, disturb my guests?"

The policemen ignore him and the inevitable knock can be delayed no more. The handle turns and I hear a deep, raspy tone: "Come out, please. Police check. Come out immediate."

"Hold on, hold on." I splash water over my face, and as I step out I am surprised to feel a certain diminishing of tension as if unburdened from my ridiculous self-imposed hiding place. There is only one officer in front of me, which is another surprise. He is thick-set, round-faced and of similar height to me, all of which is inconsequential compared with the apparent blandness of his expression. I had been anticipating a more intense greeting for someone investigating the disappearance of a husband and father of a young child, assuming this was his purpose.

"Where do you sleep?" I am asked. I show him into my room. Matt, Andy and Clare are all bleary-eyed but otherwise untroubled. "You have I.D. card?... passport?"

"What is this, eh?" I say, trying to affect Tom's style. "What is the problem?"

"Just show 'im your passport, arse'ole," says Matt, peeping from behind his canopy. "The sooner you do that, the sooner 'e'll clear off, and the sooner we can get back to kip."

I wish getting back to sleep was my only concern, but I don't hold it against Matt. I am one of the few people here who tolerate and even pity him for his six-day toil, drink problem, and loveless bottom-bunk lifestyle. I ignore the insult and pass my I.D. card over to the policeman. I am assuming I won't see that again for a while and that I'll be spirited for questioning to the police station, for the second time in weeks. He looks at my picture and then at my face, while I keep my head down. He tells me to look up, then clears his throat, releasing his breath, while I hold mine. But nothing more is said. Instead his outstretched hand is proffering my card and his face still has that lack of urgency. If anything he appears slightly bored. He hasn't written anything down or spoken a word; nor has he called any other officer for assistance. Could it really be just a routine check? He turns and walks out of the door, and I let go a big sigh.

"What's wrong with you?" asks Matt. "You got something to hide or what?"

"No… nothing. I've… er… just got a bit of a guilt complex when I'm confronted by authority. It's the same when I go through immigration and customs. I just can't act natural even though I've done nothing wrong. Especially first thing in the morning when you're not expecting it."

"Course they took you by surprise. That's the bleedin' idea."

"What do you reckon they were looking for?"

"Usually illegal immigrants and over-stayers. They raid these mansions every few months. Just routine for us but they usually give the Pakis a hard time. They're the ones they're really after."

"Is that all?"

"Sometimes they check for drugs or stuff."

The police haven't checked any of my possessions, which is a good sign, but I still want a final confirmation. I peruse the hall to see if they're making an exit. Not yet. Two coppers are hassling one of the Africans, who is unimpressed at having his sleep curtailed at such an hour and is not afraid of telling them so. Some Pakistanis are also being thoroughly checked and I can still hear Tom's voice at the end of the corridor, remonstrating about something or other. It seems I am the last person the police want to interrogate. I test the theory by walking out of the hostel and past the lone officer guarding the door. He yawns loudly but doesn't give me a second look, indicating beyond any reasonable doubt that I am not the target.

With a couple of hours to kill before work I head over to Signal Hill, my favourite place in this chaotic district for a spot of quiet repose. It is a clear Monday morning and I find myself, just as I did soon after my arrival, looking wistfully out to the end of the airport runway in the direction of the Lei Yue Mun channel, where the eastern sides of Kowloon and Hong Kong Island almost converge. It's a fine outlook and one that positively affects my own. I feel calm now, but as I watch the planes taking off, just as I did a year earlier, I begin to feel those same restless stirrings.

Arriving at work I am hoping to find clues as to what happened to Duncan. For as long as he is missing, I can't rest. But I don't believe anything sinister is behind his disappearance. Knowing his state of mind, it is possible he has had some kind of breakdown, but just as likely, he is holed up with one of his 'friends' and will return home when he is ready. I am half-expecting him even to show up at the Club. But when I ask the reception girls and the teachers, nobody has any information.

I teach but I am detached from the class, easily distracted, failing to concentrate, repeating myself and asking questions that have already been answered. My students can tell something is wrong, but I just put it down to the police raid and a lack of sleep. Once again I am extremely glad when the four-hour session is up and I can return to the solitude of my dormitory for the afternoon.

As I go in the main door of the hostel, Tom is going the other way with a large leather bag slung over his shoulder. I am immediately reminded of his tribulations this morning, which I had given little thought to, so absorbed was I in my own personal plight.

"What happened?" I ask.

"Got rumbled by the cops again."

"No! How come?"

"Fishy, man, fucking fishy, is what it is. Some bastard only went and planted stuff in me bag."

"Fuck. What kind of stuff?"

"Dunno. Some kind of dodgy pills. Could be E's... could be fucking anything."

"And they weren't yours?"

He laughs coldly. "No way, man. Not my thing at all. How could I afford them, anyway? You know I lead a spartan existence. I just cannot understand this at all."

"You don't think the police planted them, do you?"

"No, no. This ain't Goa. They don't operate like that here. Why would they? They're well-paid and secure. They wouldn't have got much out of me, even if they'd asked. Anyway I saw him pull it out of me bag. It was already in there, unless he's a bleeding magician. No, some fucker's been in and planted it yesterday or last night. Unbelievable but there it is… no other explanation. Any ideas?"

"Not a clue, Tom. Not a clue." But then I think back to Saturday night and I have my suspicions.

Tom, seeing me in contemplation, asks, "What is it, Joe?"

"Oh nothing, really. Well, I was just wondering if you know of anyone who might have a grudge against you."

"No... no... well, unless you include Helen, none at all."

I look knowingly back at him, inviting him to dwell on the significance of the comment.

"You don't seriously think..."

"She was really upset with you last night, you know. Must admit I couldn't understand why she took it so personally."

"Well, we do have a bit of history."

"Tell me more."

"Well, we had an on-off relationship but, although she's a good-looking girl, I found her a bit intense."

"So you ended it?"

"More or less, yeah."

"Well, that explains everything."

Tom snorts dismissively, shaking his head.

I can't believe his naivety. He had – however unintentionally – embarrassed a proud and strong-willed young woman who already harboured personal bitterness after their relationship, and he didn't seem to regard that as significant.

"I think you ought to confront her," I say.

"No, let sleeping dogs lie, what's done is done. I can't prove anything anyway, and until such time I prefer to assume she's innocent."

Despite his predicament he still seems as calm and content within his own mindset as ever, but I wonder if his overwhelming self-belief may have left him insensitive to the feelings of Helen and the effect he has had on them. Still, I can't help liking Tom. Even after the hand he has been dealt he seems to bear no malice and is not intent on digging out the dealer of his sorry hand. And I admire him. For him the incident is just another of life's obstacle courses to be negotiated with the equanimity of crossing a road.

"So where are you off to, then?"

"Can't say, my friend. Can't hang around here, though. Fuck it, they don't mess around with repeat drug offenders here, you know. Could be heading for a lengthy term if I don't make it."

"Haven't the police charged you yet, then?"

"Yeah, they took me to the station, questioned then charged me. I got the feeling they didn't disbelieve me, but what does that matter when they've got all the evidence they need?"

"So when are you scheduled to appear?"

Moving toward the door, he says, "Tomorrow morning... so you can appreciate the haste."

"One last thing, Tom. Didn't the police take your passport?"

"No, no." He laughs self-consciously. "Only my I.D. card."

I call down the walkway as he departs, asking him to get in touch if he makes it. He waves in acknowledgement but doesn't turn.

The next evening, everyone in the dorm is wondering what happened to Tom, and so I reprise.

All are silent and shocked except for Matt, of course, who reckons, "The stupid fucker had it coming."

"How do you work that out?" I demand.

"Well if you'd been cautioned for possession in a country where the drugs laws are strict, would you a) carry on as before? b) stop? or c) if you can't stop, move on? He 'ad the choice and blew it."

"I already told you, someone planted the drugs in his bag. He wasn't using them."

"And you believe him?" laughs Matt. "Don't be a mug."

Disillusioned, I am temporarily at a loss to reply. But Clare isn't: "I didn't particularly like Tom but at least he had a life and a personality..."

Matt is poised to react to Clare's insinuation when the door is flung open and in comes an irate-looking Andy.

"Has anyone seen me passport? It's gone. Has any of you seen anyone suspicious around me room the last couple of days? I left it in me rucksack there."

"Now there's a bloody coincidence, innit?" announces Matt, with an inappropriate degree of satisfaction. "What with Tom disappearing at the same time. Well, I said he was a bad 'un. But would they listen?"

It all adds up. Of course the police would have confiscated Tom's passport and, aside from any thoughts of retribution, Andy's passport was the most logical one to opt for. It was easily accessible and, more important than that, he bore a similar swarthy complexion, with dark brown hair and a roundish face not unlike Tom's. Trying hard not to smile, I mention to Andy the police find in Tom's luggage early that morning, then mischievously ask if he thinks the two incidences are related.

"Don't care about him. Got enough to worry about," he replies dismissively.

After he leaves I decide to broach my conspiracy theory with Clare and Matt. The latter, who always believes the worst about everyone, immediately endorses my theory, thereby nullifying his prior allegation and scathing disparagement of Tom. He switches the blame easily and naturally onto Andy and Helen, quite unperturbed by his judicial inconsistency. "I never liked them either," he says. "Wouldn't trust 'em an inch. I saw Andy moving his stuff into Helen's room earlier. They're a team now. I reckon they are capable of stitchin' Tom up."

Clare speaks as if she's trying to convince herself as much as us of Helen's innocence. "You don't seriously think Andy and Helen would frame Tom just because of that argument?"

"I think we both know there was a bit more background to it than that," I say.

"Hell hath no fury…" starts Matt.

"Shut up, you," snaps Clare.

I remind Clare about Helen's personality, her politics and how much they mean to her; how she'd blown me out several months ago, and most saliently, how offended and hurt she felt under the weight of Tom's polemic.

"Sorry but Helen is a good friend and you're just throwing out these idle accusations and rumours without any proof whatsoever. I just don't think they're capable of doing something like this."

I say, "If they'd been sober you might have a point, but they were stoned out of their heads the other night, remember."

Helen looks pensive for a moment, then aggressive once more as she glares at me. "You need to stop casting aspersions around when you don't know all the facts. I suggest you keep your suspicions to yourself before you get yourself into trouble."

She is right, of course. I know too much; the elation I felt on learning of Tom's master-stroke is fading, and now it's my turn to be pensive.

DUNCAN'S WIFE

I seldom receive telephone calls at the hostel (or if I do, nobody tells me, because that's how things work here). However, on picking up the phone, the first thing I notice about the female voice on the other end of the line is that it's not Wendy's.

"Who's speaking?"

"This is Jane. Are you Joe?"

I am not in the mood. "Sorry, Joe is not here."

"Oh... erm... you sound like Joe. Can you ask him to call me later?"

As I come out of work after the morning session I find myself face to face with Jane. She looks stern as she asks, "Why didn't you speak to me last night?"

I deny knowledge but I can tell she knows I am lying. "Would you like to talk now?"

It is raining hard and she gestures for me to shelter under her umbrella. I don't want to be seen huddling together with her at this time in this place. Rumours already abound, with teachers and students speculating over Duncan's disappearance and its probable cause. They cite his depression as a likely factor, with suicide a possibility; that he had a girlfriend in Thailand or the Philippines and had gone to join her; or, most disturbingly, that he had been murdered by his wife. This last theory, barely whispered early on the first day, has been gaining credence among the scandal-mongers. Several people have retold Duncan's tales of domestic abuse at the hands of his spouse: "She threw a frying pan at him... she tried to stab him with a carving knife... had to defend himself with a chair... she's a psychopath..."

Despite the gossip, I don't believe that Jane had anything to do with the disappearance of her husband when it is apparent that she is searching for – rather than attempting to hide – the truth. But now, standing so close to her in public, in full view of anyone going in or out of the Club, I am uneasily aware that not everyone would see it that way.

"Can we go somewhere?" I ask.

"Follow me."

I don't care where as long as it is away from here and quiet. I'm more afraid of being seen with Jane than what she might do or say. She may have been violent with her husband on occasions, but that could in part be explained by his neglect. Duncan often returned home late, drunk, and sometimes not at all if he had a better offer. For a proud and beautiful woman like Jane the situation must have been more than she could bear.

We walk away from the main drag and the neon along a dingy back street, past a small market and a number of little restaurants and noodle shops. This is a typical West Kowloon neighbourhood, featuring rows of grubby, run-down eight-storey buildings, ubiquitously illuminated by yellow and pink lights at the entrance. These indicate that they are brothels, but there are no girls hanging around, no pictures, only a few signs written in Chinese to show the price. The international red-light symbol of this kind of business is curiously absent. A tourist strolling down here would be none the wiser. Bangkok it ain't. (I remember discussing the Hong Kong nightlife with Will, the little sandwich seller, and being told that once on entering one of these establishments he was immediately turned down and shown the door. Whether it was his appearance that put them off or just the awkward inconvenience of dealing with foreigners, I wouldn't know. But I could relate to it, having on occasions been rejected by a barber and shunned by waiters. It isn't common, but it happens. My students find excuses for their fellow citizens by citing cultural and linguistic barriers, but in other Asian countries like India and Thailand such issues are easily overcome. Here in Hong Kong – where shyness of foreigners is combined with everyone making enough money – the rules are different).

We pass by a *dai pai dong* – a makeshift street-food restaurant held together by corrugated iron and flapping tarpaulin covers – which is one of the last commercial premises in the area, then turn down another street of tenement buildings, as dull and colourless as the sky. There are few people around now as the rain angles down, soaking my shoulders and legs despite the umbrella. The weather renders us quiet. I wish we were making small talk to lighten the oppressive air, but all she says in reply to my question of what she wants from me is, "Be patient." Through the hush I can feel a serenity of purpose about this woman, and it makes me uneasy. She is not like other Asian women who are so often passive with foreigners they don't know. We cross a road and she links arms like we're a married couple on a Sunday afternoon stroll. This is her way of affirming control of the situation. I glance at her implacably collected features, wondering what is going on inside that mysteriously beautiful head. I can only speculate in silence and on edge, as we continue our way through the clammy gloom.

Unable to contain my insecurity any longer, I ask, "Where are we going?" *Where the fuck are we going?*

"*Cha um dowla.* Do you know what that means?"

"Sorry, my Chinese isn't what it should be."

"It means *nearly there.* Don't worry, Joe."

Finally we stop at a traditional open-fronted Chinese tea shop. Ornate, ebony tables and stools, delicate China crockery, a pot of sweet lychee tea, and a beautiful companion, but I'm in no mood to appreciate any of it. I just wish she would get to the point.

She doesn't share my sense of haste, however. "Oh, what weather!" she sighs. "It never stops raining these days. It seems like God is crying over the return of Hong Kong to China…" She pauses, taking in my sceptical expression. "…Yes, I believe it. It is a terrible shame because Britain and Hong Kong make a perfect partnership, I think. But I am Chinese so I should be proud, right? But I don't trust the Chinese government, you know? I think the British should stay. Sometimes I think that the British believe they are superior, like my husband, but then I meet others who are quiet and gentle… like you perhaps? This is the typical English gentleman, I think. I hope." She laughs with abandon, but I have no time for her flirtations.

"Okay Jane, let's get to the point."

"You look uncomfortable, I think… I'm not surprised." She pauses, deliberately studying me for a reaction. Her voice is calm but she is glaring. Classic passive-aggressive.

I feign indifference and again tell her to stop playing games. Still she says nothing.

"Well?"

"Joe, you were there on Saturday night. I am waiting for *you* to tell *me* what happened."

"Since you've obviously spoken to Curt, you know as much as I do."

"How did you guess?"

I say nothing, but am quietly impressed with this Mainland Chinese woman's use of sarcasm in her third tongue. She continues: "He told me you and Duncan was together when he left the club. Also he thought you were both up to something, taking drugs maybe." Again she fixes me stonily and, with a grave tone, "You were the last person to see him, Joe. What happened next?"

I had not come with the intention of telling Jane everything, but she has a steely resolve and, I suspect, with it a forensic thoroughness that would not be sidetracked by any concealment on my part. Regardless of that, I owe nothing to Duncan, and as for the drugs and the girls, it will scarcely be a revelation to her. Conscious of the fact that I know little more than she already suspects and aware that she expects more, I tell her every detail of the evening's events to the best of my recollection.

Still she looks unimpressed.

"Have you been to the police?" I ask.

"Of course, but they are not really interested as no crime has been committed. They say it is not that unusual anyway... he will come back when he is ready."

"So the detective work is left to you." Then, without thinking, I say something – "Why don't you go to the club itself and look for some clues?... Ask around a bit" – I almost immediately come to regret.

"That's a good idea, Joe!" For the first time she sounds animated, excited even. "We can go tonight!"

"We?... we?... I meant you!"

"You just asked what you had to do to convince me you were telling the truth, well, now is your chance! Why wouldn't you come unless you have something to hide?... Look Joe, I don't even know exactly where the club is. I don't know where he was sitting, I don't know who served the drinks, I don't know any of the girls he may or may not have gone with. You on the other hand..."

She has a point – several in fact – but I am weary and in no mood for Wan Chai tonight. "Tomorrow would be better, I think."

"No! What is that English phrase? You should strike the iron while it is hot!"

"...Something like that." Then it occurs to me: "Tomorrow is actually a week to the day since he disappeared, so there is more likelihood of meeting the same clientele and staff who were there last Saturday." The fact that I would be finishing work earlier and had nothing otherwise planned had nothing to do with it.

She pauses briefly. "Your idea is good," she says, very matter-of-fact. "You will not let me down, Joe."

BACK TO WAN CHAI

Walking the short distance from Wan Chai MTR, through the dank backstreets of Wan Chai, with Jane once again firmly linking my arm to hers, feels like *déjà vu*, that sense of foreboding as apparent as the night before, only now more contrary. Being with her at this time and this place is absolutely the right thing to do, so why doesn't it feel it? For all her intelligence, good looks and difficult circumstances there is something about her – a coldness, an invulnerability – that does not easily lend itself to sympathy.

It is nine-thirty when we arrive and the club is still quiet. This gives Jane the opportunity to approach all the bar staff – a cosmopolitan mix of Chinese, Filipinos, Nepalese and Europeans – to show a picture of Duncan. I don't recognise any of them and, judging by the blank expressions and shaking of heads, they are indicating a similar response to the photo. Not that Jane is despondent or in any way deterred. She gestures for me to join her as she turns her attention to a cluster of Filipina girls, then another, and then another, as each time she is met by polite negatives.

I have a feeling this will be the recurring theme of the night and that my presence will be futile. A change of tactic is required and Jane guides me to the entrance, advising me to look out for anyone I or Duncan might know. As she continues to display the picture to each arrival, I scan the faces carefully, and as I do so, my feelings of uselessness are magnified as I realise that even if the last woman seen with Duncan were to appear I'm not sure I would recognise her.

During a lull in intercepting the arrivals I admit to Jane that I don't think I can really help and that it was too dark in the club for me to have got a clear impression of anyone, not least being half-inebriated. I expect an abrasive response, but instead Jane's voice is soothing: "Don't worry honey, you may not have a picture in your mind but if you see anyone from that night I am sure it will jog your memory."

"No, I don't think so... I wish I could help you, but I think we're just wasting our time, to be honest."

"Oh don't say that Joe! I couldn't do this without you. Even if we don't find out anything, just having you here is a great help and comfort."

I'm beginning to see Jane in a different light. And she doesn't miss a thing. "Penny for your thoughts?"

"What?... nothing... nothing worth repeating."

She looks at me with an expression half-smiling, half-quizzical. "Joe?" Her voice is slow and rich, ever-so-slightly teasing. "What do you think of me, Joe?"

She is focused on me to the exclusion of all else, as self-possessed as I am self-conscious. I would rather not be having this conversation. But Jane's uninhibited transparency is infectious. And she is staring softly at me.

"Erm... I was just thinking, I've never met a woman like you before, and certainly not a Chinese woman."

She smiles confidently. "That's because you've never been to Shanghai. Hong Kong people, despite being open to the world for lifetimes, are much more conservative than urban mainlanders."

"How come?"

"I think Hong Kong people, since they were ruled by the British, always tried deliberately to maintain their Chinese ways. They respected British democracy and rule of law but culturally they did not want to be British, they had to maintain their own native identity, so they are more closed, more defensive. People in Shanghai on the other hand, they were brought up through the Communist system, so the young people they feel more rebellious against that establishment, so they are actually more outward-looking and more willing to embrace Western ideals. But in Hong Kong the establishment is Western, so you see... the difference."

I had never thought of it like that. In one paragraph Jane had summarised the cultural outlook of Hong Kongers in a way that I had never extracted from students in day after day of classroom conversations.

"But Shanghai is distinct from other places in China, right?"

"Yes of course," she laughs proudly. "You see, Beijing may be the political capital of the nation, but Shanghai has always been the commercial and cultural capital. People in Beijing are more loyal to the government for that reason. In Shanghai there is more tradition for dissent. We are the city of writers, philosophers, poets, musicians. We are outward-looking and liberal, and we do not respect the establishment."

"Sounds like a great place to be. So how come you ended up in Hong Kong?"

"In twenty or so years' time Shanghai will overtake Hong Kong, I am convinced. It is still developing, though, with great infrastructure projects planned and so much potential. I would like to return, but for now at least Hong Kong offers more opportunities with jobs and pay. It also gave me the chance to improve my English and find a husband."

"No regrets?"

"I have a good job here, make more money than I could have in Shanghai and I have a beautiful son. What have I to regret?"

"Duncan?"

She looks momentarily perplexed, pained even, but it is a look motivated more, I suspect, by my question and my need to ask it than any emotion for her missing husband. She is utterly enigmatic, but before I have the chance to study her expression further or ask more, her composure is restored as she gets up and announces she is going to buy me a drink. The vulnerability I had for the briefest of moments managed to elicit is gone as Jane once more takes control of the situation.

I am left pondering the complexities and contradictions of this extraordinary woman and it almost makes me breathless. Normally, in the presence of such beauty, intelligence and charisma, I would be striving, and no doubt stumbling, in my attempts to impress. But this is different. She is the one looking for affirmation, attention or... what? My experience is that Chinese women can sometimes be more open with a Western man – or at least this Western man – than they are with their countrymen, and my ego allows me to consider the possibility that she is motivated by attraction. But at a time like this? There has to be more to it. And another thing bothers me. And the more I think about it the more it bothers me: that is the contradiction between Duncan's description of his wife and the reality I am finding. Certainly he alluded to her beauty, but he also made much of the cultural differences, as if she were a poorly-educated, unsophisticated Mainlander with broken English, when the very opposite is true. In almost every way I could conceive, Duncan was punching above his weight, and yet he still wasn't satisfied. But then I think of Jane's powerful assertiveness and recall Duncan's description of how it manifested itself domestically and I realise that any feelings of dissatisfaction were, in all likelihood, mutual and probably justified on both sides. I am minded also of Duncan's comments about her potent irresistibility in the early stages, and even given what he would later discover, he would still in the same situation probably make the same mistake again, such was the powerful hold she exerted. I am wary, determined not to compromise, but at the same time fascinated by this woman and intrigued by what she knows and what she wants from me. The fact that I am willingly waiting for her in this place, knowing what I do about her and aware that my guardedness is about be challenged by alcohol is, I suppose, already Round One to her.

She comes back with the drinks and I suggest we sit at a prominent table with an unhindered view of the bar and dance-floor. But as we chat I notice Jane has stopped looking at the new arrivals, the girls dancing, or anyone except me. She is asking lots of questions about my background, family, former jobs, and all the while looking at me as if I am the only person in the room. Her delicate hands are mostly clasped together, occasionally flicking at her hair, but her eyes never stray from mine. I feel some stirring,

but I am wary of the potential and decide that this will be my f.
and last drink of the night.

"What are you drinking?" I ask.

"Coke. I don't need alcohol. I like to be in control at all times."

"I had noticed," I laugh.

"Duncan always said I was a control freak."

"You control-freaked him out!"

It is a bad joke, particularly given the circumstances, but as with my previous comment, Jane sees the funny side. I can do no wrong in her eyes now, it seems. And the fact that she has brought Duncan's name into the conversation motivates me to ask: "Do *you* have any idea where he might be?"

"Joe, I have no idea. I am desperate. That is why I came to you for help. That is why we are here now."

Her tone is more persuasive than affronted, which I take as a green light. "I appreciate that but there are just, I don't know, a lot of things that don't add up."

Her eyes narrow. "For example?"

This is potentially awkward and I am struggling to say what I want to say tactfully: "Well, it's just... erm... you say you are desperate, but... well... you don't really seem it."

I am braced for a backlash and for Jane to at last reveal something of that notorious temper of hers, but once again she is a picture of calmness and tolerance. "I am desperate to find out, Joe, not desperate to have him back. There is a difference."

"Do you think he will come back?"

I am looking at her closely for signs of emotion or fallibility (culpability even), anything that might lend credence to my theory that Jane is concealing something, but her demeanour

 _ains as imperceptible as ever. "He will come back as long as _othing bad has happened."

"Nothing bad?"

She answers slowly, deliberately, choosing her words carefully. "Yes. You have confirmed he was taking drugs, which I already suspected. But where did he buy them? Who did he know? What if he owed them money? Then there are the girls... You told me one of them had a grudge and made a scene last week."

I have no time for Jane's theories and tell her so. When it came to drugs, I am convinced Duncan was strictly small-time, just buying enough for his own occasional recreational pleasure, and the idea that a dealer would provide him with an IOU is laughable. The girls' conspiracy may be more plausible, but I cannot shake the feeling that the woman with the biggest grudge, the greatest sense of betrayal and, therefore, the strongest motive is Jane herself. Not that I can say. Not that she would listen. She is still regarding me as if we are on a date, and her attentions are becoming increasingly unambiguous. Although I am slightly aroused and flattered, predominantly I am suspicious and uncomfortable. And I need to get away. "I think we should go."

"What?! It is not late. What if one of the women turn up? No, stay, Joe."

"But you've stopped checking anyone coming in! I don't know what we're even doing here."

"I'm just trying to fit in like all the other couples here. I don't want to look suspicious, don't want anyone to notice us now."

"Very convincing," I say with a sarcasm for once lost on Jane.

"You, Joe, you are the one who should be looking all the time, you have the knowledge, not me."

A compromise is agreed and we stay for one last drink. We put

on a front of vigilance, which succeeds in reducing Jane's fl▪
and the conversation becomes more neutral and, for me at le
more relaxed.

During a rare lull in the conversation I ask who is looking after
her son tonight.

"He is at home with our maid."

"Did you never worry about Duncan and the maid being
together in the same household?"

"No, she is an old maid."

I laugh and Jane looks nonplussed, which pleases me in a
perverse way.

I finish my drink before midnight, while Jane takes another
fifteen minutes. As soon as her glass is emptied I am up and
motioning towards the door, thankful there has been no suspicious
arrival to detain us and keen to get out before she can develop a
new strand of conversation.

I walk briskly to the station and keep communication to a
minimum. Once on the train, however, I have nowhere to go and
Jane is back in charge. She is tactile and effusively complimentary,
telling me she has had a lovely time and that it was just what she
needed to take her mind off things. She wants me to return the
tribute, I am sure, but I am reluctant in the circumstances.

"Why are you so… conservative, Joe? I know you have enjoyed
yourself tonight… you like my company, right?"

"Well… yes."

I continue to do my best to neutralise Jane's attentions until
our train starts decelerating towards Tsim Sha Tsui station. Jane
takes my right hand and clasps it tight within her two hands. "Let
me come with you, Joe. I don't want to go home now."

My conscious head is urging me not to, against the advice of reacherous instincts. But however untrustworthy my visceral inclinations may be, they are as nothing compared with the dangerous potential of Jane. And for that reason I do something I have never done before: I spurn the advances of a beautiful woman. She looks pained and vulnerable as I depart, before she collects herself with that familiar self-assured smile, the mask restored. I try to make amends by insisting we will meet again.

Later in bed my head is alive, reliving the evening's events, trying in vain to read Jane's intentions, wondering if I made the right call. I refer to Walsh's Code, a set of personal ethics I try to live by where relationships are concerned. Not perhaps as virtuous as it sounds, when sleeping with Jane would scarcely have violated any of its key principles. True, it does stipulate you *do not go with a friend's partner*, but then Duncan is hardly a friend. And, even if he were, would his behaviour and infidelity have justified the withholding of loyalty? The pursuit of a married woman is also forbidden, but when the roles are reversed it is a rule-changer surely (under my flexible interpretation at least). Then there is a directive straight out of a PG Wodehouse novel, which insists it is ungentlemanly for a single man to reject the advances of a single woman. Even allowing for the fact that Jane is married – and the Code thus not infringed – did not necessarily make this easier. For me, Bertie Wooster and, I suspect, most men, it does not come naturally to be the quarry, going so against our social and cultural conditioning and experience that the act of rejecting is harder than that of being rejected. Under other circumstances – that is circumstances free of mysteriously missing husbands and suspicious wives – I know I would have acted differently. Indeed I have acted differently in the past, including with women I would have rather avoided; anything to avoid the social awkwardness,

anything to avoid seeing the expression of hurt bewilderment th
Jane so fleetingly revealed as I alighted from the train.

Nonetheless, I wake in the morning convinced I have done the
right thing and feel somewhat proud of myself for standing firm.
The feeling is quite liberating and proof perhaps that I am growing
up. Normally the prospect of good sex – and that is probably
to undersell Jane – trumps everything. But had I surrendered I
would now be full of regret, mired neck-deep in Jane's world,
whatever the hell that entails, and hostage to her whims. Any pity
I feel for her – and I do – is assuaged by the knowledge that she
has the supreme self-confidence and mental resilience to cope.
And it is an opinion that is proved rather more emphatically and
sooner than I would have cared for.

The phone rings at the unmanned reception. I take it and
immediately recognise the calm, measured tone of voice and the
pureness of vowels. As she talks – at me, not to me or with me – I
am aware that there is little purity elsewhere and feel even more
vindicated that I made the right call last night. Jane speaks non-
stop, telling me – not asking me – that she will call round later this
evening to collect me. She has a lead on one of the Filipina girls
apparently and needs my assistance. Although there is nothing in
her tone of voice that betrays her, I don't believe a word.

She hangs up, the date arranged, without my being able to
utter a word of confirmation or anything else, and I feel as if I
have been mugged off. It is nine on Sunday morning and the
hostel is unusually quiet. No one is up except for me. I decide to
go back to bed, take advantage of the peace for another doze. But
as soon as I lie down I realise it is not going to happen. Jane has
got under my skin again, that much is clear. And the worst thing
(apart from the very worst thing, which is Jane herself, of course),

that I have no one to share it with. Wendy is otherwise occupied and, in any case, would struggle to understand the complexities of my dilemmas, morally as much as linguistically. And she wouldn't be any different from any other woman I could think of when it came to judging my tormentor. For Jane is no girl's girl or woman's woman. If she had any female friends she never mentioned them, and if such a friend existed she would have to be very tolerant or eccentric, or indeed both. Any normal woman would be scathing about Jane and would advise me to be ruthless with her, because that is how they would handle an awkward man in a similar situation. I could mention that some men are incapable of dealing with women with the insensitivity with which many women treat men, and mention the skill of manipulation that Jane possessed in her exchanges with me, but they wouldn't get it. And why should they? I am the mug after all.

Even the men at the hostel would not understand. Matt would just say 'What's all the fuss about? Tell her to fuck off'. Andy would be more subtle, but with so many other options at his disposal and a history of promiscuousness, he would not dwell on Jane. I wish I could say the same. It is not that I like her, trust her or want her (not long-term anyway), but she has an intrigue, a twinkling charisma, an intelligence and an easiness on the eye that is uniquely attractive but, with respect to her marital circumstances and untrustworthiness, not irresistible. That much I had proved. But if she were to keep on pursuing, keep on subjecting me to her alluring chemistry, I don't know if I could resist forever. There are one or two of my teaching colleagues whom I believe would empathise but I cannot afford to tell them a thing. Tom is the one person I could talk with about these things. He would understand

and would not be reluctant to give his opinion, which would
considered not necessarily right, but always worth listening to.

I spend a quiet Sunday to myself, not sharing my issues with
anyone and decide early on that I am going to stand Jane up.

By early Monday morning, with the kind of irony or
serendipity of fate that sometimes seems too commonplace
to be mere coincidence, I am thinking about Tom as I give up
attempts at further sleep and wander out into the corridor and see
a postcard under the letterbox on the floor. A picture of a couple
of sun-tanned Oriental babes in front of the classic palm tree
and beach scene, and on the back, a Thai stamp and in scrawling
handwriting:

> *Greetings from Thailand (I hear it's very nice there this time
> of year!!)*

> *Well I made it Joe, begging, borrowing and scrounging to
> survive – haven't resorted to stealing yet. But who cares?
> Mere inconveniences in the great scheme of things. Good to
> be reminded of the value of liberty from time to time. Never
> take it for granted. Love life, live long.*

> *Meantime, Happy Handover! (If you survive HK until
> then)*
>
> *T*

> *p.s. Please send my regards to Helen and Andy (love and war
> and all that…)*

Ah, the fast-approaching handover… I had hardly given it a
moment's thought in the preceding days. It means nothing

...ne now, but hearing from Tom is just the tonic and I can't ...op smiling at the thought he made it and got one over on the conniving couple. I wonder where he is really, but again it hardly matters: he is once more free as a *jerk jai*, as he put it, while I am confined to a putrid, cockroach-infested hostel, being hounded by a beautiful, psychotic woman with a potentially dangerous secret, and working at a teaching sweatshop on minimum pay, with job satisfaction diminishing by the day.

The message seems just the omen I need. But first I have a stomach that needs filling. I head over to Ollie's, the only place in Hong Kong I know, outside of the overpriced hotels, that serves something resembling an English breakfast (albeit with inferior frankfurter-type sausages). I have adapted to the Cantonese cuisine, but when you are as hungry as I am, sweet bread and milk, or ham and egg in a light noodle soup will not do at all.

The staff at Ollie's are usually friendly and polite, but tend to lack initiative. Last time I was here the lad serving me was reluctant to give me any HP Sauce before consulting with the manager, because HP Sauce is supposed to be for bacon, not sausages, apparently. Another time I asked for a refill, which is allowed up to eleven o'clock. The server looked anxiously at the clock, which said one minute past. My cup was on the counter waiting emptily, the pot of tea was in his hand, the manager nowhere to be seen. But I was still left empty-cupped. Today, keen to avoid any unnecessary contention when I have so much else on my mind, I make do with one cup of tea and breakfast without brown sauce.

As I eat I am mulling over the last few extraordinary weeks of the most extraordinary year of my life; a last few weeks beset by drama-on-crisis-on-drama on top of exhaustion, and I

can't compute it all. Stuff is happening on a daily basis, but .
is happening to me; I am not making the happening happen. I
feel I have been driven down a trail with unwelcome diversions
at every turn. *Been driven* (grammar: passive voice) rather than
driving (grammar: active voice) with no control over journey or
destination. And I realise it is time to take back control, time to
drive again, time to rediscover my active voice.

I leave Ollie's and head straight over to the Kowloon English
Club for the last time. I see Robert, as ever assiduously preparing
for his morning lesson. He tells me he is also planning on leaving.
"This place is cursed, or, if it ain't, it sure has bad karma. First
there was Harry, then poor Jamie, Fraser and now Duncan. Who's
next? You're sure making a wise move, Joe." (Harry and Jamie
were before my time. Harry was an old boy, famous for spouting
about the importance of healthy living, exercise and diet, who
dropped dead from a heart attack in front of his students last year;
Jamie was tragically killed a few weeks later in a shark attack at
an isolated beach in the rural northeast, with only his upper torso
ever recovered.)

I tell Maxine I have to leave Hong Kong due to family issues
and I don't know when I will be back. Of course there is no
sympathy from her and I have to forego a week's pay. But it is no
use arguing and risk the rest of my month's salary.

I take my cheque to the local bank, but they won't cash it
because my name on the cheque, Joe Walsh, isn't the same as
'WALSH Joe Raymond' on my I.D. card. I try to convince them
that middle names are seldom used by Westerners and that we
don't usually write our surnames first as the Chinese do, but she
just shrugs and gestures to the next customer.

By the time I have been to the KEC to get a new cheque and

ack, a queue is stretching out of the door and along the street. It is a common-enough scene and seems to epitomise the attitude and priority of Hong Kong's largest bank (British-owned, as it happens). They are quite happy to leave their customers broiling in the tropical sun or dripping under tropical downpours instead of providing a couple of extra tellers if it means saving a handful of dollars. I am sweating and fuming and cursing those penny-pinching bankers. But I am alone. Asian forbearance is very much in evidence as I look at the people around me and find not an ounce of indignation or impatience. How do they put up with such service without complaining or taking their custom elsewhere? They are mistreated by a company they financially support, but one that regards them as expendable. Go to a branch in Central, where all the big investors work, and witness the difference in service quality and waiting time. It is another case of a company making so much money that it doesn't care. Mention these things to Mr or Mrs Hong Kong, though, and all you will get is a shrug like my teller's and something to the effect of, 'So what?' I'm left wondering if people back home would put up with such service, then I'm reminded of what London commuters have to put up with and I doubt the people of Hong Kong, accustomed to one of the world's most reliable, efficient and cheapest transport systems in the world, would be any more accepting.

After that annoying fifty-minute wait, I am served, this time without ado. I take the money and immediately head for Time Travel, emerging some ten minutes later and fifteen hundred Hong Kong dollars lighter. I walk back to my hostel, feeling brighter and more sanguine than at any time in the last four days. I pack, settle up with Akram, giving him an awkward manly hug on the way, and leave.

I feel burdened, not just by my heavy backpack but also by thought that I am not leaving on my own terms. I find my looking in all directions, ready to take flight in the unlikely ever of Jane showing up. I berate myself for worrying when I know she has nothing on me whatsoever. Not, I suspect, that it would make any difference to her. If she could see me now heading for the airport with my baggage, I wonder at the response. All I know is that it wouldn't be a peck on the cheek and 'Bon voyage'.

As my bus arrives I feel a loosening of anxiety, and I take that as some justification for my drastic move. Further pressure is released little-by-little as we exit Tsim Sha Tsui district and join the airport expressway, then as I negotiate the terminal, check-in, customs, passport control. By the time I am seated on the plane I feel a sense of calmness I haven't felt in months.

The aircraft taxis, turns and halts at the end of the runway, jet engines silent for a moment before whirring into action. Normally my levels of apprehension at this point would be high, but I realise Hong Kong has extracted so much of my nervous energy that I have none left. Even a recent aviation nightmare born of those last stressed-out days of Kowloon life does not play on my mind. In that disturbing dream I was standing by Victoria Harbour, waiting for a plane to come and pick me up (unquestioningly, so of course a dream). A British Airways 747 came cruising out of the blue, silently somehow, ever so gently, gliding on approach, then skimming the dark waters, the nose breaking the surface, followed by the fuselage then, almost in slow-motion, slipping beneath the swaying waves, sinking, leaving only the tail visible as it cut through the surface like a huge metallic shark fin, until it too succumbed to the depths. The water eerily reverted to a calm and pacific state, concealing its catastrophic consumption as if it never been. I stood alone in silent disbelief. No one else saw what I saw. No rescue services would come, no onlookers, no journalists. This was my own personal drama, in a dream of such incandescent clarity that, on waking with a start, it felt almost like a premonition.

Now, sitting comfortably, I am too emotionally spent to dwell on its significance and, in any case, I have another theory. If dreams are supposed to represent our deepest hopes and fears, I suspect that airliner was the embodiment of home and my diminishing prospects of seeing it again if I remained in the grip of a place and a person that I could love and hate and know I will miss but yearn to be free of.

Taking off is a straightforward affair compared with landing: straight out and over the sea which, from this elevation on a shiny afternoon, glimmers silver prisms of light. We swing slightly to the right and virtually the whole city becomes visible. Hong Kong is putting on a good farewell show. The mountains are lushly green from early summer rains and stand graphically against an uncommonly haze-free, azure sky. Below the ridge, Hong Kong-side twinkles like a million jewels, whilst across the 'Fragrant' Harbour its poorer neighbour Kowloon appears a truncated entity of concrete blocks and greyness, to all appearances a different city.

Looking across from Lion Rock to the Peak, and Kennedy Town to Siu Sai Wan, it seems almost impossible to grasp that all that has happened *could* happen in such a small urban space. Hard too to accept that I may never again see it and live it. Already I feel a heavy sense of nostalgic loss for the times and the places, the lives and the loves, fading with the view. I recall the pride and relief I felt as I survived then thrived on the challenge of teaching English, and the privilege of meeting a people who showed me and welcomed me into their lives and culture. And then the harbour disappears and they are gone.

For barely a minute we fringe the rural east coast of Hong Kong Island, rising all the while skywards over the wide expanses of the South China Sea. Outside Hong Kong jurisdiction and we are not going to crash – at least not in Victoria Harbour – but the consolation is scant and my earlier satisfaction is waning under the influence of an irrational and melancholic desire to return to that unceasing flow of life and sudden death, where the conflicting forces of greed and generosity, loyalty and apathy, lust and chasteness, ambition and acceptance, tolerance and intolerance are all played out every day. Like anywhere else. Only more so.

But it cannot be.

I think of the Duncan and Jane scenario and others I would wish to avoid, such as Helen and Andy.

I consider the prospects of work in a post-British Hong Kong.

I think of all the other places in the world waiting to be discovered and recall the words of my grandfather advising me always to move on, never to look back.

Then I recline in my seat, shut my eyes, and relive once more the experiences that define the time of my life... and I am not so sure.

THE END

Epilogue

Post-handover Hong Kong would prove a very different place. Most of the Brits were gone, tourists were few, and economic confidence was shot. A flat, oppressive and loveless mood pervaded the city. The old vibrant haunts – the hostels, hotels and bars of Tsim Sha Tsui, and the Chungking Indian restaurants – were virtually empty; the Kowloon English Club was struggling for survival and most of the sandwich delivery companies were no more.

Without the competition of British newcomers, opportunities actually increased for English teachers (whose pre-handover I.D. cards were still valid for work) in contrast to the employment prospects of almost everyone else. Many of Joe's teaching colleagues had found new and better teaching jobs while, curiously, their old jobs were often filled by laid-off construction workers.

Duncan would never return to the hallowed halls of the KEC, and although he slunk back to the matrimonial home after a week's absence with his new girlfriend, his lies and excuses would be rejected by Jane. He would end up in the Philippines while Jane was heading back to her beloved Shanghai.

Those who stayed had witnessed history with the changing of the guard, and although it would rain on the handover parade –

and rain and rain and rain – it was undoubtedly a monumental occasion to mark the end of an era and the dawn of a new one.

Wendy was there, of course, and although Joe had left in a hurry without saying goodbye, they would stay in touch. Within a year Wendy would be married and expecting a baby daughter to whom Joe would be godfather.

Joe had missed the wedding and indeed the handover, but he was there when it mattered. And before those memories could fade, he would relive the best and worst of times by jotting down what he could recall of the places, passions and personalities. The result of those labours is not history but his story in the making, a tale that may not even have been told had it not culminated in dilemma and departure. Most likely Joe would have strolled on without pausing to chronicle those halcyon, tumultuous, wonderful and dreadful times when – in the words of Will – Hong Kong really was at the centre of the universe.

EXPLORE ASIA WITH BLACKSMITH BOOKS

From bookstores around the world or from *www.blacksmithbooks.com*

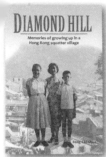

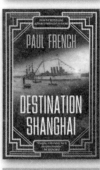

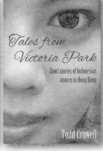